"Ahoy, there."

Jason watched as the sailboat's captain stepped onto the dock. He caught a glimpse of a face, and realized the sailor was a woman. A woman he knew.

Piper strode toward him. "Good morning, Mayor."

He couldn't help but stare at her dark hair. He'd dreamed about that hair. He swallowed, rejecting the flash of interest that prickled whenever he talked to her.

"You'll need a car, Miss Langley. Serenity Bay's public transportation isn't up to big city standards."

"Please call me Piper," she said. "I'm familiar with the need for wheels around here. I lived in Serenity Bay years ago. They were some of the best times of my life."

Then she smiled and it was a glorious thing. Her gaze held his. A zing of awareness shot between them.

"That explains your enthusiasm for this place, then," he said. "So what do you have planned for Serenity Bay, Miss Langley?"

"You're the boss. Shouldn't you be telling me, *Mr.* Franklin?"

Books by Lois Richer

Love Inspired

Love Inspired Suspense

†Faith, Hope & Charity
*Brides of the Seasons
‡If Wishes Were Weddings
**Blessings in Disguise
††Serenity Bay
‡‡Finders, Inc.

LOIS RICHER

Sneaking a flashlight under the blankets, hiding in a thicket of Caragana bushes where no one could see, pushing books into socks to take to camp—those are just some of the things Lois Richer freely admits to in her pursuit of the written word. "I'm a book-a-holic. I can't do without stories," she confesses. "It's always been that way."

Her love of language evolved into writing her own stories. Today her passion is to create tales of personal struggle that lead to triumph over life's rocky road. For Lois, a happy ending is essential. "In my stories, as in my own life, God has a way of making all things beautiful. Writing a love story is my way of reinforcing my faith in His ultimate goodness toward us—His precious children."

His
Winter Rose
Lois Richer

Steeple
Hill®

Published by Steeple Hill Books™

STEEPLE HILL BOOKS

Steeple
Hill®

ISBN-13: 978-0-373-87421-7
ISBN-10:   0-373-87421-9

HIS WINTER ROSE

www.SteepleHill.com

Printed in U.S.A.

So whenever you speak, or whatever you do, remember that you will be judged by the law of love, the law that set you free. For there will be no mercy for you if you have not been merciful to others. But if you have been merciful, then God's mercy toward you will win out over his judgment against you.

—*James* 2:12-13

This book is for Judy, Ken and the kids.
Thanks for introducing me to cottage country.

Prologue

"**M**s. Langley? Piper Langley?"

"Yes."

Maybe it was the suit that took his breath away—a tailored red power suit that fit her like a glove. But he didn't think of power when he looked at her. He thought of long-stemmed red roses—the kind a man chooses to give his love.

Maybe it was the way she so regally rose from the chair in Serenity Bay's town office and stepped forward to grasp his hand firmly. Or it could have been her hair—a curling, glossy mane that cascaded down her back like a river of dark chocolate.

His sudden lack of oxygen wasn't helped by the megawatt smile that tilted her lips, lit up her chocolate-brown eyes and begged him to trust her.

From somewhere inside him a warning voice reminded, "Trust has to be earned." Immediately he recalled a verse he'd read this morning: Commit everything you do to the Lord. Trust Him to help you and He will.

"I'm Piper." Her words, firm, businesslike, drew him back to reality.

"Jason Franklin," he stated. "Would you like to come through to the boardroom?"

"Certainly." She followed him, her high heels clicking on the tile floor in a rhythmic pattern that bespoke her confidence.

Inside, Jason introduced the town's councillors, and waited till she was seated. Only then did he take his place at the table and pick up her résumé. It was good. Too good.

"Your credentials speak very well for you, Ms. Langley."

"Thank you."

He hadn't been paying her a compliment, simply telling the truth. She was overqualified for a little town like Serenity Bay, a place in Ontario's northern cottage country.

"I don't think we have any questions about your skills or your ability to achieve results." He glanced at the other board members for confirmation and realized all eyes were focused on the small, delicate woman seated at the end of the table.

Piper Langley had done nothing and yet they all seemed captivated by her. Himself included.

Careful! his brain warned.

"I'm happy to answer anything you wish to ask, Mr. Franklin." She picked an invisible bit of lint from her skirt, folded her hands in her lap and waited. When no one spoke, she chuckled, breaking the silence. "I'm sure you didn't ask me here just to look at me."

So she knew she drew attention. Was that good or bad?

"No, we didn't." He closed the folder filled with her accomplishments, set it aside. "It's obvious you have what we're looking for, but I can't help wondering—why do you want to leave Calgary? Especially now, after you've worked so hard to build your reputation, finally achieved the success you've earned? Why leave all that to work in Serenity Bay?"

She didn't move a muscle. Her smile didn't flicker. But

something changed. If he had to put a name to it, Jason would have said Piper-the-rose grew prickly thorns.

"Several reasons, actually. As you noted, I've been working in the corporate world for some time now. I'm interested in a change."

That he understood. He'd come here to seek his own change.

"I was intrigued when I heard about your plans for Serenity Bay. The town has always been a tourist spot for summer vacationers."

"Lately the year-round population has been in decline," he admitted.

"Yes." Her gaze narrowed a fraction. "If I understood your ad correctly, you're hoping to change that." She glanced around the table, meeting every interested stare. "I'd like very much to be a part of that progress."

Nice, but not really an answer to his question.

Why here? Why now?

Jason leaned back in his chair and began to dig for what he really wanted to know.

"How do you view this town, Ms. Langley?"

"Please call me Piper." She, too, leaned back, but her stare never wavered from his. "I don't want to hurt anyone's feelings, but to me Serenity Bay looks like a tired old lady much in need of a makeover. The assets are certainly here, but they're covered by years of wear and tear. I'd like to see her restored to a vibrant woman embracing life with open arms. I have some ideas as to how we might go about that."

Piper elaborated with confidence. Clearly she'd done her research, weighed every option and planned an all-out assault on the problems besieging the Bay. But she didn't stop there. She offered a plethora of possibilities Jason hadn't even considered. Two minutes into her speech she had the board eating out of her perfectly manicured hand. None of the other candidates had been so generous in sharing their ideas.

Jason was left to find a hole in her carefully prepared responses.

"You're used to large budgets, Ms. Langley. You won't have that here."

Her brown eyes sparked, her perfectly tinted lips pinched together as she leaned forward. So Miss Perfect had a temper. He found that oddly reassuring.

"Money isn't always the answer, Mr. Franklin." Her fingers splayed across the shiny tabletop, her voice deepened into a firmness that emphasized the sense of power that red suit radiated. "Yes, it will take some cash to initiate change. It will also require hard work, forward thinking, a vision that reaches beyond the usual means to something new, untried. There will be failures, but there will also be successes."

"I agree."

She stared at him hard, her focus unrelenting, searching. Then she nodded, just once.

"It will also take commitment. By you, your board, the community. No town gains a reputation for great tourism through one person's actions. It takes everyone committing to a common goal and pushing toward it—no matter what. It takes teamwork."

Jason hoped his face remained an expressionless mask, but his heart beat a hundred miles an hour. Of everything she'd said, that one word had made up his mind.

Teamwork.

It was what he'd been cheated of before.

It was the one thing he'd demand from the town's newest employee.

"Unless anyone has another question, or you have something more to say, Ms. Langley, I believe we're finished. Thank you for making the trip." He rose, surprised to see more than an hour had passed. "We will notify you of our decision by next week."

"It's been my pleasure." She worked her way around the table, shaking hands, flashing that movie-star smile. "Regardless of whom you chose as your new economic development officer, I wish you much success in your endeavor. I look forward to coming back in the summer to see the changes you've wrought."

Jason ushered her out of the room, back into the reception area.

"Thank you again," he said, holding out his hand toward her. "You've obviously put a lot of thought into how you'd do the job, Ms. Langley. We appreciate your interest."

"It's Piper," she murmured, shaking his hand. "And the pleasure was all mine. It's been good to see the town again." She picked up a long, white cashmere coat and before he could help she'd wrapped it around herself, fastened the two pearl buttons in front.

A winter rose.

He got stuck on that thought, gazing at her ivory face rising out of the petal-soft cashmere.

"Mr. Franklin."

"It's Jason," he told her automatically.

"Very well, Jason." She inclined her head, flicked the sheath of sable-toned hair over one shoulder, shook his hand in finality. "Thank you for the opportunity. Goodbye." Then she turned toward the door.

Jason kept watch as she strode to her car, a grey import

rental. He waited until she'd climbed inside, until the quiet motor glided away from the town office.

She was wrong about one thing.

It wasn't goodbye. He knew that for sure.

Chapter One

"A toast to each of us for thirty great years."

Piper pushed her sunglasses to the top of her head, protection not only against the March sun's watery rays, but against the reflected glare of those highest peaks surrounding the bay where traces of winter snow still clung to the crags and dips.

She held her steaming mug of tea aloft, waiting to clink it against those of her two friends in a tradition they'd kept alive since ninth grade.

"Happy birthday, ladies. May we each find the dreams of our heart before the next thirty years pass."

Rowena Davis drank to the toast, but her patrician nose wiggled with distaste at the mint tea. Rowena was a coffee girl, the stronger the better. She quickly set down her mug before studying the other two.

"We'll hardly find any dreams here in the Bay," she complained with a motion toward the thick evergreen forest. Her dubious tone mirrored the sour look marring her lovely face.

"Don't be a grump, Row." After a grin at Piper, Ashley Adams sipped her tea, savoring the flavor thoughtfully. Ash always took her time.

"A grump? Wake up, woman." Rowena shook her head. "I can't imagine why on earth you've moved back here, Piper. Serenity Bay isn't exactly a hot spot for someone with your qualifications."

In unison they scanned the untouched forest beyond the deck, its verdant lushness broken only by jutting granite monoliths dotted here and there across the landscape. Beyond that, the bay rippled, intensely blue in the sunshine with white bands of uninhabited beach banding its coastline.

"Maybe Serenity Bay's not a hot spot, but it is calm and peaceful. And she can sail whenever she wants." Ash turned over to lie on her tummy on the lounger and peered between the deck rails, down and out across the water.

"True." Rowena laid back, closed her eyes.

"Peace and quiet are big pluses in my books these days. I may just come and visit you this summer, Pip."

The old nickname had never died despite years of protest. Strangely enough, Piper liked it now; it reminded her that they cared about her, that she wasn't all alone.

"You'd leave the big city, Ash?" Piper struggled to hide her smile. It was impossible for her to imagine her friend ignoring the lure of the galleries and new artists' showings she adored for more than a weekend.

"Yep. For a while, anyway." Ashley's golden hair swung about her shoulders as she absorbed the panoramic view. "I'd forgotten how lovely it is here. No haze of pollution, no traffic snarls. Just God's glorious creation. This invitation to join you and Row for our annual weekend birthday bash has reminded me of all the things I give up to live in my condo in Vancouver. Especially after soaking in your posh hot tub last night! The stars were spectacular."

"Total privacy is a change, too." Rowena sighed as the sun

draped her with its warmth. "You know, Pip, Cathcart House could bring in millions if you turned it into a spa."

"It already is one," Ashley joked. "Welcome to Piper's own private chichi retreat. Which I'll happily share whenever she asks."

"Anytime." Piper chuckled. "I recall you were always partial to my grandparents' home, Ash."

"No kidding." Rowena snorted. "I think she spent more time on their dock than in her own backyard those summers on the Bay."

"My grandparents never minded. They loved to see you both." The pain of their deaths still squeezed Piper's heart, though time was easing the sting of loss. It helped to recall happier times. "Remember the year Papa bought the sailboat?"

"Yes. I also remember how many times we got dunked before we figured out how to sail it." Rowena's face puckered up. "The bay never gets warm."

"But didn't it feel good to whiz past the beach and know the summer kids were envying us? We wowed 'em that year." Ashley leaned over, laid a hand on Rowena's shoulder. "In retrospect, they weren't all bad times, Row."

"No, they weren't." After a long silence, Rowena managed to summon what, for her, passed as a smile. "I had you two to go with me to school. That meant a lot."

Rowena tossed back her auburn hair as if shaking off the bad memories, then took another tentative sip of tea.

"Now tell us, Pip. What exactly are you doing back here? Besides hosting our birthday bash, I mean."

Piper leaned back, her gaze on the bay below.

"I've accepted a position as economic development officer to organize Serenity Bay's tourism authority," she told them. Stark silence greeted her announcement.

"Economic development?"

"Did she actually say that?"

Rowena looked at Ashley and both burst into giggles.

"What development? The place looks smaller now than when we used to live here. A few cottagers, some artists, a defunct lumber mill. What's to develop?"

Just as she had when she was fourteen and frustrated by their inability to see what was so clear to her, Piper clenched her jaw and grumbled, "You have no vision, Philistines."

"Oh, boy, that takes me back." Ashley laughed out loud. "Okay, David. Tell us how you're going to conquer your next Goliath."

Piper took her time, gathering her black hair into a knot and pinning it to the top of her head while making them wait. It was an old trick and it always worked. Their interest had been piqued.

"Spill it, Pip." Ashley wasn't kidding now.

She took a deep breath and began.

"It may interest you to know that Serenity Bay has a new, very forward-thinking mayor."

"Oh?"

Now they were curious. Good.

"He has plans that include making our lovely bay into a tourist mecca. And why not? We're sitting smack-dab in the middle of the most gorgeous country God ever created. All we have to do is tell the rest of the world about it."

Utter shock greeted her words. Piper knew the silence wouldn't last long. She leaned back, closed her eyes, and waited.

"You're kidding. Aren't you?" Uncertainty laced Ashley's whisper.

"She's not." The unflappable Rowena was less surprised. "Our Pip has always had a soft spot for this place. Except—"

Piper didn't like the sound of that. She opened her eyes. Sure enough, Rowena's intense scrutiny was centered on her. Faking a bland smile, Piper watched her hazel eyes change shades as quickly as her friend's thoughts. It wouldn't take Row long to home in on what she *hadn't* said.

"This new mayor you're going to be working for—"

"Aha." Ash leaned forward like a cat waiting to pounce.

"Tell us, Pip. What *exactly* is he like?" Rowena tapped one perfectly manicured fingertip against her cheek, eyes narrowed, intense.

Piper couldn't stop her blush as a picture of Jason Franklin, tousled and exceedingly handsome, swam into her brain. A most intriguing man.

To hide her thoughts she slipped on her sunglasses.

"What's he like?"

"Don't repeat the question. Answer it."

"I'm trying." Piper swallowed. "I don't know—like a mayor, I guess. He owns the marina."

"Short, fat, balding fellow, happily married with six kids?"

"Grease under his fingertips?" Ashley added.

"N-no. Not exactly."

"How 'not exactly,' Pip?" The old Row was back in form, and she was enjoying herself. She held up her fingers and began ticking them off. "No grease?"

"Uh-uh."

"Not short?"

"No."

"Not fat?"

Piper shook her head. That definitely didn't apply. Jason was lean, muscular and more toned than the men she knew who regularly worked out in expensive gyms.

"Balding? Six kids? Married?"

Flustered by the incessant questions about a man she hadn't been able to get out of her thoughts, Piper decided to spare herself the onslaught of questions and explain.

"He's—I don't know! Our age, I suppose. A little older, maybe. Tall. Sandy blond hair. Blue eyes. Good-looking."

Ashley and Rowena exchanged a look.

"Ah. So he's a beach boy."

"Beach boy? No. He owns the marina." Piper decided to change tactics. "I didn't really notice that much about him. He's just the mayor."

"Didn't notice much. Uh-huh." Rowena sniffed, checked with Ashley. "Thoughts?"

"'The lady doth protest too much, methinks,'" the blonde quoted.

"Methinks that, too."

"Look," Piper sputtered, regretting her choice of words. "It's not—"

"Maybe he's why she came back." Ashley frowned. "Either that or—" Her forehead pleated in a delicate frown. She focused on Piper. "Or there's another reason you're here."

They knew her too well.

"Is it your father? Is that why you left Calgary?"

Might as well admit it.

"Indirectly."

Both women sighed, their glances conveying their sympathy before Rowena deliberately shut down all expression. She had good reason to remember the past and even more to forget it.

"I knew it wouldn't be a young, eligible male that brought you back here." Ashley's eyes flashed with anger. "It has to be your old man at the bottom of this sudden change. How typical."

"What has the great Baron D. Wainwright done now?"

Piper didn't blame Rowena for the spite in her tone. Row

and Ash had been there for her ever since that first summer when her angry father had repeatedly ordered her back to the house where her mother had died. When she'd refused to return to a world she hated, a world where he'd become so demanding, so strict, so unlike the loving mother who'd shielded her, these two had consoled her.

Her father's angry denunciation of her still stung today, even after so many years. And then of course there was the other.

Piper pushed that away.

"Pip? Please tell us what's wrong."

They'd always listened. She could trust them.

"It's not what he's done, it's what I think he's *going* to do. The company's conducted some research on the Bay's waterfront. Past experience tells me he intends to build one of his mega hotels right on the shores of Serenity Bay."

"Oh, no." Ashley couldn't hide her dismay. "Pavement, parking lots, bars open all night? It'll ruin the place."

"Like Baron cares about the ambience of Serenity Bay." Rowena sniffed. "I'd guess he's well aware of your mayor's plans and is trying to one-up him before you can get this tourism thing organized."

Piper nodded. "My thoughts exactly."

"So your mayor isn't the only one who's seen the potential of the area." Rowena's brows drew together. "I wonder who else is involved?"

"Jason's not *my* anything," Piper insisted as heat, which had nothing to do with the sun's rays, scorched her cheeks. "I don't think either he or the other council members know about the hotel. Not yet. That's not the way Wainwright Inc. works." She paused, then copied her father's brusque tones. "First buy up the land, then dazzle the locals with lots of promises. If that doesn't get you what you want, initiate a lawsuit."

Piper pushed her chair back into the upright position, picked up the plate with her slice of birthday cake on it and took a bite. "But that's not the only reason I decided to move back."

Ash and Row stared at her.

"Dare we ask?"

"I needed to come home. The house, these cliffs, the meadow—I spent some of my happiest times here."

They nodded, each transported back to carefree summer days when life's decisions were so much simpler. Ash, Row and Piper had walked every inch of this land many times, consoling each other through puppy love, acne and a host of other trials. No matter where they went, they always came back.

"I'm tired of the nonstop meetings, of cutthroat marketers trying to outdo each other to get another star on their A-list. I guess I'm tired of the rat race. None of it seems to matter much anymore."

"And this will?"

"I think so." Piper saw the concern in their eyes and knew they were only pushing because they cared. "I have such precious memories of this place, of my grandparents and you guys, of coming home at Christmas, watching fireworks displays from Lookout Point. I want other kids to have that."

"The past always looks rosy in hindsight," Rowena muttered. "Except for mine, that is."

Ashley patted her shoulder but kept her focus on Piper. "Serenity Bay may have changed," she warned.

"Trust me, it has." Piper turned her chair so she could look across the water toward the town. "I did a little research. There's barely anyone left that we know. After the lumber mill shut down I guess folks had to move away to find work. There are more than a hundred cottages for sale."

"A hundred?"

Both wore the same stunned expression she'd had the day she'd driven around the town.

"More than. I'm sure lots of people come back in the summer but the number of permanent residents is sinking fast. I'm guessing that's why the mayor thinks the town has to act now, before it's too late."

"Back to the mayor." Row and Ash exchanged looks, then watched her, waiting.

"Why are you looking at me like that?"

"Are you sure this mayor didn't have anything to do with your decision to move back?"

"No." Piper sighed, recognizing the futility of trying to withhold anything. "I've actually been considering it for a while. After Vance died I poured myself into work. I didn't want to think about God taking my husband—or anything else."

"And work hasn't been enough?" Ashley asked softly.

"For a while I thought it was. But this birthday has me thinking, I'm not getting any younger."

"Neither are we. But we're not closing up shop and moving back here." Rowena's voice sounded harsh, but her eyes brimmed with pity. "Have you been so unhappy?"

"That's not the right word, Row. I've been rudderless, without any real goal. Serenity Bay is offering me a chance to stretch, to think outside the box. I need that challenge."

"Need?"

Piper nodded.

"Need. I want the Bay to prosper, to grow, to provide years of fun and joy for other kids, for other families—just as it did for us." She waved a hand. "This is where I want to spend my days, maybe someday raise my kids. I might even get back into Papa's gold studio during the long, frosty winter nights, see if I can create again."

"You always did have a flair for the unusual," Rowena said. "People still stop me to ask where I got this." She fingered the four-inch gold mask brooch she wore on her lapel.

"If it doesn't work out or I get tired of the solitude, I can always go back to the city. But moving here, this job—I have to try."

"Cathcart House is the perfect place to do it."

They sat together, each musing over the changes that had come into their lives.

"I keep expecting your grandmother to bring out a jug of hot chocolate and tell us to button up." Ashley sipped her tea, a half smile curving her lips.

"Last night I thought I heard your grandfather's snores." Rowena shrugged at their surprise. "What? Even I have normal dreams sometimes."

"They left Cathcart House entirely to you, Pip? You don't have to share it with your brother or anything?"

"They left Dylan cash. He never seemed to like the Bay, remember?" Piper shrugged. "I never understood that but he seemed happy enough with his share when I talked to him after their wills were read."

"Was your father at the funeral?"

"No." Piper swallowed hard. "At least, I didn't see him."

"It would be a bit much to expect him to show sorrow, wouldn't it? As I recall there was no love lost between your grandparents and him." Rowena tossed the rest of the tea over the side of the deck. "Though I must admit, I never heard them say a word against him."

"Gran always said God would handle him so she didn't have to worry."

The three remained silent for a few moments in sober remembrance.

"So you're not too concerned about your father or his plans?" Ashley asked, her forehead pleated in a tiny furrow.

Concerned, worried and a whole lot more. But Piper wouldn't say that or these two friends would fuss about her. She didn't want that.

"I want to be here to help with development if I can. That beach is glorious. There's no way I'm going to sit back and watch a Wainwright hotel ruin it."

"You're sure that's his plan?"

Piper nodded. "One of them."

"And if he sways the council to his way of thinking? What will you do then?" Ashley pressed, her face expressing her concern.

"Pray." Like praying had saved Vance's life. Piper pushed down the anger. God's will, not mine, she reminded herself.

"Changing Baron Wainwright would take an act of God, all right." Rowena snorted. "Other people's plans have never mattered to him. Did you hear about that Wainwright project in London? There are rumors that officials received bribes to pass some inspections."

"I hadn't heard." Piper sloughed off her gloomy feelings, determined that nothing would spoil her joy in having her friends visit. "Anyway, I'm going to do what I can here. This job means I'll be kept abreast of everything that goes on in Serenity Bay so, hopefully, I'll be one step ahead."

"Ever the optimist, that's our Pip."

"It's not optimism, Row. It's determination." She narrowed her gaze trying to make them understand. "I want to prove something and this is the perfect place."

"You don't have to prove anything to us, honey." Ashley rose, moved to fling her arms around Piper. "We already know you can do anything you set your mind on."

"Thank you." She hugged Ash right back. "But I have to prove it to myself, here, in this place. I didn't come back to see my grandparents as often as I should have when they were here. Maybe I can keep their dreams for Cathcart House and the Bay alive."

"Do it for yourself, Piper. Don't do it to prove something to your father," Row warned. "We all know he's not worth the effort, not after his behavior toward Vance. Just know that if this is what you want, we're behind you all the way."

"She's right. The Bayside Trio takes on tough challenges and rides 'em out no matter what. We're fearless females just waiting to vanquish our foes." Ashley thrust her arm above her head in the charge they'd chanted since grade nine. "Onward and upward!"

"Onward and upward," Piper and Row repeated, grinning as if they were fifteen again and the world was just waiting for them.

"Here's to your thirty-first year, Pip. You go, girl."

Rowena dumped a splash of the hated tea into her cup and the three friends held up their mugs in a toast. Their admiration went a long way toward reassuring Piper that she'd made the right decision. She drank to her own success, giggled at Rowena's jokes and answered Ashley's questions as best she could.

But that night, after the party was over and her friends had left to return to their own lives, Piper lay alone in the big house and let her thoughts tumble into free fall. It was time to face the truth.

She'd told Ashley and Rowena that she wanted to help the Bay grow, and that was true. But more than that, she wanted to stop her father from ruining the one place she called home. And he would ruin it. He ruined everything he touched. Her childhood, her relationship with her brother. Every summer that she'd returned here from boarding school he'd arrived to make a scene about her coming back to live with him. She'd gone back twice—and regretted both. She'd even tried to work with him once. He'd ruined that, too, treating her like a stupid child. So she'd left Wainwright Inc., built a name for herself.

And even after that she'd given him one more chance, a chance to make the difference between life and death, a chance to prove he loved her. He'd blown her off, refused to help.

Well, he would not ruin Serenity Bay. There would be none of the gaudy neon lights his hotels boasted, no famous rock bands blaring till four in the morning and leaving mayhem behind, nobody wandering the streets at all hours, causing a disturbance. Not here. Not while she could stop it.

Curious sounds so different from the city noise she was accustomed to carried down the cliff's side on a light breeze that fluttered the bedroom curtains.

Piper got up for a glass of water, and noticed someone moving across her property toward the peak of the cliff. At a certain point he or she stopped, removed something from a backpack and knelt down. A second later the figure had disappeared.

Lookout Point had always been a place where teens met for a good-night kiss. That's probably who was out there now.

She stood watching for a moment, her thoughts drifting to the mayor and the many plans he had for the direction the town should take. She'd never had a problem working with anyone before, but something about the way Jason Franklin had watched her respond to the council's questions made her wonder if he was as confident of her abilities as he'd said.

In her past jobs she'd been given a mandate and left to accomplish it, filing the paperwork, making her reports at the appropriate stages. But primarily she'd been her own boss. A tiny voice in the back of her head told her this job wouldn't be like that. Mayor Franklin had an agenda. He wanted the Bay to start growing and he wanted it to happen his way. From what he'd said, Piper was fairly certain he wanted it to happen yesterday. It might be hard to appease him when developers didn't immediately respond to her initial probes.

She smothered a yawn and padded back to bed.

Whatever happened, happened. She'd deal with it.

Maybe in doing her job she could coax Jason's diamond-blue eyes to come alive, maybe get him to loosen up a little. Piper had a hunch that somewhere under all that grit and determination, a guy with a sense of humor lurked.

Maybe the girls were right. Maybe Jason Franklin would turn out to be more than the mayor.

Maybe she could finally come to terms with why God had taken away the only people who'd loved her and left her with a father who couldn't see beyond his money to the daughter who wanted to be loved.

Chapter Two

When he'd handed in his resignation in Boston, he'd been told he wouldn't last a year in the sticks.

A lot they knew.

Not only had he endured, he was thriving.

Jason swallowed the last of his morning coffee, certain he'd never tire of this view. He had no desire to go back. Not to traitors....

Don't think about it.

He jerked to his feet. In his haste to escape what he couldn't forget, he almost crashed the foot of his chair into the Plexiglas panel surrounding the deck.

"Calm down," he ordered his racing pulse. "Just calm down. Forget the past. Let it die."

Easier said than done.

Originally he'd thought living on top of his marina store was the kind of kooky idea one of his former high-flying clients might have come up with. But after two years in Serenity Bay, he still relished his perch high above the water.

His neighbor to the left was an age-old forest whose trees

sheltered him from the wind. On the right, Jason shared the view with the docks and a public beach.

Nobody watched him, and he only watched the water. A little lonely, perhaps. But then again, he'd come to Serenity Bay for the solitude. At least that's what he told himself.

Today the sun shone, the water sparkled and sent the wind skimming over the land in a faint caress. Serenity Bay looked picture-perfect.

He squinted across the lake. That early sailor with two sheets billowing in the wind was bolder than most. The fun seekers he'd once hung around with wouldn't have endured more than five minutes of this cool April breeze blowing off the barely thawed lake before they'd turn back.

But this sailor didn't hesitate. The craft continued on a clear, invisible course directed by sure and steady hands, straight toward Jason. The streamlined hull pointed into the wind with gutsy determination. He liked the brashness of it— thrusting ahead on an unswerving course to get where you were going, no matter what.

That's what he was doing.

Fresh air, pure sunshine and a landscape only the Creator could have fashioned was about all anyone could ask.

Just about.

"Lucky guy." He wasted several minutes watching the pristine sailboat flit across the water like a butterfly set free from the cocoon of winter. Then he decided it was time to get to work.

He balanced his last cinnamon bun and a thermos of coffee in one hand, pulled the door closed with the other and descended the circular stairs into his office, unable to resist a glance through the wall of windows that overlooked the lake.

The sailboat was making good time. Obviously whoever was operating her knew exactly what he was doing.

At the height of summer when the days were heavy with heat and the promise of cool lake water beckoned, Jason often envied the freedom and peace a sailboat offered. But he freely admitted his knowledge lay in engines, the kind that sent speedboats tearing across the lakes, towing skiers or tube riders through the water. Or the kind that powered fishing boats and let them troll at a leisurely pace. Engines he understood. He could talk motors with the best of them.

But sailing? You needed money for beauties like that sailboat, and men who built marinas in small lake towns that development hadn't yet reached seldom found cash to spare.

A noise drew his attention to the dock and he stepped outside.

"Hey, Andy. Did you get those rentals all cleaned up?"

"Yes, sir." Andy saluted him, then grinned. "You find the customers, I've got the boats spick-and-span."

The kid looked like a double for an actor on *Gilligan's Island*. That effect was enhanced by a kooky sailor cap Andy loved, but which always slipped to one side of his shiny head.

"Ready to roll, boss. I also swabbed the decks, checked the minnow stock and measured the gas tank. We're good to go on all counts. Now I'll get at that painting."

"Good job." The boy was an employer's dream. He took pride in accomplishing his duties before being asked.

Andy reminded Jason of himself, long ago, before he'd learned that fresh-faced eagerness wasn't necessarily an asset in the corporate world.

"You see that?" Andy's gaze was also on the trim red craft and the pristine sails. "She's a beauty, isn't she?"

The sharp bow cut cleanly through the crest of waves, zooming ever closer, sails puffed out smooth. As they watched, the boat tacked left, turning in a perfect half circle as it headed into the harbor, straight toward them.

"I hope he knows how to bring her in. It'll cost a fortune if I have to get those docks redone."

Andy grinned, shaking his head.

"Don't worry, boss. The way that beauty's moving, there's no novice at the helm. Man, I'd love a chance to go out in her."

Who wouldn't? Jason pretended to busy himself, but he kept close watch as the sailor trimmed his sails perfectly and the delicate red hull slipped easily into dock. He turned away, refusing to let the owner of such magnificence witness his jealousy. Someday, when he retired, maybe he'd get a boat like that.

Someday.

"Ahoy, there. Mind tying me off?"

That voice was familiar. Jason twisted around, watched Andy snatch the line tossed at him and fasten stem and stern so that the sailboat was perfectly docked against Styrofoam buoys that would keep its hull mar free. Golden letters in a delicate font shone from the bow. *Shalimar*.

The sailboat's captain accepted Andy's hand and stepped onto the dock. Once the thick coat was unzipped and he caught a glimpse of her face, Jason realized the sailor was a woman.

Piper Langley.

She tossed her coat inside the hull, then drew the red knitted cap she was wearing from her head and flipped it into the boat, allowing her glossy black curls to dance in the breeze.

"Thank you, kind sir." She curtsied to Andy, then strode toward Jason. "Good morning, Mayor."

"Good morning."

He couldn't help but stare at her bouncy haircut. It had been a long mane of ebony when they'd first met. He'd dreamed about that hair. He couldn't decide which style he preferred.

Her ice-blue shirt and matching slacks managed to look

both businesslike and chic. The wool jacket added to her polished look, though her eyes weren't businesslike at all. He swallowed, rejecting the flash of interest that prickled whenever he talked to her.

"I didn't realize—that is, er…" He hesitated. "You'll need a car, Miss Langley. The area is large and our public transportation isn't up to big-city standards."

She frowned, obviously trying to decipher his curt tone.

"Please call me Piper," she begged. "I don't get to sail very often so I thought this would be the perfect way to commute across the lake. I left my car here." Her gaze brushed over the boat in obvious fondness, then she focused on him and the brown eyes darkened to almost black.

"I paid for the berth. Yesterday."

Andy hadn't told him. Jason wished he could time-warp back about an hour and do this all over again. Though it was a little late to explain, he gave it his best shot.

"I wasn't implying anything. I just wanted to be sure you knew you'd need a car." Idiot! How old was he that her appearance could knock him for a loop?

"I don't know whether or not I explained to you when we talked before, Mr. Franklin, but years ago I lived in Serenity Bay. I'm familiar with the need for wheels around here."

She smiled and it was a glorious thing. Her skin glowed, her eyes shone and her curls danced in the breeze. She was more beautiful than he remembered.

"No, I don't believe you mentioned that." *Otherwise, I wouldn't have made an idiot of myself talking about public transportation.*

Her gaze held his. A zap of awareness shot between them.

"Well, I did. Six summers, actually."

"Really?"

"They were some of the best times of my life."

Which meant—what? That she was here to recapture the past? That her life had taken a downturn and she'd returned to start over?

"That explains your enthusiasm for this place then." And her knowledge of the economic possibilities in the area.

"I guess." She continued to watch him, her scrutiny unflinching.

"What do you have planned, Miss Langley?"

"You're the boss. Shouldn't you be telling me, Mr. Franklin?" Heavy emphasis on the *Mr*.

"Actually I didn't think you would start till Monday."

"Why wait?"

She stood tall and proud, head tipped back, face impassive as her glance clashed with his. She shifted as if she were eager to get on with things.

Something was tapping. Jason looked down, noticed that her blue shoes matched the blue of her suit perfectly, and that the toe of one was rapping impatiently against the dock.

During his Boston years, Jason had known a lot of women. But he'd never met one who couldn't stand still for even a few minutes. Piper Langley pulsed with leashed energy.

She cleared her throat. "Mr. Franklin?"

"I prefer Jason. We're informal around here. Okay, Piper?" He smiled, showing there were no hard feelings. "Now perhaps—"

"Wait a minute. Jason. Jason Franklin. Man, I'm slow." The whispered words slipped through her lips on a breath of recognition.

He froze.

"There was a rather well-known Jason Franklin who gained the reputation of finding fantastic recreation property that developers could evolve into spectacular tourism centers. He worked for a company called Expectations in Boston." She paused, searching his face while she waited for his response.

"Guilty," he admitted, heart sinking. "But that was in the past. Now I'm my own boss." *And I like it that way, so don't ask any more questions.*

"Of course." She nodded, obviously receiving his message loud and clear.

Immediately Jason wondered exactly what she'd heard, and from whom.

"It's a wonderful marina," she murmured. "We never had anything like this when I was here."

"Thank you. I've enjoyed putting it together."

Then in the blink of an eye, Piper Langley became all business.

"I've done some preliminary work since you offered me the job of economic development officer. I hope that's all right?" One finely arched eyebrow quirked up, daring him to say it wasn't.

"Great."

"Nothing too risky, but I thought one way to begin getting Serenity Bay on the map might be to initiate a fishing tournament, with a rather large prize. I realize it's only the first of April, but these things take a while to publicize and we don't want to miss the season." She glanced around, took in the lack of customers. "Do you have time to discuss some of my plans now?"

As mayor, he'd made her the offer on behalf of the town council, agreeing to hold the position until she was released from her current job. Her eagerness to get started was a far better beginning than Jason had dared expect.

He'd known she was the right one at their first meeting. Looked as though he was about to be proved correct.

"Now's a bad time?" The toe was tapping again.

Jason considered his schedule. Saturday. There would be very few people looking for a boat to rent this early in the season. Maybe a couple of guys would drop in looking for new rods and reels, but the majority of the cottagers hadn't opened up their summer homes yet and those year-round residents who weren't enjoying the sunshine were more likely to be planting what little garden they could, rather than visiting his marina.

"Now is good," he agreed. "Why don't you come inside, into my office? I've got some coffee already made."

"Great." She followed him. "Thank you."

Early on in life Jason had learned that tidiness was an asset with inestimable value. Today it proved its worth, especially when he found himself oddly confused by her presence in his personal space.

"Great office."

"Yes, it is." Jason checked for sarcasm but her appreciation seemed genuine. He castigated himself for suspecting her motives. Not everybody was insincere.

"I chose this side of the building specifically because of the natural woodlands next door. I don't have to worry about neighbors building over my view, or at least I hope I won't. The council hasn't approved the zoning yet."

"From here you can see across the entire store and down the marina." Piper trailed one finger over the metal filing cabinets that bordered his office, but did not obstruct his view. "Smart man. Do you live upstairs?"

"Yes." Why the sudden curiosity?

"It must be a dream to wake up to this view every morning."

"You wake up to the same thing, don't you?" He nodded toward the lake.

Her eyes widened in surprise. "Yes, I guess I do." She chuckled. "I keep forgetting that I'm here for good. Which reminds me—do you know what's happening up on Lookout Point? I went walking yesterday and noticed someone's been doing some digging."

"I have no idea. A telecommunications company has a tower near there, don't they? Maybe it's something to do with that. We've been begging them to install a higher tower to improve cell phone coverage."

"Maybe that's it." The brown eyes sparkled with interest. "You've put a lot of thought into a variety of aspects of development."

"Yes, I have."

"Good. You can give me some ideas." She rubbed her cheek with her thumb, then shrugged. "Seems a shame for land like Lookout Point to be used for something as mundane as a tower. It has spectacular cliffs and a view to die for. And some of the best wild strawberries you've ever tasted."

"I haven't been over there much. You're staying nearby?"

"At Cathcart House. It was my grandparents' and they left it to me. The land from Lookout Point once belonged to my Gran's family."

Jason hadn't lived in Serenity Bay for two years without hearing some of the old-timers rave about the parties at Cathcart House. There was a private beach, private docks, an oversize boathouse and a gazebo for parties on the lawns.

Piper Langley came from money. He probably should have figured that out, given her chic clothes and perfectly styled hair. It made her presence here in the backwoods even more curious.

"The house is far too big for one person, but—" she shrugged "—I love it. Every room is full of memories."

He envied her that strong sense of family identity. He'd never had it. Maybe that's why he pushed so hard for Serenity Bay to be the kind of place families could be together.

Most of the time the land acquisition team he'd been part of at Expectations seemed a thousand miles away, part of the distant past. Then he'd remember Trevor and that horrible feeling of being duped and he was right back there. Once he'd almost been willing to sell his soul to buy a piece of Expectations—so deep went his need to be part of something important and fulfilling.

Jason blinked back to reality when Piper swung a briefcase onto his desk. He hadn't even noticed her carrying it.

"I took the liberty of drafting up a few ideas for you to look over, Jason." She took a quick look at him over one shoulder as if to check he was listening, then spread charts and graphs across his desk. "I've been talking to several corporate heads and put together a list of those who might be willing to chip in as sponsors for different events I've planned for the summer."

The woman twigged his curiosity. According to her résumé, she'd had a great job in Calgary. Her boss had told him confidentially that when she'd resigned, she'd refused a substantial raise to stay, even given them rather short notice to come to Serenity Bay. Yet no one Jason contacted had said anything negative about her. Rather, they were very vocal with their praise of her skills.

Cathcart House couldn't be the only thing drawing her back. She could have kept that as a summer place, visited during her vacations. Instead she'd made a permanent move from the city to the middle of nowhere.

Stop questioning your good luck, Franklin.

"As you can see, I've scheduled events throughout the

summer and fall. That way we can maximize the exposure without running ourselves ragged."

Jason hadn't heard all of what she'd said, but what he had absorbed told him her plans were ambitious. And clearly thought out.

"Piper. Why are you here?"

She feigned composure, but Jason caught the slight tremor in her hand, the way her eyes flickered before she glanced down.

"I'm here to do a job, to help make Serenity Bay a desirable getaway for those who want a healthy, natural vacation." She looked up, met his stare. "Isn't that what you wanted?"

Her voice was quiet, relaxed. And yet something nagged at him.

"Yes, it's what we want," he admitted.

"Do you want me to leave?"

"Of course not. We're delighted that someone with your qualifications is willing to take on the project." He paused, unsure of exactly the right words that would voice his feelings.

"You have doubts about my ability."

"Not really. It's just…I can't help speculating why you chose to return at this particular time. Your grandparents—?"

"They moved into a nursing home in Toronto about three years ago. They've since passed away."

"I'm sorry."

"Thanks." Piper's clear skin flushed. "If there's a problem with my references—"

He shook his head. "No, there's no problem."

She frowned, lifted one palm. "Then—"

He was an idiot to question the best thing that had happened since he'd been elected mayor. Everything he'd learned said she was great at what she did. That should be enough.

"Forgive my question. I've been told I'm a little obsessed

when it comes to our bay." He smiled, hunkering down to peer at her work. "This looks very aggressive."

Piper didn't answer for several minutes, but when she did, a guarded note edged her voice in cool reserve.

"I thought that was the point. Didn't you want to start showing the world what treasures you have here in cottage country?"

"Yes, of course. Could you explain the first step?"

"It will be a weekend extravaganza, to whet appetites so people will want to come back."

Maybe Serenity Bay was her escape, too.

Jason nodded as if he'd understood. But he hadn't. Especially about that winter festival. He'd been thinking about promoting the Bay as a summer resort town and now she was talking about year-round development.

"Is there anyone you might know who could offer me some input on current local activities?"

He thought a moment, then nodded.

"The artists' guild is meeting this afternoon. They're the primary draw for outsiders at the moment. We have quite a number of local artisans. Weavers, painters, potters, stained-glass artists. Several earn a living from their work but most of them have to go to the other towns to capitalize on the customers that flood in during the summer."

"If we bring people in here, that will change. I can understand why they live here. The beauty stimulates your creative genes."

"Are you an artist, too?" He somehow couldn't imagine her spattered in paint.

"My grandfather was a goldsmith, my grandmother a jewelry designer. They taught me. I'd like to get back to it one of these days."

Gold. Yeah, that fit her perfectly.

"I see you have a tour program proposed," Jason said.

"Some of the guild members would certainly go for that. Why not ask for volunteers to help with the extravaganza thing? That way you'd get to know them sooner."

"Yes, I'd thought of that." Her eyes glittered like black onyx. "This is going to be a very exciting time in Serenity Bay, Jason. I can't wait to see what happens."

"Neither can I." He cleared his throat.

"But?" She frowned.

"I'd appreciate it if you'd keep me in the loop about what you're doing. The council has several ideas of their own. We don't want to overlap."

"Don't worry, I'll keep you informed of whatever's happening. Thanks for your support." In a flash she gathered her papers and replaced them in her briefcase.

Five minutes later Piper Langley was walking down the pier toward a small red compact that sat in the parking lot.

Jason waited until he saw her taillights disappear, then he picked up the phone.

"Hey, Ida. How are you?" He chuckled at the growl from the town's secretary. Ida's bark was always worse than her bite. "Yes, I do know you're off work today. I just want to ask you something. Our new economic development officer is officially on the job. Can you let me know if she asks you for anything special?"

"Asks me for something? Like what?" Ida Cranbrook never skirted an issue. She claimed she was too old for that. "Pens? Paper?"

"You know what I mean. I just want to make sure she and I are on the same channel," he muttered. "We haven't got much of a budget. I don't want to see it squandered."

"You think she'll do that? A woman with her reputation?"

"Well—"

"You don't have to spell it out. I get it, Jason. You want to approve everything before she does it."

"You make that sound like a bad thing." Silence. Jason sighed. "I just need to know. Okay? Satisfied?"

"Not nearly." She cackled at her own joke. "You're the boss, Jason. If you want me to spy on the girl and give you daily reports, I suppose I'll have to do it. But I won't like it."

"I'm not asking you to spy on her."

"Ha!" Ida Cranbrook was no fool.

"Never mind. Sorry I bothered you, Ida. Especially on your day off."

"Doesn't matter a bit. Harold's nodded off to sleep in the middle of one of those car races, anyway. I just started spicing up some ribs for dinner. You interested?"

Interested in Ida Cranbrook's specially prepared, mouth-watering ribs? Was a fish interested in water?

"Just tell me when and where." His stomach growled at the thought of those succulent bits of artery-clogging pleasure.

"Six o'clock. And bring the girl. From what I saw at the interview, she looks like she could use some meat on those bones. Besides, then we can all watch her, make sure she doesn't pull a fast one on us." Ida barked a laugh, then hung up.

In one weak moment he'd confided his past and the betrayal that had precipitated his leaving Expectations. Now Ida could read him like a book—which Jason found extremely disconcerting.

So was inviting Piper Langley to go with him to Ida's. Piper of the iceberg-blue suit and immaculate makeup. He just couldn't envision her dripping in barbecue sauce and grease. Seemed a little like casting pearls into the mud to him.

Good looks and nice clothes had nothing to do with the person inside. He'd learned not to judge by exteriors and he couldn't afford to forget that lesson. Besides, he'd never yet met a person who didn't love Ida's ribs. Between Ida, Harold and himself, they should be able to find out more about the new owner of Cathcart House.

Jason drank the coffee he'd forgotten to pour for Piper wishing he'd told her straight up that he intended to be involved in every part of her plans.

Jason had compared her to a rose, but roses had thorns that could draw blood, cause pain. Fine. He could deal with that. But Serenity Bay's development was his chance to put his mark on the world, and he wasn't about to let anybody ruin that.

Jason had survived the shame of being duped by someone he trusted, had weathered whispers, mended broken relationships with each of his clients while he worked out his notice at Expectations and left a job he loved. He'd endured the sly looks at a wedding that should have been his by planning a new dream and praying for forgiveness while he struggled to trust God for a new plan for his future. He still wasn't certain he was where God wanted him, though he prayed about it daily.

Putting Serenity Bay on the tourism map without input from the major developers he'd once worked with would show anybody who doubted him that he could still make it in the big leagues.

He'd been duped once. But nobody, including Piper Langley, was going to fool him into trusting wrongly again.

Chapter Three

"I'm glad you asked me to join you tonight. I've never met Ida Cranbrook. At least, I don't think I have. I'm sure she wasn't around when I lived here before."

"She and Harold have only been here a little longer than me."

Piper climbed from Jason's truck and walked toward a cottage that looked like Hansel and Gretel's gingerbread house. She sniffed the air.

"Oh, that aroma is marvelous. I love ribs."

"You'll like them even more after you taste Ida's. She has this secret recipe. Every year more and more people try to copy it."

"Maybe I could wheedle it from her for the good of the town. You know, 'Come to Serenity Bay and sample Ida's ribs.' Something like that." Piper smiled at Jason, liking the way his hair flopped across his forehead. He was so different from the corporate stiffs she usually worked with.

"Nobody has managed to get it out of her yet, so you'd have a coup if you did." His fingers grazed her elbow as he directed her up the two steps to the front door.

"Hmm. I'll try hard, then."

"Ida's also the sounding board for the entire community. She knows everything about everything. What she doesn't know, she'll find out."

"Ah, an unimpeachable source. Good."

He laughed, rapped the door twice, then opened it.

"We're here," he announced in a loud voice, then motioned for Piper to precede him inside.

A man emerged from the room beyond, ducking his head to walk beneath the low, exposed beams.

"Don't call her," he murmured, shaking his head as he beckoned them inside. "She's at the crucial stage."

"Of what?"

"I don't know, exactly, but she says it's crucial." He held out his hand, smiled at Piper. "I'm Harold Cranbrook, Ida's husband. And you're the lady who's going to put the Bay on the map. Come on in."

"Piper Langley." She shook his hand. "And I hope you're right."

"Jason hasn't steered us wrong yet."

As far as she could tell, everybody liked Jason. That would make it easier to work for him. She hoped.

Piper glanced around. It was like walking into a doll's house. Everything seemed so tiny. How did a man as large as Harold endure living among all this china, crystal and dolls?

"Ida's out on the deck. Is it too chilly for us to join her?"

"Let's do," Piper agreed, relieved they'd be away from the fragile objects, at least for a little while. She eased left, leaving a wide gap between her leg and the tiny, blue china ladies perched atop a table, then blushed when Jason winked at her and followed suit on tiptoe.

"Hey there! I didn't hear you arrive. Come on out." Ida slid open the patio door, then wrapped her tiny arms around Jason in a hug. She did the same to Piper. "I'm glad you could come, Miss Langley. Welcome to Serenity Bay."

"Thank you. It was sweet of you to invite me."

"Jason told me you used to live here. We only moved here two and a half years ago, so I didn't know your grandparents, but I've heard a lot about Sara and Gordon Young from the old-timers on the Bay." She basted the ribs, pushed a fork against the meat, then shook her head and closed the lid. "People used to talk about how he'd sail her around the coves in that cute little sailboat. What's it called—*Shalimar,* that's it. Such an unusual name." Ida glanced at Jason, raised one eyebrow.

"Papa said it sounded like a faraway place you'd escape to. That's why he chose it." Piper noticed some kind of under-current running between the mayor and his office helper. She decided to wait and see what it was about.

"Piper uses *Shalimar* to get to work." Jason's gaze remained on the sizzling barbecue.

"Only when it's good weather," she said.

"Like today. I heard you've been talking to the guild." Ida glanced at Jason as if she knew something. "So has Piper given you her report yet?"

"What report?" Piper glanced back and forth, even checked Harold's expression. "Did I miss something?"

"Jason here is a bit obsessive when it comes to business in the Bay. Scratch that. He's a lot obsessive. Not that he doesn't have a good reason. Betrayal by your best friend is never nice." Ida patted his shoulder as if he were six. "If my hunch is right, and it is, he'll want to know exactly what you did this afternoon."

"But he already knows. I told him my plans this morning." Piper accepted a seat on a wicker chair, then glanced at Jason. He was frowning at Ida. Piper didn't blame him. Being betrayed by your best friend sounded horrible.

Maybe that's why he'd come to Serenity Bay, to prove to the powers at Expectations that he could handle more than one aspect of development. Maybe he hoped his work here would push him up their career ladder faster. *Please, not another Baron.*

"I am not obsessive."

"Ha!" The tiny woman sat down, crossed her arms over her thin chest. "You like to pretend you aren't, but you're totally obsessed by the Bay's future." She looked at Piper. "Controlling, too."

"Stop badgering the boy, Ida. We elected him to be concerned about Serenity Bay. I'd say he's doing his job perfectly." Harold turned to Piper, lowering his voice. "They're like two five-year-olds in a school yard. Best to change the subject. You got a boyfriend?"

Piper gulped. What ribs could be worth this?

"Don't answer that. Harold fancies himself a matchmaker. You give him the least bit of information and he'll go hunting up a beau for you." Ida poked Jason's leg. "You read those test results?

"What tests? I go to the boat show in Toronto for two days and you've got people doing tests?"

"I do my job," the older woman sniffed. "Public health said we had to have a water check. I got it done. No problem there."

"Good."

Ida stood and peeked under the barbecue lid, adjusted the heat.

"Ribs need a few more minutes," she explained. She wiped her hands on a towel hanging on the front of the barbecue. "Water's okay, but we do have a problem with some of the campsite facilities. He's going to let you know."

"Fine." Jason switched subjects, but he didn't meet her

stare. "Piper thought someone was working up on Lookout Point. Know anything about that, Ida?"

"Nope. But the telephone people visit it in the spring and the fall. Could be them." She turned to Piper. "What was Serenity Bay like when you used to come here?"

"Pretty much the same. Maybe there were a few more people but then I was mostly here in the summer. In the winter Gran and Papa went to Florida but only after we celebrated Christmas together at Cathcart House." She didn't want to talk about the past. "About the summer people—do you know the kind of radius you're drawing from?"

"We've done some surveys." Ida prattled on about the city dwellers who came north to get away.

"Would you be able to get me a list with addresses? I'd like to get an idea of our current market."

"Sure." Ida shrugged as if it wasn't important. "I'm in Tuesday."

"Do you always take Mondays off?"

"Unless there's something pressing. The town hasn't got enough money for full-time office staff in the winter." Ida plunked down on one of the patio chairs. "I'll start working full-time after Easter."

"Is there any new industry in the area?" she asked, looking for something to hang her plans on. "There used to be a sawmill—"

"It's been closed for years." Harold pulled out a map. "I heard that years ago some folks found a nice vein of copper up past the mill road—about there," he said, pointing. "Purest ever seen, according to the stories. Shone in the sun as if it had been molded into those rocks forever. People used to stop by, take little pieces of it. Few years of that and it was gone, too." He shrugged. "But it brought the place a minute or two of fame."

While he'd been speaking, Ida had hurried away. She now returned with a platter and scooped the ribs off the barbecue onto it and handed it to Harold.

"Time to eat," she announced.

Piper followed Ida to the dining room, where a long buffet table, six chairs and a huge black table were set.

"Piper, you sit there. Jason can sit across from you and Harold and I will hold down the ends. Good. Now, grace, Harold."

Harold gave thanks, then picked up one of the plates stacked in front of him and began to load it with ribs, creamy mashed potatoes and bright green peas.

"Oh, my!" Piper gaped when he placed it in front of her. "It looks delicious, but it's way too much. Perhaps you can make me a smaller plate."

"Nonsense! You get started on Ida's ribs, you won't stop."

Piper looked at Jason while searching her brain for some way to make them understand that she would never be able to eat what she'd been served. But Jason was busy eyeing his own heaping plate and spared her only a quick grin as he picked up a rib.

"Try them first," he advised, then bit into the succulent meat.

Since everyone else had begun to eat, Piper followed their lead. She picked up the smallest piece between two fingers and nibbled at the end. The spices hit her tongue like those candy Pop Rocks she and her friends used to buy for a quarter and leave on their tongues while the flavors fizzled and hissed.

Only better. Much, much better.

Silence reigned as the four of them enjoyed their meals. Piper waited until Ida had coaxed everyone into seconds before she asked her, "Have you noticed anyone looking around the town recently?"

"Oh, we get Looky Lou's all the time. Never amounts to a

thing. Funny fellow with big glasses was in the office when Jason was away. Biggest brown eyes I ever saw. Wanted to know about the beach. It's sand. What more could I say?" She croaked a laugh at her own joke.

So Wainwright Inc. *had* sent someone to check things out. It was strange Dylan was doing on-site research these days.

Piper realized Jason's blue eyes were on her. A smear of sauce dotted his cheek.

"Something wrong?" he asked.

"Not really. I just wondered if a corporation was already interested. I didn't see a hotel in town—"

"Exactly what I've been telling the council," Jason exclaimed. "The no-tell motel is hardly the kind of place we want to showcase, though it's clean enough. But Bart doesn't think there's any point in painting or modernizing the place, especially since business has been so slow. If he heard he'd have some competition, I imagine he'd sink some cash into his outfit pronto."

"So nobody's talked to you about building a hotel?" Piper had hoped for nonchalance but knew it hadn't quite come off when Jason's curious stare stayed on her. He couldn't know why she was asking, could he?

"To me personally? No." He turned toward the older woman. "Ida, you didn't get the name of this man, did you?"

Ida set down her fork, her forehead wrinkled.

"He gave one. I just don't remember what it was. Young fellow, really friendly. I might have written it down. I'll check on Tuesday." Her scrutiny shifted to Piper, grew more intense. "Why are you so interested in this guy?" she asked.

"If he was scouting locations, I'd like to talk to him," she ad-libbed. "Maybe the town can dangle a carrot that would encourage someone to build."

"We don't have much to dangle," Ida mumbled, her face

skeptical. She forgot the subject they'd been discussing, until later when Piper was drying dishes beside her.

"You know who was here snooping around don't you?"

"I could guess. I have a few feelers out with friends who suggested a company but I'll have to do more checking." She kept her attention on the glass she was drying.

"He kept asking about bylaws to do with the beach. You think someone wants to put a hotel right on it—like in Hawaii?" Ida swished the suds down the drain, then hung her dishcloth over the sink. "That might not be a bad idea."

Piper set down the last dry dish, searching for a way to express her concern.

"It could work, with a lot of input from the town council. But we don't want such a beautiful beach to be ruined."

"By pollution, you mean?" Ida shrugged. "I'm sure the government has lots of laws to control that sort of thing."

"Not just pollution. The wholesome atmosphere of the town has to be protected if we want to attract families. We don't want a bar near little kids playing in the sand."

"Goes without saying." Apparently her explanation satisfied Ida, who then busied herself filling the coffee decanter with water. "Stays light longer now. Would you like to join us outside and watch the stars come out?"

"They are beautiful, but don't make any coffee for me. Thanks, Ida. I have to be going. I sailed over and I need to get back before dark."

"Harold and I probably shouldn't be drinking coffee before bed, anyway. Harold always dreams." Ida pulled open the fridge and took out a jug of red juice. "Can I interest you in some cranberry juice? Made it myself."

"Could I try it another time?" Piper glanced at her watch, unwilling to believe the time on the kitchen clock was correct.

"You're welcome anytime. Bring Jason with you. He says he likes his own cooking, but he doesn't cook much. Gets most of his nourishment from those cinnamon buns he buys at the farmers' market. I try to fatten him up."

If Piper was any judge, the fattening up would take a while. Jason Franklin didn't have a spare ounce on him. Rather, he had a polished, muscular look that made her think of a jaguar. From the state of his sneakers, she suspected he jogged to stay in shape. No wonder he could eat cinnamon buns whenever he wanted.

"Thank you very much for dinner. It was so delicious, I won't have to think about another meal for days. And if you ever want to let me in on your secret rib recipe…" Piper let the sentence trail away when Ida shook her head firmly.

"Can't do that, but you're welcome to share them anytime."

"Thank you. And you and Harold are always welcome at Cathcart House."

The dock was only a few minutes' walk from Ida's, but Jason insisted on driving Piper.

"I would have walked here with you, but I wanted to drop off Harold's motor." He hoisted the machine out of his truck bed and stood it against the workshop where Ida's husband waited beside the birdhouses he'd carved from driftwood.

They thanked the couple for the meal, wishing them goodnight before riding back to the marina. Silence stretched awkwardly between them. Piper couldn't think of a thing to say.

"Are you going to be able to get back safely?" Jason asked as he unfastened her boat from its moorings.

The evening had grown cool and Piper tugged her coat from its hiding place in the hatch of the sailboat. "Oh, yes. I'll be fine."

Jason scanned the sky.

"There's a storm blowing in," he told her. "You could get swamped."

She tried to explain that she'd been sailing many times, and had handled her fair share of rough weather, but he refused to listen.

"I'll tie your boat behind mine. I've got an inboard that can weather anything. It won't take long to zip across the lake. Besides, I'll feel a whole lot better if I know for certain that you're home, dry and safe. The lake water is too cold to capsize in."

She couldn't talk him out of it, and so a few moments later Piper found herself seated beside him in his boat, watching the familiar coastline fly past. Truthfully she enjoyed the feeling of knowing someone cared. It had been a long time. Another thing she'd prayed about and it was still unanswered. Did God want her to remain single?

Jason asked her questions about her meeting with the guild and she told him some of what she'd learned and how she intended to use it.

He was obsessive, about the town at least. Well, maybe she could use that to her advantage.

They arrived in her little cove twenty minutes later, just as the last flicker of light sank behind the jagged cliffs of Paradise Peak. As she peered up through the gloom, Piper could see little of the familiar landmarks because the dock lights hadn't come on.

"Will you come up for some coffee?" she invited, once her sailboat was secured.

"Only if you make it hot chocolate," Jason said. "After Ida's high-octane sauce, my stomach will go into convulsions if I add coffee."

"Sure." Funny that his agreement brought such a flush of

relief. She'd never worried about coming back late before. Piper led him off the dock and up the path to her home.

"You need some automatic lights. With all the clouds, it's quite dark along here. The trees keep out the moonlight."

She was suddenly aware of why she'd felt so uneasy. It wasn't just the dock lights that were out. There were no lights along here, either.

His hand grazed her shoulder.

"Piper? What's wrong?"

"I do have lights." She looked up, pointed. "There's one."

"Well, it's not working."

She raised one eyebrow. "Yes, I'd noticed. Thanks."

He grinned, then glanced around. "Looks like they're all out. What do you suppose happened to them?"

"I have no idea. Fortunately, I'm very familiar with this path." She turned and began striding along, confidence growing with each step she took. The next moment she was on her knees. "Ow!"

What was the willow chair her grandmother had always kept on the porch doing here?

"Whoa!" He was there, grasping her arm, helping her stand, his grip strong, reassuring. "What happened?"

"My pride just took a beating." She brushed her palms against her legs, feeling the prick of pebbles that had dug into her skin.

"Maybe I should lead." He lifted the chair out of the way.

"You've been here before?" she asked, staring at him.

"Good point. You lead, I'll follow. Just go a little slower, okay?"

"Right." Embarrassed, she picked her way up the path, her mind busy with the light question. "Maybe a breaker's flipped or something."

"Maybe."

When she stumbled again, he took her hand, his warm, strong fingers threading through hers. "Let's just go slowly, make sure we don't *happen* over anything else."

At that moment the moon slipped out from between two black clouds and provided just enough light for her to see a shape move through the brush.

"Do you see him?" she whispered.

"Who?" He glanced at her. "I can't really see anything."

Then moonlight was gone. So was the shadow. Maybe she'd imagined it. Piper shook her head.

"Never mind. It's not far to the house now. This leads to the garden. Once we're past these roses, we take two steps up onto the deck." Her eyes were adjusting now, discerning familiar landmarks. "See? There's the arch into the garden."

He probably didn't need her directing him, but she did it anyway until finally they stood before her door.

"Now if I can just get the key inside." She slid it into the lock and twisted, unlocking the door and pushing it open. With one flick of her wrist the house entry and deck were illuminated. "Come on in."

She turned on lights as she walked into the house. Thank goodness she'd cleaned up the kitchen this morning.

"So all the power's not out. Just those lights." He raised one eyebrow. "Where's the breaker box? I'll check it, if you want."

"Thanks." Piper showed him the panel in the basement, then left him, intending to return to the kitchen and put the kettle on. Halfway up the basement stairs she stopped, taking a second look.

The old wicker furniture her grandparents had replaced several years ago still sat down here because Piper had hopes of locating someone who would recane the seats and backs. But the furniture had recently been moved, and not by her.

Someone had been in her house.

"The breaker was off, all right." Jason slapped the metal door closed. "If you've got a timer, you'll have to reset." He stopped speaking, looked at her more closely. "Something else isn't right?"

"I'm not sure." She went back down the stairs, stepped between the two love seats and stared at the thick wooden door she always kept locked. When she tried to open it, the dead bolt held, but she could see faint marks on the wood where it looked as if someone had pried a screwdriver. Had it been done tonight?

"Where does that door lead to? A secret tunnel?"

"Kind of. I told you my grandfather was a goldsmith, didn't I? Well, he kept a workshop here after he retired." She saw the interest flare in his eyes and hurried on. "I've been catching up on what he taught me. Because of the chemicals we use, he always insisted his work area be kept hidden and locked up. I'm the same way."

"Sounds interesting."

"It is." Piper didn't want to say any more right now. She wanted to think about whether someone could have gone through her house, and why. "Thanks for fixing the breaker. It'll be nice to have lights again."

"Yes." He kept looking at her, though he said nothing more. He didn't have to; that stare sent a funny kind of zing up her spine.

"Let's go have that hot chocolate," she murmured, tearing her gaze away.

"Sure."

Jason followed her up the stairs to the kitchen and perched on one of the breakfast stools, watching as she put the ingredients together.

"Are you telling me that you are a goldsmith, also?" he asked when the silence between them had stretched to discomfort.

"No. I just putter at it. Gifts for friends, things like that." She held out a mug. "Would you rather sit outside? There's a space where we'll be protected if it rains. We could watch the storm, though I'm sure it will only be a tiny one. The wind isn't blowing hard anymore."

"Outside sounds fine."

Before she could lead the way, the phone rang.

"Hey, there. I tried you earlier, but no answer. Were you out on a hot date with the mayor?"

"Um, I'll have to call you back, Ash. I've got company right now."

"So I was right! Rowena owes me ten bucks."

"Lucky you. Bye now."

Knowing full well that her friend would immediately call Row and the two of them would discuss her visitor made Piper uncomfortable, especially with the subject of their conversation so near.

"Sorry, that was a friend of mine." She pushed open the door. "You didn't have to come over here with me. The sailboat does have a motor."

"I'm glad I came. I was curious to see where you lived." He followed her through the French doors and sank down onto the chair nearest hers. "It's a beautiful view."

She tried to see the garden through his eyes. Her grandmother had ordered small, shielded lights installed high up which cast a wash of illumination over her favorite gnarled oak trees. Accent lights hidden by boulders would soon show off the glorious blues of delphiniums, bright-red poppies and candy-pink carnations. Buried in the beds of the soon-to-be fragrant and colorful rose garden were soft, romantic lights, and along the path oversize mushroom lights showed the next step on the path down to the lake.

"Sitting up here, it feels as if the world is far away. It must be a wonderful place to come home to."

"I never get tired of it." Piper wished he could see it on a summer day when Cathcart House was at its best. "Every day I thank my grandparents for leaving this to me."

"How did they die?"

"They moved to Toronto when Papa's heart needed an operation. But he was too frail to recover. They died within months of each other."

"I'm sorry."

"So am I."

"You didn't come back?"

"Not for a while. It hurt too much."

Low, growling thunderclaps rumbled their warnings across the water, and every so often a jagged slash of silver-blue lightning illuminated the rich, black-green forest across the lake for one brief space in time. A few droplets of rain spattered on the flagstones.

Why didn't he say something?

"When I sit out here and see all the beauty God's created, I can't help but think of that hymn, 'How Great Thou Art.'" It sounded silly, but Piper chalked her uneasiness up to the odd situation with the lights and the feeling that someone was watching them.

"I feel the same way," Jason admitted. "There are so many lovely places around Serenity Bay. That's one reason why I want to stay on top of the development we let in. It would be terrible to see the forests cut, the lake polluted and the coastline ruined in the name of progress. Know what I mean?"

She nodded. "Yes, I know. It's like we've been entrusted with something precious, and while I do want others to see and appreciate it, I also want it to be here a hundred years from now."

"For your grandchildren," he teased.

"Yes," she whispered. But Piper didn't laugh.

Ever since that horrible afternoon she'd kissed Vance goodbye, she'd never allowed herself to think about kids. That only brought stabs of regret for what could never be. Her mother had clung to enough regrets for all of them. At twenty-three, when she'd left Wainwright Inc., Piper had made up her mind that she would never end up like her mother, pining for a man so consumed by making money he didn't know what his own family was doing.

To love someone so much and have him ignore you—until you lost the will to live— No!

Love best suited people like her grandparents. Vance's death proved that. Since he'd been gone, Piper had built a wall around her heart. She'd talked to her minister about it, talked to God about it, but somehow she couldn't risk letting anyone get too close in case she got hurt again. Maybe that's why she couldn't trust God when it came to her father. God's ways were slow and she had to stop Baron now.

"This has been great, but I think I'd better go now that the lightning has stopped. It's getting quite late." Jason stood, smiled down at her.

"You don't have a light on your boat?" Piper asked, rising, too.

"Oh, yes. I won't have any difficulty getting back."

"Oh." Obviously he was simply anxious to get away from her.

"I teach some boys a Sunday school class and I like to bone up on my lessons on Saturday night. They always have questions." He stepped down off the deck, then turned back. "You're very welcome to join us, if you'd like. It's Bayside Believers

Church, about half a block from Ida's. If you meet me on the dock at nine-thirty, I'll give you a ride. It's always easier to go somewhere new with somebody else, don't you think?"

His thoughtfulness touched a chord inside her. How was it he'd managed to read her so easily while he remained an enigma to her?

"Thank you. I'd like that. I'll be there."

"I'll wait for you then. Good night."

"Good night." Piper stood on the deck, watching as he wound his way down the path and climbed aboard his boat.

When he looked up, she waved, waited for the sound of his powerful motor to recede then picked up the two mugs and walked inside, carefully locking the door behind her.

She rinsed the mugs, but left them in the sink until morning. Right now there was something else she needed to do.

Piper quickened her step down to the basement. She grabbed a nearby flashlight and shone it on the door. Yes, those were tool marks. And they were new.

She moved back upstairs, checked the back doorknob. No marks. Same thing on the front. No sign of forced entry. Her entire body slumped in relief.

"Thank you, Lord."

Then she remembered.

"If you ever come and can't get in, we'll have a key hidden right here. Nobody will know about it but us."

Piper flicked on the outside lights, unlocked the door and stepped onto the deck once more. She trod lightly across the deck, stopped in one corner. Her grandmother's wishing well sat there, unused after the cold winter, cobwebs, dried leaves and dust frills gathered around the bottom.

The day she'd arrived she'd discovered one of her grandfather's diaries was missing. It contained her grandfather's thoughts from the last year of his life and it was the only one she hadn't read, thinking she'd leave it until the grief wasn't so fresh and it didn't seem as if he were sitting there, saying the words to her.

Piper bent, tilted the well and slid her fingers beneath, searching for the key. Nothing. She pushed and shoved the heavy wooden piece, propped it up with a piece of wood, then shone her flashlight beneath.

There was no key.

She'd come here once after her grandparents had gone into the home and again after they'd died. The key had been there then. So had the diary. She could close her eyes right now and see the gilt letters etched on the leather cover.

Someone had taken the key and the journal.

Someone like Baron Wainwright?

After a hasty survey of the garden, Piper stepped back inside, closed and locked the door. She made sure all the windows were secure before she phoned the police. Piper felt certain they would find little and she was right. The police left no wiser than when they'd arrived.

Even so, Baron was the top suspect on her list. He'd hated her grandparents because they'd shielded her when he'd tried to force her back home years ago. He'd hated her because she'd told him the truth—that her mother would never have condoned his hateful behavior toward them, threatening them with legal action and lawsuits, but stood up to him and demanded he leave them alone or she'd disown him. And because she wouldn't bow to his wishes.

Was taking Papa's diary his way of denying her the solace she might have found in those last beloved words? Or was it a trick, a way to get her to call him and beg for what was rightfully hers?

If he thought she'd come crawling to him, he was in for disappointment. Piper had nothing more to say to her father.

Soft rain began falling, muffling the world outside. Piper lit a fire and curled up in her grandfather's chair. She opened her briefcase and focused her attention on her plans for Serenity Bay.

But her thoughts kept returning to the tall, handsome mayor and the sense of gentleness she'd felt when he escorted her home.

Jason was a nice man. If she didn't disappoint him about the Bay they could be good friends. But that's all they'd be. Her heart couldn't risk anything more.

Chapter Four

Piper Langley was no slouch.

Except for weekends and the busy summer days when rentals were in demand and tourists milled around everywhere, Jason preferred to come in to the town office early to check on happenings from the day before. But on both Monday and Tuesday mornings Piper arrived before him. Today she was already on the phone.

"I know it's early for you, Jeff. But it's even earlier for me." Her light, musical laugh carried through the general office to the reception area. "I need to know if you're interested in making an investment. Serenity Bay. I sent you a fax. Of course you haven't heard of it yet. I haven't started publicizing it yet. But when I do—"

Jason moved quickly into his own office, sorted through the files Ida had left for him and began dealing with his workload. Piper's melodic voice carried to him periodically, her laughter bubbling out like a brook released from winter's grip. From what he'd overheard, she sounded awfully friendly with this Jeff person. But then someone who looked like her wouldn't be alone for long.

Checking the direction of his thoughts, Jason plowed through the pile of manila folders, then decided to start the coffee. Ida preferred hers the consistency of tar and wasn't averse to tossing out anything she declared dishwater. He needed a cup before she came in.

He walked to the kitchen, filled the coffeemaker and waited for the water to drip through the grounds.

"Tomorrow? Fantastic. Thanks a lot, Peter."

When the coffee was finished, Jason poured himself a cup, added some sugar and carried it toward his office. He was almost there when Piper flew out of her office and ran smack-dab into him. He jerked back to protect her and caught his breath as hot, dark coffee slopped over the rim and across his chest.

"Oh, I'm so sorry. I didn't realize anyone else was here. Come on, we need to get some cold water on this or it will stain."

She grasped his arm and half led, half dragged him toward the ladies' room. Bemused by her quick actions, Jason dug in his heels before she got him through the door.

"Umm…Piper…" he muttered.

Piper followed his stare to the sign on the door, blinked. "Oh, yes, of course," she murmured. "Just wait here and I'll get something."

She returned moments later with a wad of wet paper towels which she applied directly to his sweater.

He jerked back as the icy water contacted his skin.

"Hold still," Piper ordered.

"There wasn't any warm water in the tap?" he grated, watching as she dabbed then blotted the mark, her head tilted to concentrate on the task at hand.

"Cold works better." She kept up the routine until most of the color had been absorbed by her paper. "Just a little bit more," she said. "Stay here."

She disappeared into the ladies' room again before he could argue that it didn't matter. Seconds later she was back and the routine began again.

The dark curls of her hair bobbled and danced in the light from above. A tiny pleat marred the perfection of her forehead, her eyebrows drawn together in serious concentration as she assessed her work.

"I think that's the best I can do," she murmured, tipping her head back to look at him.

Jason got caught in her fragrance, a soft, light scent that brought to mind warm summer nights when you could smell roses bursting with beauty.

"Excuse me!"

Jason jerked back to reality, grimacing. Ida.

"I think your shirt's all right now." Piper acted as if she hadn't even noticed Ida's appearance.

Jason knew he should have warned her about the woman's tendency to gossip. He loved her dearly but Ida took great pleasure in being the first to know anything. And to share it with everyone.

"I spilled coffee on my sweater. Piper insisted on cleaning it up."

Piper winked at him then turned to face Ida.

"Actually, he's being gallant. I came rushing out of my office and forgot to check for cross-traffic. Not a very good way to impress the boss, is it?"

"If it was that dishwater he usually makes, it wouldn't have stained anything." Ida examined Piper's cream sweater and slacks admiringly. "You're an early bird, too?" she asked.

"Not really. I'm half-asleep most mornings. But there was so much I wanted to do today—" she smiled "—I couldn't sleep for ideas that kept bubbling up."

"Looks like they hired the right woman for the job then. We could use some new ideas around here." Ida undid her jacket. "About time I got to work, too." she said. "Otherwise somebody will want to dock my pay." She cackled then walked away.

"Sorry," Piper apologized. "I didn't mean to embarrass you."

"I'm used to it. That's Ida's favorite pastime." He grinned to show there was no ill will. "What are you working on this morning?"

"Sponsors for the fish derby. So far I've got three."

"Anyone I know?"

"Could be." She turned toward the staff area where the coffee machine was. "I think I'll get a cup of that. Want me to pour you a fresh one?"

He handed over his mug, trailed behind her wondering why Piper hadn't told him who the sponsors were. Was it a secret?

"Just in time," she mused as Ida picked up the pot. "If you're going to dump it out I'll have some first."

Ida poured both cups, made a face at the liquid. "Not a bit of body," she grumbled and tossed the remainder down the sink.

"Ida, could you get me a list of the dates for town council meetings?"

"Why do you need that?" Jason asked, accepting his mug.

Piper's surprise was obvious.

"I'll need approval from them, won't I? I mean, I can't just go ahead and put my ideas into action without some communication. We'll want to work together to make sure everyone is on the same page."

He felt like an idiot. Of course she would attend council meetings. He was getting paranoid. But that seed of distrust from the past still lay rooted inside, warning him not to be tricked again.

"Yes, of course. I wasn't thinking clearly," he told her. "Lack of coffee."

"My fault." She grinned, excused herself and went back into her office.

"Why are you acting so suspicious?" Ida scolded him. "The girl's trying to do her job, that's all."

"I'm not acting anything."

"Yeah, you are." Ida's gaze narrowed. "You're going to have to get used to working with her. It shouldn't be too hard. She's pretty."

"I never noticed."

"Liar." Laughing uproariously, Ida began filling the carafe with fresh water. "I saw the way your mouth was hanging open when she was cleaning your sweater. At church on Sunday when the pastor was talking about loving your neighbor, you kept sneaking looks at Piper. Never noticed, my foot!"

Jason sighed.

"Ida?"

"Yeah?"

"Get to work." Irritated beyond measure, Jason walked back to his office and this time he closed the door to shut out that laugh. But it took him a long time to read through the first sheet of paper.

A very long time.

"I love it, Ash." Piper leaned back in her chair and closed her eyes. "It's the most perfect job."

"With the most perfect boss."

"I'm not too sure about him," Piper admitted, remembering their encounter this morning. "One minute he's really friendly, the next he looks at me as if he suspects I'm going to walk out of here with the town payroll. It's weird."

"Especially after he took you to church and everything." Laughter lay beneath Ash's quiet voice.

"He didn't take me. I went with him. He introduced me around. But, yes, he was friendly then. But this morning—" A knock on her door cut short her conversation. "I've got to go. I'll call you later, okay?"

"Sorry. I didn't realize you were on the phone." Jason stood in the doorway.

Piper prayed he hadn't overheard that crack about the payroll.

"Is this a bad time?"

"No. It's perfect." She motioned toward the chair. "Have a seat."

"Thanks." He sat, his attention riveted to something on the floor.

"Something special you wanted to see me about?" she prodded, wondering about his stern look.

"I got a call this afternoon. At the marina. It seems you were talking to one of my suppliers about sponsoring one of your events—some kind of cup, I think he called it."

"The Vanity Cup is my working name for the project," she explained. "Yes, I did make some calls. Is there a problem?"

"I don't know." He named a well-known boat manufacturer. "Peter Evans. Yes, I called him. Is something wrong?"

"Not *wrong*, exactly." He looked bemused, as if whatever he'd learned confused him.

To keep her hands still, Piper clasped them in her lap, waiting for the explanation. She couldn't have blown it twice in one day—could she?

"He wants me to arrange for a display of his boats near the marina this summer. His cost. If we sell them, he'll pay a hefty profit." Jason frowned. "Whatever you said to him must have impressed him a lot. He's never been willing to consign so much before."

"I take it that's a good thing?"

"Very good."

"Then I'm happy. Now if we can just get him to commit to some sponsorship stuff, I'll be even happier."

"He said to tell you 'yes,' whatever that means." He blinked when Piper let out a whoop of excitement.

"It means that I've got somewhere to start, a concrete commitment toward the boat and motor we're going to offer as a grand prize for the Vanity Cup," she explained. "It's not difficult to bring others on board when someone's already committed. Getting the rest of the prizes should be easy. I'll need some money to get the publicity rolling. I've worked out some figures if you want to take a look. Also, I want to get some advertising prepared."

A burst of excitement surged inside her. She'd prayed Serenity Bay was the right move for her and if this first success was any indication, God approved. Maybe He'd also help her stop Baron.

"Uh, yeah, I can take a look. But it's after six. Don't you want to get home now? You've been here for almost twelve hours."

"Really?" She checked her small gold wristwatch. "So I have. I guess it can wait for tomorrow."

At that precise moment, to her very great embarrassment, Piper's stomach growled loudly.

"Sounds like you're hungry." He chuckled.

Her cheeks burned. She picked up her jacket and thrust her arms in, surprised to feel his hands on her shoulders as he helped with her coat.

"Thank you." Her purse lay on the credenza behind her desk. She slid the strap over one shoulder and stepped toward the door.

"I don't suppose you'd want to share dinner? We could talk then."

Piper paused, surprised by the offer.

"The Lakeside Diner serves a great lasagna." He leaned against the doorjamb, waiting for her response.

"You're sure it's not an intrusion giving up part of your evening for work?" she asked, noticing that he'd changed his coffee-stained sweater for a gray one that emphasized the silver glints in his blue eyes. "Or maybe I should have said *another* evening. I'm sure that acting as mayor requires a lot of your time."

"Some months are more hectic than others. But developing Serenity Bay is important to me. I think it will be interesting to hear your plans."

"Great." But as she walked out of the building, women's intuition told Piper that Jason Franklin was more than just interested in what she'd planned.

"Do you mind walking?" He locked the door behind them then shrugged into a light windbreaker. "It's just a couple of blocks."

"Sounds great. I could use some fresh air." She turned her face into the wind, let it soothe the day's tension as she walked beside him. "The Lakeside Diner used to be a pizza joint when I lived here. We used to call for delivery so we could ogle the delivery boys."

"Your grandparents?" he asked, one eyebrow raised.

"No, silly, my friends. The Bayside Trio." She giggled. "We're still really close."

"And the delivery guys?" His eyes were bluer now, sparkling in the sunlight that still glittered on the water.

She grinned at his dour look. "None of us ever got up the courage to ask one of them out. We were really brave when we were talking about it, but once they showed up, our tongues got all twisted."

"Typical teenagers. Do your friends still live here?" Jason held open the door of the restaurant to allow her to walk through.

"No. We've all moved on. I did see them a few weeks ago, though. We make a point of getting together for an annual birthday bash. This year I hosted it here."

"Sounds like fun."

"Do you ever see any of your former coworkers?" she asked idly, taking stock of the homey interior of the restaurant. If the food went with the decor, the place must be busy in the summer.

"No."

His brusque answer surprised her. Piper studied him while he spoke with the owner. He introduced her, then followed her to the table. There were only two other tables occupied.

"I'm sorry," Piper murmured when they were alone. "I didn't mean to get personal. I'd forgotten what Ida said."

"It doesn't matter."

But it did. Otherwise why would he sound so gruff?

They ordered, then Jason leaned forward.

"Okay, tell me about the Vanity Cup. What have you lined up so far?"

Piper explained how she envisioned the plan working.

"I think we should make the Vanity Cup the final part of the Serenity Bay Fish Festival." She leaned back, waited for his response.

"But I thought the intent was to make this a family vacation spot. If we're catering only to fishermen—"

"We're not. We're going to have something for everyone. The events I'm planning will last throughout the summer— I've named it Summer Splash. Each weekend the art guild has agreed to sponsor a sidewalk sale in what I hope will soon be known as the town square. I have to talk to you about that."

He didn't look happy at that prospect but Piper plunged on, outlining events that would bring visitors in through the spring, summer and into the fall and engage people of all ages in ongoing contests, games and a host of other activities.

"The fall events will be connected under the banner of Fall Fair. That gives us Spring Fling, Summer Splash and Fall Fair. I'm thinking maybe Winter Festival, too. What do you think?"

He was spared an answer by the arrival of their food. Piper wasn't sure she could eat anything. Waiting for his response was like sitting on pins and needles.

"Smells great." He bowed his head for a moment. Piper followed suit, said a quick plea for help. Then Jason picked up his fork, then glanced at her, one eyebrow raised.

"Yes, it does." If he wanted to play it cool, she'd follow along.

"I like the ideas you've proposed," Jason said five minutes later. "There's a real diversity that will mean people want to keep coming back. But I'm somewhat concerned that you've contacted so many people without running this by me first."

"But you knew the basic idea," she said, stunned by his objection. "I showed it to you that first morning."

"This sounds much bigger than we first thought."

"That's the nature of tourism. It grows and changes." She sipped her water and tried to think of this from his perspective. "Some things that we try this year won't work the way we expect and we'll have to revise plans, even change midstream sometimes."

He nodded but she could tell he wasn't convinced.

"Is there something specific that bothers you?"

He lifted his head, stared at her. "Do I sound critical? I'm sorry. It's just that it's all a little overwhelming."

Piper nodded. "That's because I'm trying to get the ball rolling without the six to twelve months of prep work that should have gone before. We don't have time to lose if we want to see results this year." She fiddled with her napkin absently. "That is what you wanted, isn't it?"

He nodded. She continued.

"It's going to be hectic, but it's doable. Don't worry about details right now. It's more important to get the big picture in place. Once we've got things nailed down, once we know exactly what we can handle this year, who will sponsor what and how we'll handle whoever comes to town, that's the time to start getting the details in sync."

"But some of those details are going to affect what we can do this year. For instance, a hotel. We have a couple of motels, an RV park and a number of campsites, but we just can't handle the influx of people you're talking about without a major hotel developer."

"Yes, we do need more accommodation. But I doubt anyone can get a hotel built and operational before summer so we won't have to concentrate on that just yet."

"But that's the thing," he insisted, laying down his fork to accentuate his point. "Building a hotel takes time. I want to recruit a company who can provide the kind of amenities we're asking for quickly."

"Once Serenity Bay takes off, there will be any number of prospective developers knocking down your door. But most of them want to see some of the potential first. I'm sure you know that from your work at Expectations." One glance at his face had Piper wishing she hadn't said that. "There are lots of hotel builders, Jason." She heard a wariness creep into her own voice and paused. He didn't need to know her worst nightmare.

"There are. But I don't want just anyone. If we show them

your plans, perhaps we can lure one here." Jason reached into his jacket pocket and pulled out a paper. "I drew up a list of those I think would do a good job for us."

Piper took the list out, read the first name and swallowed.

"I think we can cross off Wainwright," she murmured.

"But they are my first choice." Jason was clearly not pleased by her comment. "They've done lots of developing, they know how to make a project take off, they've got enough resources behind them to keep their commitments."

"They've also had trouble on several projects recently," she told him, remembering what Rowena had said about the London undertaking. "I don't want us to get tied up with a company that's dealing with serious legal issues elsewhere."

"Who are you suggesting, then?" he demanded, his gaze narrowed.

"I'm still checking into that. Ida mentioned a couple of local people who may be interested."

"Locals?" Jason's forehead furrowed. "I was hoping for someone with enough resources to make a big impact. I'm not sure a small local venture is—"

"It might be exactly what we want. The personal touch and all that. Besides," she reminded him, "we can hardly turn away their request for development. We don't want to be guilty of bias. The friendly, small-town aura a local would offer could be an asset, don't you think? Wainwright is known for their big, expensive hotels. Intimidating to some."

He didn't look convinced.

Piper changed the subject and by the time the meal was finished, Jason had completely forgotten about Wainwright— she hoped. She insisted on paying for his meal. After all, he'd listened to her ideas. She could tell Jason wasn't happy about that situation, either.

"I'll agree, as long as you let me buy next time."

"Agreed. Thank you." So there'd be a next time? Piper checked her watch. "I'd better head home. I've got a lot of notes to make. I don't want to forget anything we've discussed."

"You really get caught up in a project, don't you?" he asked, head inclined to one side.

"What can I say?" She grinned, spread her hands. "I love my job."

He walked her to *Shalimar,* waited while she stowed her briefcase. But the engine wouldn't start.

"That's odd. It was working well this morning."

"I didn't notice you sailing over," he murmured.

"You were probably still sleeping. I was in a bit of a hurry to get to work." Casting all your cares on Him for He cares for you. It was a promise of God's and yet she couldn't just leave her father to Him, could she? She had to stop Wainwright cold—before Baron got a foot in the door. She pushed the start button again. Nothing. "I wonder what's wrong."

"Can I take a look?"

"You don't mind?"

"Truthfully?" He waited for her nod, then climbed aboard. "I've wanted to check this baby out since the first day I saw her."

She unlocked the door to below, waved a hand, then chuckled at the speed he used to uncover and display the motor.

"I never would have guessed you were interested in her. Well?"

"When and where did you last fuel up?" he asked after tinkering a few moments. He touched a spot of something, rubbed two fingers together.

"Yesterday. At home." She saw tiny bits of grit on his fingertips. "What's that?"

"If I was guessing, I'd say sugar. Or salt. Whichever, it's

going to have to be cleaned out. Thoroughly. You can't go home in her tonight for sure."

"How would salt or sugar get in my gas?"

Jason held her gaze, his own open, thoughtful.

"Someone put it there."

"Someone...?"

He shrugged. "I doubt it happened here. Andy or someone would have noticed." He checked the lock on the boat's entry door to below. "Doesn't look like anyone's tampered with this. Maybe it's your tank at home."

"The whole tank?" She stared at him. "I just had it filled."

"Do you keep it locked up?"

"Of course. In fact, it's inside the boat shed. You have to have a key to get inside. Besides, I did cross the bay this morning. Could I have done that if it had been in the tank from Cathcart House?"

"No," he admitted with a frown.

Piper didn't like where this was leading. First someone had been in the house. Now her fuel had been sabotaged. She'd have to call the police again.

"Do you want me to run you home?" Jason closed up the motor and replaced the door, sealing it from the rest of the boat. "It's no problem."

"That's kind of you. But I have my car. I'll drive." She dug through her bag for her car keys. "Would you be able to fix the motor, maybe tomorrow? I've really begun to enjoy those trips across the water."

"Sure." He held out his hand for her to grasp, waited till she'd stepped on the dock, then accepted the key for the boat after she'd locked up. "I'll get at it tomorrow morning."

"Thanks." His hand still held hers and Piper decided she liked it. Part of her wanted to keep her hand in his but the other part told her to act like a businesswoman. So she drew her fingers away. "Let me know when it's ready."

"I will." Jason's gaze held hers. An odd light glinted in his blue-grey eyes. "Drive carefully," he murmured.

"Uh-huh." Feeling utterly self-conscious, Piper walked across the lot to her car, unlocked it and stepped inside. She adjusted the rearview mirror, saw Jason had remained where she'd left him.

Calling herself a fool, she shifted into First and pulled away, but couldn't help fluttering her fingers in a last wave. Jason remained where he was.

Watching.

Piper drove the switchback road as twilight fell on the greening hills. As she gained the last crest, a small deer bobbed out from the bushes forcing her to slam on the brakes. Startled and slightly unsettled, she paused to draw a deep breath and settle her nerves before moving on.

Below her, Cathcart House lay nestled into the crook of the hill. The yard lights switched on as she watched, illuminating the budding rose garden her grandmother had coaxed to beauty each summer. Piper was ready to employ the lessons she'd learned to woo the biggest blooms from those bushes.

Her hand touched the gearshift just as Piper glimpsed a shadow by the hot tub move. Her breath caught in her throat as the figure lifted the lid, dumped something inside, then set the lid back in place. A moment later the intruder slipped into the darkened woods leaving no trace of a visit.

Call the police? Or check out the tub first? If it was nothing, just a nosy neighbor, she'd rather find that out for herself.

But a neighbour would have asked to use the tub first.

Piper sat in her car trying to imagine who would sneak into her yard. It had to be the kids from Lookout Point.

She put the car in gear and slowly glided down the hill.

"I'm an idiot, God. It's gotten so I suspect everyone. I want to get over that but with dad—it's hard. Please help me."

She pulled into the yard. The place looked the same as she'd left it this morning.

Piper unlocked the door, carried her things inside, then moved to the deck. With a flick of a switch the entire area was illuminated.

No one.

"I need to soak in that tub and do some serious praying," she muttered.

She lifted the cover of the tub to turn on the jets and immediately stepped backward as a pungent odor filled the air.

Just then she heard a rustle behind her.

"You can come out now, Dad. And you can quit playing these silly games. It doesn't matter what you do. I'm not leaving Serenity Bay."

Piper waited for Baron to slip out from the shadows. Nothing could have prepared her for the sight of Jason.

Chapter Five

"What are you doing here?" Piper asked, her voice ragged, harsh-sounding in the quiet of the forest surrounding them. The tremble of her voice bothered him.

"After you left, I spotted some unusual lights flashing over here. At first I was going to ignore them, but then I thought about the salt in your tank and decided to check things out. Didn't you hear my boat?"

"No. I didn't hear anything." She sounded odd—confused as she glanced around as if searching for something—or someone.

"What happened?" He took her arm, guided her toward a chair and when she was seated, squatted in front of her. "What's wrong?"

"What makes you think something's wrong?"

He raised an eyebrow, glanced at her fingers clenching the side of the chair. "Call me intuitive?"

She made a face, then explained about the shadow and the excess chlorine. He noticed the strong odor as well.

"If you breathe in too much of the fumes they can do damage," she whispered. "Not to mention the effect on the skin."

He watched as she opened the small door of a niche, pulled out a plastic box which held various chemical bottles. She chose a pack of test strips, threw open the lid and when the cloud of steam disappeared, dipped one strip into the water.

Then she compared the dark navy square with the normal shade on the bottle.

"Way too much."

He noted absently how the tub seemed to fit into the deck, as if it had been built when the original house had been erected, though given the age of the house, that wasn't likely. "Do you keep the chlorine out here?"

She shook her head. "Never."

"So they brought their own. Nice of them to think of it since they're using your tub." In Jason's opinion, Piper was too pale. "I'm going to call Bud Neely, ask him to take a look."

"There's nothing the police chief can do." She put the test strips into the box, returned the kit to its storage place.

"You don't know that." Something about her body language, the way she looked at him, pricked his curiosity. "Do you?"

He could hardly believe what he saw register on her face.

"You saw someone—a prowler's been out here before?

"Yes. A couple of times, I think."

"When?" He thought a minute. "The night I brought you home?" Every hair on his arms stood up. "You mentioned seeing a shadow."

"Yes. I've seen something several times. But it may not be as bad as it sounds. I think my visitors have something to do with Lookout Point," she told him. "There are always kids going up there to meet each other. Even when I was a teen it was a popular place. I'm sure those were the lights you saw."

"Maybe. But, Piper, this isn't just a prank. It's dangerous. If you hadn't noticed—" He stopped, hating to finish the thought.

"Not necessarily dangerous," she amended. "Chlorine is one thing you smell as soon as you open the hot tub lid. After you add it, you're supposed to leave the tub open to circulate and off-gas. Since the lid was closed immediately, the smell was kept inside. I'm sure I noticed something wasn't right as soon as I lifted the lid."

She touched a button on the control panel that soon had the jets whirring. Clouds of steam rose upward. Along with them, the odor of chlorine dissipated into the night air.

"I'm calling Bud anyway. If he can't come out tonight, he or someone from the department can make a trip tomorrow and check things out." Jason frowned as he scanned the woods, saw the flicker of lights some distance away. "I don't think it's advisable to have Lookout Point open after dark. The terrain's rugged up here."

"There's hardly a reason to have a Lookout Point if you close it after dark," she murmured. "The lure of the place is the darkness. And the scenery, of course."

"What do you mean?"

"Teenagers. Moonlight. You can't have forgotten. You're not *that* old!" Piper smiled at him, her wide mouth tilted in a teasing grin.

Jason found himself blushing as he wondered what it would be like to go to Lookout Point with Piper. "Watch it," his brain warned.

"Thank you for your concern," she said, her voice back to normal. "You came a long way just to make sure. That warrants a reward."

"What did you have in mind?" he asked, his brain still busy with thoughts of moonlight and Piper Langley.

"I have some apple pie, if you're interested. And I could make some tea."

"You don't have to." Jason stopped when she cast a look behind her at the call of an owl. She was still nervous. "But I'd love some pie."

"Great. Come on inside." She led the way into the house, turning on lights as she went. "Make yourself comfortable."

After that first interview, before she'd moved here, whenever he'd thought of Piper, Jason envisioned chrome, glass and glittering stainless steel. Cathcart House was as far from that as the prairies were from Serenity Bay.

Big, comfy chairs and couches lay scattered around a room with vistas on three sides, hidden now by the night. Jason sat down in a leather recliner placed near a fireplace and found it exceedingly comfortable.

"I love this chair," he told her.

"So did my grandfather. Some of the chintz Gran favored went to the city with them and was later sold off, but that chair had to stay here."

"You said you stayed with them?" he asked, hoping his curiosity wouldn't show too much.

"After my mother died. I came here mostly for summers and Christmas. I went to a boarding school the rest of the time."

That tiny bit of tension in her voice only added to the questions he had about her past, but before he could ask more she was carrying in a big, brown teapot and two chunky mugs to match.

"Can I help?"

"The pie is on the counter. Help yourself."

He did, then returned to his seat. Once she'd poured the tea he sat back and savored the flavors of cinnamon and cloves he tasted, watching Piper light a fire.

"Did you bake this? It's great?"

"Nope. Sorry. I went to a bake sale the art guild was having.

I wanted to buy something to support them. The pie looked good so I chose it." She sipped her tea, watching him eat.

"I missed a bake sale?" He frowned. "I never miss bake sales. It's my one rule."

"Wow, you're lucky if you have only one." She giggled at his dismay. "I think I heard Ida say something about you holding a boating class that day. Don't feel bad. You can take the rest of it home if you like. I'm not much of a pie eater." Piper leaned back in the wing chair, her face lit by the flickering fire. "I was thinking about the hotel as I drove home. I have a couple of ideas floating around."

"Shoot."

Her head jerked up, her eyes widened. "Excuse me?"

"Go ahead. Tell me what you're thinking."

The dark curls bobbed back and forth as she shook her head. "I don't know if I can."

"Why not?" Jason put his empty plate on the coffee table, picked up his mug. "Is it some kind of secret?"

"No, of course not." Piper's attention was on the fire as she spoke. Her words emerged quiet, hesitant. "It's just…my brain doesn't work the way you might expect. I don't have a hard-and-fast schedule or plan. Nothing is concrete. For now they're just ideas."

"So?" Something was going on behind those dark eyes, something that made him curious and set a peculiar little nerve to twitching at the back of his neck. As if she was hiding something. "Tell me the ideas."

"It's not quite that easy, Jason." She raked a hand through her curls, tousling them even more. "They're more like nebulous thoughts, glimmers, if you will. I have to let them mull for a while. I ask myself a question, poke around. Things start to gel and then I can really plough ahead. Do you understand?"

He didn't. Not really. But he tried to sound supportive. "Why don't you tell me about your glimmers? Maybe we can brainstorm together."

Jason watched her closely, saw tinges of red dot her cheeks. He understood her embarrassment; the scoffing of some council members when he'd first presented his plan for the Bay still rankled.

"I'm not going to laugh," he promised.

Piper studied him as if assessing his truthfulness. After a moment she let out a pent-up breath and began speaking.

"This is purely brainstorming," she warned.

"I know."

"Serenity Bay is such a perfect name for this place," she murmured. "I mean, think about it. That word conjures up peace, relaxation, no worries—all the things you want a vacation spot to be. But it has to work for everybody. Moms, dads, kids, seniors, young people, rich, not so rich."

"Yes," he agreed, liking what he'd heard so far. Where was this going?

"The beach will take care of a lot of the kids' entertainment. Then, of course, there's the miniature golf course and I expect other venues will pop up as time passes."

"But." He knew he heard it in there somewhere.

"But I got dreaming about a real golf course. Is it feasible? Could the town chip in enough land or perks, something that would make it attractive for a developer to put in his hotel, include a pool, a couple of conference rooms and maybe nine holes of golf?"

Jason stared. He opened his mouth but she held up a hand when he would have spoken. Her smile held a hint of self-mockery.

"In the beginning I thought, not too luxe. But if a businessman or woman brought their family along, while attending a training seminar in the hotel's conference rooms—wouldn't having some nearby links make sense? You know—meet for a round of golf and not feel guilty because the rest of the family are enjoying their own activities. Think about Banff. That's their draw. The scenery, something for everybody. We have that right here."

"Wow!" He couldn't help admiring her ideas.

"I know you think it's too big, nothing like you were envisioning for a start. And I agree. It's just one of those ideas that's been floating around. Still, thinking ahead could save us problems down the road, if we plan carefully."

He liked the way she included him, as if they were partners in this venture.

"Wainwright Hotels could certainly offer all of that," he murmured, assessing her reaction.

Piper's head jerked the tiniest bit. She turned to look at him but her face gave nothing away.

"They could. But right now I doubt they're in a position to commit to that much development in an untried area. And they have labor problems." She held out a piece torn from a newspaper detailing the issues. "Look at this. It's unlikely we'd command their focus at the moment. I'd prefer to look into other options."

"You keep saying that. Who are these 'other options'?" he asked. He scanned the report, recognized the facts as those he'd already researched. He set it down, feeling that she was still holding something back.

Then something clicked.

"Piper, is there something you haven't told me? Some specific reason you don't want to work with Wainwright?"

She'd been peering at a notepad on the table but now she looked at him directly and blinked. "A reason?"

"Yes." He felt slightly foolish saying this but if there was a chance… "Have you had some problem working with their team? Because—"

She shook her head, her curls bouncing wildly. "I've already told you my reasons. I don't think Wainwright is a good fit for Serenity Bay."

"Why?"

Piper fixed him with a hard look.

"This will probably sound sentimental and rather silly but this place was a haven for me. I found so much joy in Serenity Bay that I'm not sure I would have found elsewhere. I'd like to think I was passing it on." She tilted her head. "I feel like I've been given a kind of trust to help develop the Bay. That carries a certain responsibility. I don't want to ruin this beauty by allowing commercialism to overtake what God made. Do you understand?"

He nodded, feeling a hint of admiration.

"I understand very well. I think that's one of the reasons I tried so hard to interest you in the job. It's a goal we share." He kept his focus on her. "I've noticed that whatever you do, a certain flair, a special touch or attention to detail shines through. I think that's what makes each of your projects stand out from the others. You really care about the result. It's not just about money for you."

"No, it isn't. I think the same is true for you."

He nodded.

Their eyes met and held. A tiny flicker of current ran between them. Jason watched her moisten her lips, saw the way the fire caught the red undertones in her dark hair. Inside, a tiny ivy of interest sent down another root of interest and sprouted.

Piper could be trusted to help him accomplish this dream. Couldn't she?

She tried to hide her yawn but couldn't quite bring it off. Jason rose, carried his cup and plate to the sink.

"I'll go. You've got to be tired after such a long day."

"Thank you for coming to check up on me." She walked him to the door. "It wasn't necessary, but I do appreciate it."

They stepped outside into a spring fairyland. Her grandmother's lights twinkled in a misty breeze from the bay.

"I should have noticed the time sooner. I don't want you to get lost in the fog." She walked with him down to the jetty, pausing while he untied his boat. "Will you phone me when you get home so I don't worry that you're lost out there somewhere?"

Surprise ran through him. It had been a long time since anyone cared enough to ensure he got home safely.

"I'll call," he promised softly. Jason reached for her hand, held it lightly. "Thank you for an interesting evening. Whenever I talk to you I always come away thinking of more possibilities for the Bay."

"That's why you hired me, isn't it?" She chuckled, using the cover of her laughter to draw her hand away.

He didn't miss her reticence, but he didn't comment on it, either. Instead he climbed into his boat, started the engine and waved.

"I enjoyed the pie, too," he called. "Good night."

As he headed across the bay, Jason glanced back once. A single light illuminated Piper still standing at the end of the dock, facing into the breeze.

Then she quickly moved uphill and soon disappeared from sight. He revved the engine and headed home.

"As promised, I'm phoning," he told her later, relishing the low timber of her voice. "Home safe and sound."

"I'm glad."

"You're all right?" he asked. "No more visitors?"

"Everything's fine," she told him. "Good night."

But even after he'd hung up, after he'd talked to the police, after the lights were out and he was staring out his window over the water, Jason couldn't shake the niggling worry that everything was not fine.

It was more obvious than ever that Piper didn't want Wainwright Inc. involved with Serenity Bay and despite her protestations, he still didn't understand why.

"You're sure about this?" Piper held the phone pressed against her ear, desperate to hear the reassurance she needed. Even the May sun beaming through the window couldn't chase away her worries.

"As far as I've been able to ascertain, there are no concrete plans within the company to push ahead on Serenity Bay. Everything's been tabled."

"I see." Though she was relieved to hear it, questions bubbled in her mind. "Why tabled?"

"Mid-April, Baron ordered a halt on all projects until the problems in London can be investigated and settled. He flew over a week ago to do his usual hands-on checkup. He doesn't feel the company is sending the right image and you know how obsessive he is about Wainwright Inc. being the top in its field."

"Believe me, I know." Probably more than anyone realized. "You're sure he's still there?"

"Yes, of course. I've been sending my reports there every day. I'm still his personal secretary, Piper."

"And a very good one. Thank you for letting me know, Tina. I've been wondering and your call is very timely."

"Not a problem. How are you, Piper?"

A shot of warm affection went straight to her heart. Tina had always been like a surrogate mom to her, remembering her birthday, cheering her on. Piper often wondered if Baron knew how much his secretary had done for her.

"I'm fine, Tina. Thrilled to be back on the Bay. Working hard. In fact, our first big promo is scheduled for tomorrow. We're calling it a Spring Fling. We hope to get some interest from returning cottagers and those who are looking for a summer place."

"I'm glad. I just wish your grandparents could be there to witness your success."

"Me, too." The sting of loss eased a little each time she pulled out another memory, reassuring her that she'd done the right thing in coming back.

Jason appeared in the doorway.

"I've got to go, Tina," she said softly. "Thanks so much for everything. I appreciate it more than you know."

"You take care of yourself. And come visit soon. You can't keep hiding from him forever."

"I know. Bye." Piper hung up with a mixture of pleasure that Tina hadn't forgotten her, and sadness that she wouldn't be able to visit anytime soon. She wouldn't walk through the doors of Wainwright Inc. again. Not as long as this knot of anger at her father still festered inside.

Let Baron come apologize to her. She was the one who'd been wronged. *Sorry, God, but I just can't forgive him. Not yet. Maybe not ever unless you show me how.*

"You look upset. Is it because of the forecast?"

She swiveled in her chair, glancing out the window. The sun was gone. Dark, foreboding clouds were replacing the glorious blue.

"What's wrong with the forecast?" she asked, frowning at him.

"I just heard on the radio. We've got a blast of arctic air coming down. Snow tonight and tomorrow. About two inches."

"Oh, no!" Piper groaned. "We can't have snow for Spring Fling."

"Not my first choice, I agree. But guess what? We are." He looked remarkably unruffled.

"You aren't bothered?"

Jason shrugged. "We've done the best we can. I've certainly spent a lot of hours praying. But I'm not in charge of the weather. If God thinks we need snow, I guess we need snow. There's nothing I can do to stop it, and I have to trust that He knows what He's doing."

"You're right. I suppose there isn't. It's just that we've spent so much time organizing everything to the nth degree. The weather's been fantastic. Now snow? What are we going to do?"

"We're going to handle this. The barbecue will work just as well in the rink. We can get tables set up there."

"Probably the best place for the kids' games, too." She caught his spirit and began writing notes to herself. "The sailing regatta?"

"Let's just wait and see what happens, I guess."

"Agreed. The artists are all showing indoors so there's no problem there. But I was hoping to showcase the potential of the area and snow was not in my plans." Piper tapped her pencil against her cheek, thinking. "We'll have to hold some events outside, otherwise we lose our impact. What's so funny?"

Jason's chuckles grew louder; his whole body shook with laughter.

"Serenity Bay—a place for all seasons," he sputtered, holding up the logo and artwork they'd approved to go on all the town correspondence and promo material. "Bet you didn't know how appropriate that slogan was going to be."

"Believe me, I had no idea," she grumbled, irritated by his easygoing outlook on this near disaster.

He laughed harder.

"You're not helping, you know." The ideas began to whirl fast and furiously. She scribbled them down with little regard for neatness. *If you wanted to offer your assistance, Lord, we might make this work.*

"Stop laughing!" she hissed as Jason burst into another chuckle.

"Sorry. I'll try to control myself." But the grin remained firmly locked in place.

"If our Spring Fling is going to happen, I've got work to do." Piper grabbed the phone and started dialing.

"Me, too. I'll talk to you later." Jason took a note from Ida, grimacing. "This health inspector is getting far too chatty. Can't you block his calls?"

"No," Ida snapped as they left the room.

Piper concentrated on the task ahead of her. By the time Jason reappeared she had revised the schedule to accommodate any conditions the weatherman tossed their way.

"That forecast is not getting me down, you know. We'll have a snowman-building contest if we have to," she told him, leaning back in her chair and rubbing her neck to ease the knot of tension. "Whatever it takes, we'll make it work."

"Snow's the least of our problems." He leaned against the door frame, shoulders slumped in a weary pose.

"What now?"

"The campground. They're full with reservations. Some people have even begun to arrive."

"And that's a problem?"

"It will be. Their showers and bathrooms are operational only for summer. Thanks to the chill last night, the pipes froze and some burst. So far the units that have arrived are self-contained, but unless they all are, there won't be facilities for our visitors. Public health will shut the place down."

Piper winced, unable to believe that all their work would go for nothing.

"That's not the worst of it. The tenting area is completely flooded. Nobody can stay there no matter what their equipment. I've just gotten a revised forecast and more snow is due. I think we're going to have to call this off, Piper. I'm sorry."

Defeat. It washed over her in waves of disappointment and the realization that a major portion of her budget would be wiped out. For nothing.

What a waste.

"There's nothing we can do?"

"Short of tearing the place down and rebuilding it tonight, no. We'll have to cancel."

"Call me an eavesdropper if you want." Ida stomped into the room, her face more dour-looking than usual. "I can't believe you two are just going to give up."

"It's not our first choice, Ida. Piper's been on the phone all afternoon trying to work something out."

A river of warmth spread through Piper at Jason's quick defense and sturdy support. His style of management was as far from her father's taciturn orders as it could get.

"We can't manufacture bathrooms for this many people overnight, Ida," Piper murmured.

"Maybe you can't. But you've both ignored the biggest resource Serenity Bay has."

"We have?" Piper blinked, looking to Jason for answers. He shrugged.

"Serenity Bay was started by people who accepted the hardships of this place along with the beauty. People who didn't give up, didn't call it quits when the going got tough. The folks around here have hung on for a long time, hoping something would help this place." Her chin jutted out. "Jason came with his ideas and some of us caught a glimmer of hope that maybe the Bay could be a better place. Then you came along."

Piper shifted under the beady-eyed scrutiny. "Uh…"

"You put ideas in our heads. The painters and potters, the quilters and silversmiths, the glass artists—all of them, they thought maybe it wasn't too late for this place. That maybe they could live and work here, bring people in instead of chasing after a sale." Ida's bony finger stabbed the air between her and Piper's face. "We started to think big because of you."

Piper didn't know what to say.

"Do you know how many cottages were up for sale when you came? Do you know how many listings have been pulled since you got here?" Ida clamped her hands on her thin hips and glared at them both. "We had more than a hundred places for sale. That's down to less than thirty since the buzz about this place got out. People were just starting to think it wasn't quite time to write off the Bay. You quit now and you'll kill whatever morale there is in this place."

"I don't want to cancel, Ida. But what can we do?"

"Call a meeting," the woman declared, her eyes blazing. "Get the townsfolk together and decide what you're going to do. Find out their solutions. Give them a chance to be part of the new Serenity Bay."

As Piper watched the small, vibrant woman, her brain began to simmer with new ideas.

"Why not?" she asked Jason. "What have we got to lose?"

"It's their town," he agreed after a moment's pause. "It should be their decision."

They both turned to Ida.

"Where do we start?"

"I've got phone numbers here." She split the pages among the three of them. "We'll call them all, tell them there's an emergency town-hall meeting tonight at seven o'clock. Tell them it's urgent they be there. If they fuss at you, mention canceling your Spring Fling."

Piper nodded, scanned the list of names. But her mind was busy with something else.

"Let's get to work," Jason said.

Before either of them could leave, Piper blurted out her idea, the receiver still clasped in her fingers.

"Wait!" They turned to stare at her. "You do know what could solve the biggest part of our tenting problem, don't you?"

Ida frowned; Jason looked confused.

"Wingate Manor."

Both faces registered skepticism.

"Doesn't open till late May, three or more weeks from now," Jason reminded.

"But someone has been getting the place ready so I know they're around." Piper glanced from one to the other, wishing they could envision what she did. "The brothers have been doing repairs for weeks now. Someone told me about their new catering plans. I tried to get an appointment to speak with the Wingates last week. When they didn't return my call, I drove out there. Have you seen the place lately?"

Jason shook his head.

"They've built a great canopied area out in the back that I understand will be used for some kind of summer theater. It's high and dry," she said quietly, watching their faces. "Perfect for camping."

"Camping? At Wingate?" Jason didn't look impressed.

But Ida caught on. One finger tapped against her bottom lip. "Wingate Manor does have a surplus of bathrooms," she mused. "The old house was used as a training lodge during the war."

"How do you know that?" Jason demanded.

"I know a lot of things you don't," Ida told him pertly. "I've been doing a little research for a local history book I'm working on. Also, Hank and Henry Wingate have kept the ground floor bathrooms updated. Do you know why?"

"No." Jason watched her, waiting.

"Because they've got their eyes on building their business. All those fairy lights in the summer aren't just pretty. Folks wander the grounds, look at Henry's lily ponds while they wait for their reservation. They don't mind waiting when there's so much to see. And those who have already enjoyed a meal often amble around afterward to take a look at the Wingate gardens—though they're not up to much yet."

"My friend Rowena's landscaping company had a call about working on a project there," Piper murmured.

"All part of the plan." Ida looked smug. "Most everybody who goes to Wingate ends up paying to dip something into that chocolate fountain they put out on the patio. Some folks even go to Wingate specially for the high-priced desserts."

Piper's brain began to percolate.

"Not that I'm saying it's a good thing, you understand." Ida scowled. "The prices those two charge, they should have a full orchestra and black-tux waiters to serenade everybody while they throw away their money."

"Smart men! The ground-level bathrooms would make it easy for people to stay on the property without bothering the restaurant clientele. Theater groups with facilities nearby would draw even more patrons." Piper looked at Jason, who was watching Ida.

"If people come just for the desserts, they don't have to dress up for dinner so the chocolate fountain on the patio makes perfect sense." Jason nodded. "Very clever."

"And good for us if we can get them to let us use those bathrooms," Piper inserted. "Do you think the Wingate brothers will come to the meeting? I mean, they've been fairly reclusive. I'd hoped to include their place in our plans for the town but I'm not having a lot of success. Maybe if they came—" Piper glanced from Jason's sly smile to Ida's scowling countenance. "What?"

"They'll come—if Ida asks them."

"Oh?" She waited for a clue that would explain the flush of color on Ida's pinched cheeks. "Why?"

"The brothers want her rib recipe. Badly." Jason grinned when Ida smacked him on the arm. "Don't pretend it isn't true, Ida. Put them on your list to call. I'm not getting chewed out again by Hank for not repaving the road to Wingate Manor. He refuses to understand that we haven't got the funds right now."

"That's a good idea. I certainly don't think I should call, since I've never actually met them," Piper added.

"Don't think I don't know you two are in cahoots." Ida glared at them both then turned on her heel. "Fine. I'll call them. You two—start phoning," she ordered before stomping from the room.

Jason grinned. "You heard the woman," he said. "Let's get busy. Wouldn't hurt to pray while you're at it."

"I've been praying since you first mentioned snow," she told him dryly. *For all the good my prayers do. God isn't talking to me.* And she knew why. *Forgive me.* She saw him glance at her lists.

"Keep me posted," he added before leaving.

There it was again. *Keep me posted. Let me know. I'd like an update*. That constant reminder that he was always watching, always monitoring her every move irritated her.

It felt as if he didn't trust her. And that always brought to mind her father. Maybe Jason was more like Baron than she'd realized.

She was going to have to talk to him about that. Later.

Piper picked up the list Ida had laid on her desk, recognizing none of the names. She'd work from the top down and hope everybody was home. But not yet.

She set the list aside and pulled out the envelope she'd found by the deck on the far side of the hot tub the morning after the chlorine incident. So far she hadn't told anyone about this.

She pulled out the contents and unfolded them. The paper was legal size, a photocopy of detailed plans that were so small she'd needed a magnifying glass to identify the markings. What she saw made her catch her breath.

The plans bore the company stamp of Wainwright Inc. and were drawings of a hotel situated on the banks of Serenity Bay. A big, imposing edifice that would utterly block the view of anything in the immediate area.

Had her father taken a detour before going to London? Stopped by Cathcart House?

But that didn't make sense. Baron wouldn't bother to add chlorine to her hot tub, would he? He'd simply issue an edict and expect her to obey. If he bothered to speak to her at all.

Piper folded the paper, returned it to the envelope and tucked it under her organizer.

She was going to figure out what he was up to. That meant calling Tina again. And then she'd figure out how to stop her father from taking over *her* project.

No way was Baron going to horn in on Serenity Bay and spoil it like he had the other parts of her life.

Jason trusted her to find the best hotel developer. That's what she intended to do.

Wainwright Inc. wasn't even on the list.

Chapter Six

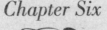

"Order. Let's come to order, please."

Jason rapped his gavel on a table, waiting for the voices to die down.

"So essentially what we're telling you is that unless we can come up with some way to look after the folks who'll show up here for our Spring Fling, we'll have to cancel the whole works. Wally's RV site just can't handle it all."

A grumbling murmur filtered through the room.

"Why didn't you think this through before you ran all those expensive ads?" someone hollered. More negative comments followed.

Jason needed to do something before this got out of hand. But he wasn't sure what. In a way they were right. They hadn't planned this out enough. But who could have expected such a huge response? Or snow?

After a moment Ida stood up.

"Order, please." Jason tapped his gavel again. "Let's be civilized about this. We have a question from the floor."

The furor died down once the group realized Ida was standing.

"Just how many people are we talking about?" she asked.

Jason could have kissed her. Ida knew the answer, of course. They'd strategized the logistics of this thing for an hour before the meeting. Obviously she hoped that getting the problem on the table would garner some fresh ideas.

"Piper, can you give us the facts and figures?"

She rose gracefully, checked the sheet in front of her then began to explain the categories of housing needed.

"At the moment we have over a hundred invitations on hold. If we're going to decline these people we need to let them know right away so they can make alternative plans."

"Don't know why we have to send away anyone who wants to see what this place has to offer," someone from the crowd said.

"Can you stand, please?" Jason asked, stretching to see the owner of that soft-spoken voice. "Ah, Henry Wingate. What are your thoughts on this?"

"My thoughts are that I've worked my fanny off for too many years trying to get folks to come to this town to see what we have to offer. Now they're on their way and we're talking about turning them away?" He shook his gray head. "How dumb is that?"

"Do you have a suggestion?" Piper asked.

"My suggestion is we welcome anyone who wants to come to Serenity Bay, just like we'd welcome our own family. Carter, you built that guesthouse of yours three years ago. Anybody ever use it?"

"Yeah, me."

The entire room burst into guffaws. Carter's proclivity for snoring, and his wife's objections, were well known all over the Bay.

"Okay, but for this weekend you rent it out. Boris, that RV of yours had been sitting in your driveway empty ever since you came back from California. It'd take care of a family for a few days. You could charge 'em if you wanted."

"Yeah, and what if they wreck it?" Boris objected.

"They want a place to sleep at night, not a party room. Keep it parked in your own yard, plug it in to your own power. You can keep your eye on it that way." Henry's quick response surprised Jason. So did the rash of responses that followed.

"I've got a couple of spare rooms at my place. I could put some of these people up. Be kind of nice to have the house full again."

"The Masons left me the key for their place. I'm sure they wouldn't mind renting it for a few days."

"I can put up some people."

Jason watched Ida scribbling down names with numbers beside them, trying to make a list. More than once she leaned over to speak to Piper, who was making her own notes.

"Okay, if that's what you want to do, we'll have Ida coordinate things. Each of you come up here after the meeting and tell her how many you can take and how much you want to charge."

"I don't want anything," Boris blustered. "This town needs a boost. If having somebody stay in my RV brings them here, I'll be glad to do it."

"He's right. This is our town. We've always pitched in to help each other out. Having all these folks show up is going to bring us business. Isn't that what we all want?"

"Long as we can make room, we won't turn anyone away." Boris grinned at Henry. "What's Wingate Manor gonna do to pitch in?"

Henry gulped, then looked at Jason. "Whatever we can," he said clearly.

Here was their opportunity. Jason glanced at Piper and caught her nod.

"We need campsites, Henry. With washrooms." He held the other man's gaze. "I understand Wingate Manor could help us out with that."

"I...guess." Fast-talking Henry wasn't quite so quick now.

"Talk to Ida about specifics." Jason scanned the room. "Anyone else have something to say?"

More people chimed in, suggesting even more ways of enhancing the town to receive their visitors with open arms.

Half an hour later they were done.

"People, you are awesome," Jason told them, meaning every word. "I can't thank you enough for pitching in this way. We appreciate all of your ideas and we'll promise to do our best to get them going. Maybe not this weekend but before the summer's out. Now we're going to need volunteers to assist Ida. If you can help, in any way at all, I want you to come up here and sign the sheets Ida's got laid out on the table. Everybody's going to have to pull together if we're going to carry this off."

He offered a few reminders, then adjourned the meeting. Two hours later the last of the townspeople had left. Piper was smiling, but she still couldn't believe what she'd just experienced.

"That was fantastic," she whispered.

"It was," he agreed with a grin. "Don't look so surprised. You prayed, didn't you?"

"Yes, I did."

"Didn't you expect God to answer?" He could see by her face that she hadn't expected what they'd seen. "Sometimes He goes above and beyond what we expect."

"Way above." She held up her folder. "I've only done a rough count, but so far it looks like we've got fifty spaces more than we need. That's quite incredible considering our position this afternoon."

"That's God for you. Never a problem too big." He saw something dark flash in her eyes, and wondered at it. "Is something wrong?"

"No, it's just—" She paused, said good-night to Ida and waited until they were alone. "Can I speak to you about something?"

"Sure." He hooked a chair with his foot, pulled it close enough then sat down. "What's the matter?"

"Nothing." She bit her lip, blinking at him as if she expected him to yell at her. "No, that isn't true." She drew in a breath, then let it out. "Tell me, have I done something wrong?"

"I don't know. Have you?" He knew immediately that his teasing was misplaced. Piper was very serious. "Why don't you just tell me what's on your mind?"

She studied him, her brown eyes dark, unyielding. Finally she spoke.

"I feel like you're constantly looking over my shoulder, checking up on me," she told him baldly. "Every time I pursue an idea or have a meeting you ask me to speak to you about it."

"What's wrong with that?" He bristled.

"I feel like I'm back in high school! You don't have to keep telling me to consult you, Jason. I have no intention of excluding you from any part of this project. But I need some space to do the job you hired me for." Her face paled slightly as her fingers clutched the black folder she held. "It's unnecessary for me to come running to you every time I speak to someone or attend a meeting and I don't think you should expect that."

"You're mad because I asked Ida to include me in your next meeting with Peter," he guessed.

"No! I'm not mad," she grated. "I just don't see the reason for your constant hovering. It's starting to feel like you expect me to cheat the town, to go behind your back or deliberately evade the truth. I thought that by now you'd know that isn't how I work."

"You haven't really talked much about your ideas beyond Spring Fling," he reminded, watching her closely.

"No, I haven't." She wasn't backing down.

"Why?"

Piper glared at him and huffed out a sigh.

"Because they're not ready. That's not how I work. I've told you this before. I have to mull things over, get a feel for how I want things to work, toss around ideas that will lead to the goal, sound out people to see if they think something is plausible."

"What people?" he asked quietly.

"Friends, former coworkers, people who are in the same business or who understand the process."

"Why not sound them out with me?"

He could see the anger build. She set both feet firmly on the ground.

"No offense, but this isn't your area of expertise, Jason. You haven't done this before so you have no experience to draw on. The people I talk to have seen what's been done. They've even had some flops themselves and can help me hone my ideas so I don't make the same mistakes."

"Isn't that dangerous?"

"Excuse me?" She stared at him, eyes wide in surprise. "Dangerous? What are you talking about?"

"What if some of these colleagues, some of these friends— what if they take your ideas and run with them?" He felt a little funny, saying it out loud like that. But Jason was determined that Serenity Bay was going to be the model, not the copycat.

"Are you serious?" she asked, then jerked her head in a nod. "Yes, I can see that you are." She sank down on one of the hard plywood chairs, studying him, her whole body an expression of dismay.

"It's a possibility. One I don't want to deal with after we've invested a lot of time, effort and especially money into a promotional campaign for the Bay. I don't want someone to make us look like the stepchild of a bigger, brighter plan."

"If that wasn't funny, I'd be really angry," she told him softly.

"Go ahead, laugh at me. But the point is valid."

"No, Jason, it isn't." Her back straightened, and she set the folder down on the table, folding her hands in her lap.

He tilted his head, waiting for an explanation.

"This is what you don't understand. First of all, if I had gotten as far as a full-scale campaign, you can rest assured that nobody outside of a select few, you included, would know the particulars. But it's a bit too early for that."

He glanced at the notes he'd scrawled on a yellow tablet in his hands. "I thought that's what we've been doing for the past several weeks."

"No. At the moment we're trying to put on a few events, get a feel for what the area can handle, what goes over well, what doesn't. We're figuring out our market. All of that is going to impact our later decisions."

"And if someone copies us?"

She shrugged. "So what? By then we'll be on to something else. I've never been short on ideas, but if I were, I'm sure time and some deep thinking could generate new thoughts. Look how the problem with the tent sites and campers got solved tonight."

He nodded. "Yes, but—"

"No buts," she interrupted, stemming his words with a shake of her head. "I have to know that you trust me, that we're in this together, or I'm out of here. I will not work under a microscope, constantly being checked. You're going to have to believe that I'm looking out for the best interests of Serenity Bay. If you have a question, fine. I'll answer whatever you need. But I'm wasting time, your time and mine, by constantly reporting every time I take a baby step."

"I didn't mean to make you feel as though I don't trust you," he apologized honestly, wishing he'd been more careful to stem his questions. "I'm very sorry that my concerns came across as suspicions. It wasn't my intent."

"I know." She smiled. "I understand that this project has been your baby for a while and you're overprotective. I get that. But you have to back off now and let me do my job so that you can get on with yours."

"I do want to be kept abreast of what's happening," he said and then realized he'd just repeated the words that had irked her in the first place. "From time to time."

His word adjustment was not lost on Piper, who smiled again. But her eyes held no mirth as she assessed him.

"Of course. When I have something new or something concrete, I'll let you know. I promise. My reputation is riding on the success of Serenity Bay, too, Jason. I'm not about to jeopardize that by trying to pull some kind of a fast one."

"No. That would be foolish," he agreed. He rose, motioning toward the door. "I guess we'd better get out of here. It's getting late."

"Yes. By the way, I'll be going out of town tomorrow. I've got a meeting." She picked up her folder, walking with him to the door.

Jason couldn't help wondering where she was going. Nobody had said a word to him, including Ida, who was usually bursting to talk about Piper. Seemed curious that she'd plan an out-of-town meeting just two days before their big Spring Fling.

As he watched her car's taillights disappear into the dusk,

a prickle of foreboding nudged him. He shoved it away and walked home. She was right—he was getting paranoid. Not everybody was like Trevor Johnson, pretending to be his pal while he secretly wooed his girlfriend and stole his accounts. Certainly Piper wasn't like that.

"Good to meet you, Mr. Gordon."

"Please, call me Ted." Ted Gordon motioned Piper toward a white leather sofa, and waited until she was seated.

"I can't tell you how much I appreciate this meeting."

"I owe your former boss a couple of favors so it's no problem." He sat down across from her and leaned forward. "Besides, I'm a little curious about this new job of yours. You've got a lot of people talking. Nothing like what you've done before, is it?"

"Not at all," she agreed with a laugh. "Which is probably why I'm enjoying it so much. We're aiming for the best of the best in Serenity Bay. That's why I wanted to offer Gordon Developments a chance to work with us."

"We usually develop our own sites," he reminded her, scratching his chin. "And we always want them to be year-round."

"I'm aware of that. We anticipate year-round activities as part of our plan."

"Really? So what do you have in mind for us?"

She'd rehearsed this carefully on the drive into Toronto. Now Piper laid out her pitch, emphasizing each detail that made the proposal worthwhile for his company.

"A golf course, huh?" He grinned at her. "You've got your conference market researched. Meeting rooms?"

"Of course. There are at least three conventions I'd like to approach. All of them would need meeting rooms. Once a hotel is in place, the possibilities for bringing in guests are endless." She let that statement dangle for a moment.

"I notice you've also included a spa in the workup. Are you sure that would be viable in a place like Serenity Bay?"

"Do you play winter sports, Ted? Ever pulled a muscle skiing? Spent the day ice fishing? Or snowmobiling? Doesn't a massage sound good?"

He burst into a guffaw of laughter. "I can see why Calgary didn't want to let you go." He chuckled. "You're good at persuasion."

"I just want you to consider all the angles."

He grew serious. "I'd heard Wainwright Inc. was interested in building there."

Piper caught her breath, turned it into a cough. Who was spreading that rumor?

"We've had no formal presentation, or any contact with Wainwright, as far as I'm aware," she said quietly. "Confidentially, I have some reservations about their ability to meet our timelines given their current…difficulties."

"Wainwright's had a spot of trouble but that won't stop them. Baron Wainwright always makes his deadlines," he said. "I've known him a while and I can tell you he's not a man who breaks his word."

You haven't known him as long as I have.

Piper did not want to go into her father's supposed virtues, nor did she want to talk about Wainwright, especially now. So she remained silent and after a moment he changed the subject, questioning her thoroughly on every aspect she'd thought of and some that she hadn't. An hour and a half later he finally rose.

"It's an interesting proposition, Piper. Very interesting." He watched her rise, motioning toward a board behind his desk. "As you can see, we're heavily invested in the Caribbean at the moment. We've got three new complexes going up."

"So I've heard."

"It would be pushing to start another venture before at least one of the others is complete. But what you're proposing is appealing. Very appealing."

"Then you'll think about it?" she asked, crossing her fingers behind her back.

"I will," he agreed.

"If you want a taste of what we're doing, come down for a day this weekend. We've planned a number of events as a first step to drumming up interest in the Bay. You can see our vision at work."

"I might just do that."

It was risky to invite him. Who knew what could happen with the weather and their constantly evolving plans. But they needed a hotel if they were to start fine-tuning their plans and Gordon Developments was top-notch.

He walked her to the door, sharing a story about her former employer. As they moved toward the elevator, Piper seized her opportunity.

"I have just one request," she murmured, glad no one else was nearby.

"What's that?"

"Everything I've told you is confidential. If you're not interested in the project, I want the opportunity to go in fresh to others. I'd appreciate it if you could keep my ideas and plans to yourself."

"Going to scoop them, are you?" He grinned. "Don't blame you a bit. Jason did a smart thing in recruiting you. Not that I'm surprised. That guy has his head on straight. Couldn't have survived and started building an empire for himself after that mess at Expectations if he hadn't."

"You know Jason Franklin?" Surprise rushed over her.

"I should. I worked with him for a number of years. He's responsible for finding our properties in New Guinea and Bali, to name a couple." Ted rocked back on his heels. "Top-notch locator until that friend of his stabbed him in the back."

"Really?" Piper wondered if he'd explain.

"I don't suppose he's talked about it much. Can't say I blame him." Ted pressed the elevator button before continuing. "Trevor Johnson wasn't nearly as good at his job but Jason used to help him out, do extra research, suggest stuff for Trevor's clients. They were friends, had been since high school. Room-mates in college. I guess Jason got used to helping."

"There's nothing wrong with helping a friend, is there?"

"Not a thing. Not until Trevor approached me for a kickback. Claimed he'd done the finding, that Jason took the credit for work that wasn't his."

This was far worse than anything Piper had suspected. As her stomach sank to her toes she struggled to keep her expression neutral.

"But our Trevor made a mistake trying to shake down Jason's clients. Developers have been around the block before. Most of us had been working with Jason long enough to know he was a valuable asset on our team. I'd been trying to coax him to come over for ages, but he was a loyal soul. Claimed Expectations had been good to him, that he liked working with his friend. He's not the type to claim credit for something that's not his."

"No, he's not." Piper couldn't imagine being in such a situation. "The whole thing sounds horrible."

"Believe me, it was. One of Jason's other clients contacted me, asked if I'd been scammed, told me the lies Trevor was spreading. He said the company was going to sack him and leave him with a ruined reputation if somebody didn't do something. He wanted permission from all of us who had been approached. Before he phoned Jason, told him what was going on." He shook his head. "Wainwright was furious and he let the powers that be at Expectations know it."

"Baron Wainwright told Jason the truth?" She could hardly imagine her father doing such a thing.

"Yes. The guy's reputation was on the line and Wainwright said he wasn't going to let it go down without doing something." Ted shook his head. "All that talent—it was sad. The treachery devastated Jason but he faced his best friend, got a retraction about the lies. Wainwright and the rest of us backed him up. Not that it did much good. Trevor's father was on the board. It was clear Jason couldn't work there anymore. Anyway, I think the fun had gone out of it for him."

"So he went to Serenity Bay." No wonder he'd spent so much time keeping track of her, following her every move. If you couldn't trust your best friend, who *could* you trust?

"I'd hoped he'd come to work for me. I know Wainwright approached him, along with a couple of others. But when Jason found out the rest of the story, he decided to get out of the business and lie low."

She was stunned that her father had done such a thing. But then he'd always been more generous with strangers than with his own family.

"Found out the rest of what?"

Ted shook his head. "I've said too much already. It's Jason's business. Ask him."

As if to end the conversation, the silver elevator door slid open.

"Thank you so much for your time," she murmured as she stepped inside. "I'll be happy to answer anything else you need to ask. My card's in the folder I've left. I hope you'll come down this weekend."

"We'll see. Thanks for the heads-up. I'll do some thinking. Goodbye, Piper."

Please let him sign on as the hotel developer. The prayer became a chorus that circled round and round in her head as she drove back toward the Bay.

She understood now why Jason wanted Wainwright. He felt he owed Baron. But if Ted Gordon took over the hotel project, Wainwright would leave the Bay alone and she wouldn't have to worry about her father anymore.

Her cell phone suddenly rang.

"Hello?"

"Hey, Pip. Just wanted to confirm that Ash and I will be there on Friday evening. Don't worry about us. You're busy and we know it. We just want to see what you've been up to. Help out if we can."

"I'm so glad you're coming, Rowena. Bring warm clothes because we're supposed to get a snowfall."

"How will that go over?"

"We'll manage." Something unspoken hung between them. Since Rowena never minced words, Piper knew it was bad. "What's wrong?"

"Tina's been trying to contact you for the past two hours. But your phone was off so she called me."

"About?"

"Apparently Dylan told her Baron is going to be in Serenity Bay this weekend. He's flying into Toronto tonight."

"But why?" Piper asked, her fingers tightening against the steering wheel as panic washed through her in a tidal wave. "What is he coming for? What does he want?"

"Like I would know how the great Wainwright's mind

works?" Rowena barked a laugh. "I just wanted you to be prepared."

"I'm not sure that's possible. But thanks, Row."

"You're welcome. Take care, Piper."

"You, too." She closed the phone and set it on the passenger seat as her mind entertained a thousand possibilities.

"What are you up to now, Daddy Dearest?"

Baron Wainwright wasn't coming to applaud any success she might have, that much was clear. There had to be some other reason to bring him to Serenity Bay, a place he had no love for, on the same weekend she'd spent weeks planning for. Had Jason invited him?

Immediately she pictured the paper she'd found, the drawing of Wainwright's hotel concept. Obviously Baron had decided to go ahead, to offer the town a proposal for his glitzy, Vegas-style hotel. One that would send the council members' eyebrows right into their hairlines, one that was as far from what she'd envisioned as parrots were from sparrows.

"Over my dead body," she sputtered indignantly.

"Where are you, God? Why don't you stop this? Don't you care?"

The silence was deafening.

Chapter Seven

Piper Langley was good—very, very good.

Jason stood in the shadow of the ice rink and watched as the last few stragglers arrived from the community worship service to join the lineup for burgers at the grill. When everyone had been served, he helped Ida refill coffee cups while Piper explained the treasure hunt to the kids eagerly gathered round her.

"When did that happen?" Ida wanted to know.

"About two-thirty this morning. Piper decided we needed a send-off for the kids that would have them clamoring to come back, so her friends and I stuck our heads together and came up with this."

"Smart." Ida asked someone to take over Jason's duties to free him to help Piper, then disappeared with her coffeepot, circulating among the visitors.

Jason focused on Piper.

"Each of you must stay with your leader. They're the ones to ask if you need hints or directions to a certain point. When you've located all the clues and found your treasure, you'll come back here. First team back gets the grand prize. Everybody ready?" Piper sent the children off in a buzz of excitement.

"She's not hard on the eyes, is she?"

"Ted?" Jason pumped the other man's hand knowing his grin stretched from ear to ear. "I didn't expect to see you here."

"Why not? The hype about this place is all over Toronto."

"Thanks to Piper." He motioned her over. "Piper, this is a friend of mine, Ted—"

"We've met," Ted interrupted. He held out a hand. "How are you?"

"Relieved," she told him, grinning. "That's the last event. By the time they get back we'll be ready to wave goodbye."

"Looks like you maxed out on attendance in spite of the weather."

"She's the queen of improvisation," Jason told him proudly. "We had three inches of snow the night before last, but we never canceled a thing. Modified, maybe, but no cancelations."

"We're getting requests for summer bookings, too," Piper added.

"Looking around you'd never know it was anything other than a gorgeous spring day in cottage country, except for the snow sculptures, and even they're melting fast," Ted said. "That sun's got some heat."

"Wait till summer. I hope you'll be here when we launch our Summer Splash," Piper said.

Her obvious comfort with his old friend had Jason wondering where and when they'd met. He'd have to ask her about that…later.

"If my kids have anything to say about it we will." He nodded at two teenagers, shaking his head when they loped across the street to join the last troop of treasure hunters. "I guess they're never too old to hunt for treasure. Jason, why don't you give me a tour, show me what you've got planned for this place."

"Sure." He turned to Piper. "If you need me, I've got my cell."

"Everything's under control," she said. "Take your time."

It became obvious after only a few minutes that Ted had been well informed about the Bay. His questions were pertinent and probing.

"This is where you're hoping a hotel will be located?"

Jason smiled. "I wondered if that's why you were here."

"How could I not take a look, especially after the pitch I got the other day? Your economic development officer is dynamite." Ted began to talk size, construction methods and access.

Jason had to concentrate on his answers. But at the back of his mind the questions formed—when had Piper contacted Ted and why hadn't she told him?

"Is the town prepared to offer any concessions?"

Jason focused on conveying his plan. He wasn't aware of the passage of time until his phone rang.

"You need to announce the winners and make your farewell speech," Piper reminded him.

"I'm on my way."

By the time Ted left, most of their visitors had, also. Volunteers were clearing the site, removing tables and putting the town square back to rights.

"Can I talk to you?" Jason asked Piper.

"Sure." She glanced around. "Want to find a park bench? I think I need to sit down before I fall down. Last night is catching up with me."

"Maybe we should do this somewhere private."

"Do what?" she asked, sinking onto one of the new cedar benches the town had paid for. She raked a hand through her curls. Her navy slacks and striped shirt were perfect for a day at the lake. For once she'd exchanged the heels he'd grown accustomed to seeing her in for a pair of pristine white sneakers, though how she'd kept them so clean was a mystery.

She gave him a veiled glance when he didn't say anything.

"Ted told you I went to see him," she murmured.

"He did. Why didn't *you* tell me?"

"There wasn't anything to tell. I presented the package, asked if his company was interested. He said he'd get back to me." She leaned closer, eyes sparkling. "So is he?"

"Interested?" Jason shook his head. "We won't know that for a while. Ted plays things close to the vest. If I were guessing, I'd say he hasn't made up his mind yet. I still think you should have told me."

Her eyes darkened. "We discussed this, Jason. Trust, remember?"

"Yes, but—" He decided to let it go. She looked too tired to argue. "Next time tell me before you hold one of those power meetings, will you?"

She didn't promise, just heaved a sigh and closed her eyes.

Jason reached out, lifted the strand of hair from her lips. "Your face is quite warm."

"I have no doubt. I got too much sun today."

"Piper?"

They both rose at the same time, bumped into each other. Jason reached out a hand to steady her and found himself the subject of scrutiny from two gorgeous women he now knew were Piper's best friends.

"Hi, Ashley, Rowena."

"Hey." They smiled at him.

"Listen, Pip, we've got to leave. Ash's flight goes out at seven so I think it's time we got on the road."

Something in the redhead's voice—Rowena, that was her

name—made it sound as if she was warning him. Her eyes tracked his hand to where it lay against Piper's waist. He dropped it.

"Oh, I'm so sorry you have to go so soon," Piper apologized. "I should have spent more time with both of you. It was so sweet of you to give up your weekends to come out here and all I did was put you to work on that treasure hunt."

"Don't be silly! We loved helping with everything, especially the snow sculptures. Watching the polar swim today was a blast." Ashley smiled, including Jason in her warm, affectionate grin. "I think the old Bay is going to take off like we'd never have imagined all those years ago." She reached out and enveloped Piper in a perfumed hug. "Good work, Pip."

"From me, too," Rowena added, then grimaced. "I wasn't sure I'd ever see the end of the doughnut fryer yesterday but it has to be the best cure I've ever heard of. I'll never look at them in the same way again."

Another hug.

"It was nice to meet you, too, Jason. Pip's told us a lot about you."

Like what?

"Thank you both for your help." Piper smiled at them. "I hope you'll come back again soon—to relax."

"Try and stop us." Ashley consulted the gold bracelet on her wrist. "I'm sorry, Piper, but we have to leave now. I'll call you when I get home. I love you."

Moments later the two peeled out of the parking lot, gravel rattling under their tires.

"We need to talk about getting that parking lot paved," Piper mumbled, her face a darker tint of rose now than it had been before. "And about making some walking trails through the forest."

"We will talk about it. Tomorrow." She looked weary. "Right now I think you need to come over to my place."

"Your place?" Her eyebrows rose as she blinked at him. "What do you mean?"

"I'm feeding you tonight. In honor of your grand success with our Spring Fling."

"That wasn't just me. We all worked on it." But she didn't object when he wrapped her hand in his and began leading her toward the marina that housed his business and home. "But it did go well, didn't it? No major incidents, no delays, nothing we couldn't handle."

"A testament to your foresight." He opened the door, motioning for her to precede him up the stairs. "Welcome to Chez Franklin. Have a seat."

She chose the big chair by the window that overlooked the forest.

"This is beautiful," she murmured, gazing at the scenery surrounding them. "How clever to take up residence here."

"I'm very clever," Jason responded, thinking how little effort it had taken to get her here and how he'd wasted days trying to think up some excuse to have dinner with her again.

He searched the tiny cavern of his freezer, wishing something would magically appear. But even his stock of cinnamon buns was depleted. He closed the door, glanced around the galley kitchen and spotted the phone book.

He hadn't actually said he'd cook for her, had he?

"Piper, I—" He turned to ask her if she liked Chinese food and discovered she'd fallen asleep. Thick, dark lashes rested on her cheeks, the porcelain skin now glistening a rich rose. Her tinted lips parted slightly to allow even breaths to escape.

Jason marveled that the strong, competent woman who'd just successfully put together three days of nonstop activity for a throng of tourists could look so fragile. Her hands lay in her lap, pale white against the navy of her clothes. Those hands had pitched in everywhere, from mixing juice drinks for kids, to balling snow for the sculptures. She'd done it all. She deserved her rest.

He had so many questions about her. She'd lived with her grandparents. There was a rift between her and her father, he remembered from the spa incident. Was there no one else in her life but her two friends?

At first he'd thought Piper expected someone else to show up this weekend. She'd kept checking the list of attendees, constantly scanned the crowds even after her two friends had arrived. But as Friday night turned into Saturday, then Sunday, she'd relaxed. He decided to ask her about that later.

For now it was enough to lift a soft white throw from the sofa and place it carefully over her, shielding her from the faint breeze drifting in from the windows. Piper never stirred. Her cell phone rested on the arm of the chair. He picked it up, decided to turn it off once he'd left the room. She needed a rest.

But Jason paused in the doorway, studying her beautiful face. Even asleep she was gorgeous. At last he turned away, went downstairs to turn off her phone and make his call. Forty minutes later the food arrived but Piper was still asleep.

Loathing to wake her but knowing she needed nourishment, he squatted beside her chair, touching her shoulder.

"Dinner is served, sleepyhead."

She sighed, lifted her lids and stared at him as if bemused. "Jason?"

"That's me." He paused a moment while she took stock of her surroundings. "Dinner's ready. Think you can eat something?"

"Everything," she told him with a soft, sleepy smile that did something funny to his midsection. "I'm starved."

"Come on, then." He lifted the coverlet away and held out a hand to pull her up. "I hope you like Chinese food."

"My favorite." She blinked at the table setting. "You made all this?"

"I could lie. But Ida would tell on me and then you wouldn't trust me again." He held up one of the containers. "I ordered it. I'm very good with a telephone. Have a seat."

Jason held her chair, waited till she was seated, then offered up a quick grace. Soon they were savoring shrimp chow mein.

"Good thing I'm not allergic to seafood," Piper murmured, then giggled at his look of dismay. "Just kidding! I'm not. This is delicious. There was a Chinese restaurant here when I was a kid but we didn't have it very often. My grandfather was suspicious of anything that wasn't meat and potatoes."

"Did you live with them the entire time you were growing up?" He saw her pause, noticed the way she stared at her plate before answering.

"Actually I went to live with them the first summer after my mother died."

"Your father didn't want you?" He thought she was going to tell him to back off but after pressing her lips together for a few moments, Piper answered.

"Oh, he tried to insist but he was too busy, and boarding school was easy. We didn't get along well and I found it increasingly impossible to live with him watching my every move. Every Christmas, Easter and summer I spent at the Bay." Anger tinged her tones. She stabbed her fork into a piece of chicken with too much force and sent a spatter of translucent orange sauce across the plate.

"But surely that was his job, as a parent?"

"His *job*," she snapped, "was to love me, to help me grow into my own person, to nurture me."

"He couldn't do that?" He kept his voice quiet, watched a flurry of emotions rush across her face.

"Not unless I let him mold me into a carbon copy of him. And I didn't." She speared a piece of broccoli from her plate and munched on it. Then her head jerked up, her eyes meeting his. "How about you? Do you have family?"

He shook his head.

"I wish I did but there's only me. I grew up in several foster families. Nice people, but it wasn't like having your own kin."

"But you went to college. You got your degree."

"Yeah." He grinned. "I was one of those pizza boys you talked about. I had a reputation for getting the deliveries to the destination faster than anyone else the company hired."

"Why?" She leaned forward, her face rapt with curiosity.

"Because the tips are always bigger if you deliver on time."

"Ah." She grinned. "An entrepreneur even then. Was Expectations your first job?"

Jason swallowed, wondering how much she'd heard.

"The owner was the father of a friend of mine. We worked there together." He lifted some rice to his mouth so he wouldn't have to say any more. But Piper wasn't finished.

"You must have traveled a lot in order to scout out locations," she mused, playing with her fortune cookie. "Did you travel with your friend?"

"Sometimes. What is it you really want to know?" he asked, setting down his fork.

"Was I asking too many questions?" She smiled, reached across the table and covered his hand with her own. "I'm sorry," she murmured, squeezing his fingers. "Sometimes my curiosity gets the better of me. We've been working together all this time but I don't feel like I know a lot about you. I was just trying to rectify that."

Jason turned his hand to thread his fingers through hers.

"Funny you'd say that. I think I know quite a lot about you, Piper."

"Really?" She stared at him, eyes wide with surprise but a hint of wariness lodged in their depths. "Like what?"

"I know your perfume reminds me of Persian roses I once smelled in Tangiers. I know you're a night person, that you force yourself to come in early because you don't want anyone to think you're a slacker, but you'd prefer to sleep in." He smiled at her quick gasp. "I know you don't like onions," he teased.

She glanced down at her plate and the tiny pile of onions lying in one corner. "Too obvious."

"Okay." He debated a moment, then plunged in. "How about this? I know you like your job, but I also know you push yourself harder than anyone else ever could. And I think it's because you're trying to prove something—maybe to yourself or maybe to that father you talked about. You want people to value you for your own merit."

Her lips tightened a fraction, but otherwise Piper gave little away.

"Don't you?" she asked, drawing her hand away.

"Yes, of course. I didn't mean that in a bad way. I just meant you're driven to succeed. That's probably how you've managed to make such a dent in the powers that be."

"Meaning?" She leaned back in her chair, ignoring the egg roll still lying on her plate.

"Meaning that Ted said he'd heard about your work here. I'm sure a lot of others have, too. That's because you don't aim for mediocre. I admire the way you took on my dream for this place and made it your own. It's a pleasure to work with you, Piper." He picked up his glass of ice water, clinked it against hers.

"I could say the same about you," she murmured, returning the toast.

"But you won't, because I'm obsessive and you don't want me breathing down your back."

"No, I don't," she admitted. "So...you're not angry about Ted?"

"Not angry," he agreed, savoring the last of the sweet-and-sour sauce on his plate. "Just curious about what he said. I realize I've been a little heavy-handed."

"A little?" She snickered.

"Okay, a lot." He set down his fork with a thud and glared at her. "Are you going to make me beg for information about your meeting?"

"It's a thought."

He scowled for the pure pleasure of hearing Piper's melodious laugh ring through the room.

"Seriously, there's nothing to tell. I laid it on thick with him, pointed out every advantage I could think of." Her slim shoulders lifted in a shrug. "He's going to think about it."

"He'd be a good choice, though not my first."

"I thought you said he was a friend?"

"He is, a good one. But I'd still prefer to have Wainwright on board."

She leaned forward, her face tightening. "I told you. They're not a good choice right now."

Jason nodded.

"I remember. I did some checking and while it's true that they're having financial problems with some aspects of their development, they seem like normal glitches for any major project. I don't think it has seriously hampered their ability to build what we need. I put a call in to their office when you were away. Someone should get back to us soon."

"You did what?" She flung her napkin onto the table and rose from her chair, her fingers fisting at her sidess "I especially asked you to let me handle this on my own time, Jason."

She was furious.

Jason watched her pace back and forth across his hardwood floors, and found himself grateful that she wasn't wearing heels.

"Do you think it's funny to go behind my back when I specifically asked you not to?" she demanded, eyes blazing.

"I didn't go behind your back," he said calmly. "You said you'd prefer not to work with them. I happen to feel they should at least be offered a chance to present a proposal."

She glared at him and he felt a modicum of regret that she hadn't been there when the call had come in from the company.

"Look, Piper. They've asked twice to present something. I've put them off both times because you were so hesitant. But they're eager to talk and I think that's a good sign. I want to see what they propose."

"I can tell you that without even listening to a Wainwright pitch," she hissed. "Big, splashy and out of place. This is cottage country, not the Vegas strip. We want understated, friendly, not overpowering, neon blaze."

"I'm aware of what we want." He studied her, puzzled by her burst of anger, completely unlike the easygoing Piper who'd taken everything in stride this weekend.

"Wait a minute—they've called twice?" she whispered as her face drained of color.

"Yes. Why? Is something wrong?"

"Wrong?" She blinked. "I've told you about them over and over."

"I'm not talking about Wainwright. I'm talking about you."

"I'm fine."

Sure she was. He thought about it, then decided to tread on thin ice.

"Piper, were you hoping someone special would show up this weekend?"

"W-why would you ask that?" Her voice had dropped, her gaze veering away from meeting his.

"Call it a hunch," he said. Jason rose, walking over to stand beside her. "You've gone all out this weekend. It's natural to feel a little down if you were expecting someone to see your work and they didn't show."

"It's not what you're implying," she told him, a tiny smile curving her lips. "I don't have a boyfriend who didn't show. You won't have to nurse me through a broken heart."

Relief fluttered through him at this news but he ignored it.

"You were looking for someone," he insisted. "I saw the way you kept checking the sign-in sheet, scanning the crowds."

"And you want to know who?" She dragged a hand through her hair, ruffled the tousled curls even more. "If you must know, I'd been warned my father would show up. Thankfully he did not. He would have ruined everything."

He tried to read her expression but Piper avoided him by moving back to the table.

"I'll give you a hand with the dishes."

He laid his hand on hers, preventing her from moving anything.

"Not yet."

"Oh?"

"We haven't had dessert. And then there's the fortune cookie."

She did look at him then, in disbelief.

"You're going to put your faith in a fortune cookie?"

He laughed. "No way. My faith rests in God. But I usually

find the sayings interesting. Scared?" He picked up the cookie, handed it to her.

"Why should I be afraid of a fortune cookie?"

"Because you might read a bit of truth?"

She snorted her opinion of that and sat down again. So did he. Jason waited while she cracked the cookie open and removed the small slip of paper.

"Well?"

"I think you planted this." Piper glared at him, but her eyes danced. "All right then. 'Man's schemes are inferior to those made by heaven.'"

"You see. Just because it's a fortune cookie doesn't mean it can't hold a wise saying."

"Yeah, yeah. Let's hear yours, Mr. Wise Man." She plopped her elbows on the table and cupped her chin in her hands. One eyebrow arched in a command to open his own.

He cracked the cookie, stared at the words.

"Well?"

"'War doesn't determine who is right, war determines who is left.'"

Piper burst into laughter.

"A fitting end to our disagreement on Wainwright, I think." She glanced at her watch. "Wow! I'm sorry to miss dessert but I've got to get going. I don't like driving those switchbacks in the dark." She began stacking the dishes, carrying them over to the counter.

"You don't have to do this. Go ahead. I can clean up."

"You worked just as hard as I did. Come on, the two of us should be able to make short work of this."

He didn't have a dishwasher but they worked together harmoniously, Jason washing, Piper drying. When the last dish was put away, she hung up the dish towel and smiled at him.

"This was fun. Thanks a lot."

"We'll do it again." He followed her to the door, remembered her cell phone and had to go back for it. "I turned it off when you were sleeping. I didn't think there'd be anything too urgent."

"Nothing that can't wait till tomorrow." She stepped outside. Jason followed. "My car's not far away."

"I need the walk," he told her, matching his step to hers.

"Would you believe from this warm air that we had snow a couple of nights ago?" She lifted her face, gazed at the heavens. "The sky is gorgeous. Look."

"I am looking," he murmured, but his attention was on her.

She caught him staring and turned away, quickening her step until she reached the car.

Without thinking Jason reached for the door handle. The door opened. He frowned.

"You leave your car unlocked?" he asked.

"No. I always lock it." She pushed the door closed, tried the remote. It worked. "I guess I didn't hit it hard enough this morning. I was sure it was locked."

He held the door for her, waited till she was inside, then pushed it closed. She started the engine and rolled down the window.

"Looks like you're taking work home with you," he said, leaning down to eye the brown-wrapped package on the backseat.

"What?" She twisted, blinked. "Oh, er, yes. Though I don't think I'll get at it tonight. I need an early night."

He was going to tell her to take tomorrow off, but he knew she wouldn't. So he stood there, staring at her beautiful face in the moonlight and wondering if he should follow his heart.

"Well, good night."

"Good night."

She pressed the button and the window began to move upward.

"Piper?"

It rolled down again. Her other hand rested on the gearshift. She turned her head to look at him.

"Yes?"

He could feel her breath against his skin. Her perfume filled the night air creating an intimacy that made him bold. Jason leaned in through the window, brushed her lips with his.

"You did a great job. Thank you."

She stared at him for a moment then nodded.

"You're welcome."

He stepped back, watched her car drive into the darkness. When it had disappeared he turned and strolled back to his place, the memory of her touch lingering.

It was probably not the brightest thing to do, given that he had to work with her. But he wouldn't regret that kiss.

For weeks now he'd been aware of the current between them. Tonight had confirmed that she felt it, too.

He stepped inside, whistling as he locked up.

Sure, there were some mysteries about Piper Langley. But that was going to make it more interesting to find out what lay beneath that mask she usually kept in place.

Very interesting.

Piper rolled out of town half-bemused by Jason's kiss. Every so often her hand lifted of its own volition, and her fingers touched her lips.

He was a nice guy, really nice. If only—

She glanced at the flash of lights behind her, glimpsed in the rearview mirror and saw that package lying on the backseat. Where had it come from?

She made a tight left turn, annoyed by the bright lights of the vehicle following too close behind. Edging over onto the shoulder, she waited for it to pass, but it didn't, which aggravated her even more.

Assuming it was one of their visitors who wasn't familiar with these roads she moved back into her lane and kept going, relieved when she could finally turn into her driveway.

Oddly, the vehicle turned, also, but then stopped and sat waiting when she drove into her parking space and shut off the engine. After a moment it backed out of the lane and drove away.

Disconcerted, Piper climbed out of her car and picked up the brown package. She carried it to the house, unlocked the door and laid it on the table. Once she'd slipped off her shoes and put the kettle on for a cup of tea, she began inspecting the parcel.

There were no marks on the plain brown paper, nothing to indicate either what it was or where it had come from. She slid a fingernail under the taped corner at one end and began unwrapping. Inside was a white box with the Wainwright logo on top.

She pressed her lips together and lifted the lid. A model sat inside—a hotel model. She lifted it out, found a small card underneath.

Proposed development for Serenity Bay.

It had to be her father. Obviously he'd come to town and when he'd found her car unlocked he'd slipped this into the backseat, too chicken to face her outright.

Piper set the model down, grabbed the phone and dialed the number from memory. Her father never went anywhere without his cell phone.

As soon as it was answered she burst out.

"How could you? How dare you? This is my project. Keep—" She paused.

"—leave a message," his voice ordered in that gruff, overbearing tone. A beep, then silence.

Piper thought for a moment then slowly hung up the phone.

She wouldn't give him the satisfaction. If he wanted to know where she was, his company spies would soon find her. If he wanted to talk to her, let him do the calling.

Suddenly she recalled those bright lights. Her stomach sank. It had been him. She was sure of it. He'd hung around, then followed her home. But he hadn't had the guts to face her.

She walked over to the mantel, picked up Vance's photo and stared into his beloved eyes.

"Why couldn't you have talked to me then, Daddy?" she whispered, her finger sliding over the precious cheeks, so gaunt from cancer treatments that hadn't worked. "Where were you when I needed you most?"

Several moments passed before Piper set the frame back on the mantel. Vance was gone, pain-free, in heaven, with God. And Baron was still out of her life. Apparently that's the way he wanted it. There was no point in getting trapped in the past again. She'd come to Serenity Bay in search of the future.

The kettle whistled and she made herself a cup of mint tea, pinching the leaves before she dropped them into the strainer, just as Gran always had. While it steeped, she studied the small model her father had left.

The main floor lobby lay open to the street level, a kind of piazza fronting it. She could imagine people gathered there, sipping lemonade on a hot day, admiring an ice sculpture in winter. The perfect place to hold all kinds of events.

The second floor restaurant and dining room overlooked

the water with big Palladian windows, their arches emphasized by molding that lent it a European style. Each of the rooms had a balcony large enough for two chairs and a table.

When she turned the scale view around she could see where the spa was located, the treatment rooms. An indoor pool had been included. It was bounded by huge glass doors that could open to a terrace with steps down to a rose garden and lawn below. A tiny sign indicated tennis courts, horseshoes and a golf course beyond. It was not the usual Wainwright style.

It was exactly the kind of hotel Jason wanted for the Bay.

But there was no way he could see this. To let Baron create this hotel, here, in Serenity Bay, would be a sacrilege to her grandparents. They'd savored happy times with their daughter here, stayed to mourn after her death.

This had been their paradise, a pure, unspoiled place of natural beauty untouched by greed, manipulation and anger—everything Baron Wainwright stood for. Even if he created everything he showed in the model, which Piper didn't believe he would, she didn't want him here, leaving the Wainwright impression on the only place she called home.

Piper knew she should destroy it, get rid of the evidence now and find someone else to build. But she couldn't bring herself to crush the tiny edifice that must have taken hours to create.

So she returned it to the box and stuffed it into a closet, out of sight, just as the phone rang. She glanced at the caller ID and froze.

"Piper? It's your father. Are you there?"

She couldn't move. Even her gaze stayed riveted to the phone.

"I saw your number when I turned my phone on. I'm glad you called. We need to talk."

No, they didn't. Not now. Not ever.

"I wish you were there. I have so much to say to you." Baron's voice sounded different, quieter, more introspective. "Okay, well, if you want to talk, you know how to reach me. Bye, honey."

The machine beeped then clicked off, its tiny red light flashing a reminder. In order to erase it, she had to listen to the message again. Tears welled but she gritted her teeth and got through it, then hit the erase button.

"Why, Dad? Why couldn't you have been the father I needed? Why can't you say you're sorry?"

Finally she turned and walked to her bedroom.

There were no answers.

Tomorrow morning she'd accelerate her hunt for a hotel developer.

Chapter Eight

He'd done it again!

Jason walked through the door and took his place at the meeting table as if she'd personally invited him—which she had not!

This was no time to pitch a fit but Piper decided that once they were finished she'd lock herself in her office until she came up with a plan to force Mayor Franklin to back off. His need for control exposed his similarity to her father more now than she'd ever imagined. And that was not a good thing.

She held her temper and called the meeting to order. When it was finally adjourned she was ready to hit the roof.

"Thank you all for coming. Let me know if you run into problems."

"Good meeting. This recreation board seems to be eager to get started on your ideas now that we're into the heat of the summer." Jason leaned against the board table, his smile appreciative. "You look beautiful, by the way," he said, for her ears only.

"Thank you." She felt the heat rise to her cheeks as he assessed the white silk jacket and skirt she'd chosen for today.

She needed to think of something to get him off her case and she couldn't think with him in the room.

Thankfully, Ida chose that moment to enter and hand her a pile of messages.

"The top two are urgent," she grumbled. "I'm going to lunch."

"Thanks, Ida." Piper scanned the first one, realizing it gave her the excuse she needed for privacy. "Excuse me, Jason, but I need to answer these."

He followed her out of the room, but when she turned to close her door, he stepped back, one eyebrow lifted.

"I'm sorry, Jason, but this is personal."

"Sure. When you get a minute, I'd like to talk about an idea I have. Call me at the marina. I've got bookings all afternoon."

"Okay, I'll do that." Piper closed the door, leaned against it and heaved a sigh. Then she walked to her desk, picked up her cell and dialed. "Can you talk?"

"Sure. I'm on a lunch break. What's wrong?"

"Nothing's *wrong,* exactly. Can't I just call you?"

"Sure." Rowena's voice brimmed with laughter. "But you sound steamed. So what's going on?"

"*That man* is going to drive me around the bend!"

"That man being the mayor, correct?"

"Oh, don't sound so smug." Piper swallowed her last words before she said something else to give herself away.

"What did he do now?"

"Most recently? He waltzed into a meeting I was having with a group who's thinking of establishing a summer camp for the mentally disadvantaged. Anyway, they'll be located about ten miles from town, but they wanted to see what we had to offer. Jason just sat himself down and took over the meeting."

"What's wrong with that?"

"Nothing's wrong with it, except that all the questions he asked, I already knew. I was hoping to get more details about other plans they have. Two hundred campers renting town facilities of any kind would certainly bring in some money, particularly because they have an autumn camp and a spring camp—traditionally slow seasons around here."

Piper slapped a pile of reports Ida had left onto her console in an effort to suppress her ire. "He's driving me nuts!"

"So get him something to do." Rowena's voice sounded muffled.

"Are you laughing at me?"

"Pip, would I do that?"

"Yes!" She thought for a moment. "He's already busy. The fishermen are coming by the boatload, excuse the pun. The fishing derby we sponsor seems to be a big draw."

"He's not busy enough or he wouldn't be at your meeting. Didn't Ash tell me you said he did the same thing last week, twice?"

"Yes, he did."

"But you were more forgiving then because he'd fed you dinner and kissed you, huh?"

"I wish I'd never told either of you that," she grumbled, her face on fire. If Ida walked in now—

"Too late. We know. And we're going to use it against you." Rowena chuckled. "Seriously, Pip, he seemed like a nice guy. He sounds a little obsessed, maybe, but if this is his dream, as you've said, he probably just wants to make sure nothing spoils it."

"You know, I have done this kind of thing once or twice before. And I'm working my fanny off to make sure his dream comes true. I can't make him trust me."

"No, you can't do that." The sound of a crunch transmitted over the line.

"Where are you, Row?"

"In a very posh part of Toronto, seated in the backyard, on a rich lady's lawn, eating an apple. She's watching me out the window. I think she's been on the phone to my boss but she's only emerged once and I don't think she'll do that again."

"Why? What happened?"

Rowena snickered. "I asked her to help me with a juniper. A seven-foot one. She got dirt on her fresh manicure. And on her poodle."

Piper could imagine her friend doing exactly that. She had to laugh at the mental picture it created.

"I can imagine she hightailed it out of there fast. Poor thing. Just because you like grubbing around doesn't mean everyone does."

She closed her eyes, imagining Rowena, never happier than in a garden, clad in her favorite tattered jeans and a T-shirt that said, The Earth Laughs in Flowers. After studying gardening in England, Row took a part-time job and parlayed it into manager of landscaping for a well-known nursery. Now her designs were winning awards all over.

"Don't feel too sorry for her, Pip. We finished her pool and hot tub yesterday. She can rinse her nails off in there." Rowena said something to someone then came back on. "I've got to go. A truckload of bedding plants just arrived and I want them planted in a certain way so I guess I have to do it myself. Call me tonight and we'll think up a new strategy."

"It's okay," Piper murmured as an idea blossomed. "I think you've given me the best advice I could get. Don't work too hard."

"I will. Bye."

Piper set the phone aside, pulled her calendar near and scoured it with a tiny smile.

"Mr. Franklin, you're about to become more involved than you ever imagined."

"Sorry, boss. You never said you wanted me to work today and I've got a date. Her family's here on vacation," Andy said.

"Wish I was," he muttered.

"Huh?"

"Never mind."

"Okay. See you tomorrow."

Jason frowned. The kid was far too young to date. Muttering about the irresponsibility of youth, he pulled off the top of an outboard and started tinkering with the spark plugs.

Just when he'd almost got it, the phone started ringing. Again. He turned to pick it up, knocking his screwdriver into the water.

"Franklin's," he growled into the receiver.

"Hi, Jason. Is something wrong?"

Wrong? What could be wrong? He'd been locked into meetings for four hours this morning, breathing in Piper's exotic perfume and watching those elegant fingers take notes while some company discussed upgrading the town's boat launches or the kind of seed a golf course would need or how many people it would take to rejuvenate the kiddie park.

After lunch Piper had included him in a meeting with government officials who asked a heap of silly questions ten times over, and took more notes than any bureaucracy could ever use.

He was heartily sick of meetings.

"I'm sorry if I'm bothering you, Jason." Her voice was too soft, too sweet.

"No bother."

"Good. Well, you said you wanted to be kept up to speed and I've scheduled a meeting with some magazine people who are going to help plan an ad campaign for our reunion next year. I know you want to be involved so we're thinking we'll meet about eight tomorrow morning. It's an all-day thing."

"All day?" Seventy-eight degrees, a little breeze and bright sunshine. He was supposed to toss all that to sit in an office and discuss advertising?

"Maybe two days," she corrected.

"Listen, Piper. Don't think I don't care, but we're getting into my busiest season and I have to be at the marina more. If you could handle this, I'd sure appreciate it. Just this once."

"Well," she temporized. "If you're sure. I don't want you to feel left out or anything."

Why suddenly so meek? She never…suddenly Jason got it.

"Okay, you can stop now. I'm on to you."

"I don't know what you mean."

But he heard the laughter underneath that velvet tone.

"Just for that, *you're* buying me dinner tonight."

"Well." She giggled. "If you think you can get away—"

"Six-thirty," he ordered. "Here. And don't think I'll settle for some puny salad like you're always munching on. I've been slowly dying in your boring meetings, and killing myself trying to keep up here. I need sustenance. Red meat is the only acceptable peace offering."

"Have you got a barbecue?"

"Piper—"

"Never mind. It was a silly question. How about if I pick up a couple of steaks and we grill them at your place. I don't expect you've got time to come to mine?"

"You're right about that." His mouth was already watering. "Have you got time to grill steaks?"

"Jason," she chided in a teasing tone.

He laughed. "Never mind. Silly question. Nobody who's as good at juggling seven different balls would find fitting in a meal difficult. Six-thirty?"

"Deal."

She was as good as her word. She arrived promptly at six-thirty and started grilling two steaks. She wouldn't let him help, so he fixed three engines while succulent aromas drifted to his nose.

"They're ready."

"Perfect." He scrubbed his hands, washing away the grease and oil with his special cleaner. "Another hour and the fishermen will be coming back. Lots of time to eat."

Piper had shed her jacket to display the sleeveless burgundy tank top underneath that showed off her delicately tanned arms. Her legs were bare and shoeless beneath her skirt, displaying her red toenails. In his mind red had become her signature color—the red of long-stemmed roses.

"You sit down, I'll serve."

He sat and watched, amazed by her ability to create this feast in such a short time.

"New potatoes, fresh garden asparagus, biscuits and the piéce de résistance—steak. Medium. I hope."

"Wow." He savored all of it, remembered he hadn't had lunch and that cinnamon roll for breakfast seemed a long time ago. "This is great. Where did you get all the vegetables?"

"My place. Gran always had a little garden patch so I planted a few things. I ran home and picked them up after work. I actually picked the asparagus last night."

"You planned this?" he asked, pausing with his fork halfway to his mouth.

"I was hoping you'd cave in pretty soon." Her eyes sparkled

with fun, her curls danced with an electricity that turned them as black as coffee without cream in the soft overhead light.

He opened his mouth to protest, then closed it. He'd been an idiot.

"Are you mad?" she asked hesitantly, as if afraid to hear.

"Furious." He chomped down on another bite of steak, closed his eyes and let the flavors hit his tongue. "Enraged," he added after swallowing.

"I did try to tell you," she murmured, watching him from beneath her lashes.

"Yes, you did. But I have this thing about trust. I should have listened to you. I'd get twice as much done. I apologize for ever questioning you."

"You don't have to." She picked at her own meat, a tiny portion a quarter the size of his. "It's just—" She laid down her fork, looked him straight in the eye. "It's important to me, too, Jason. I won't do anything to jeopardize Serenity Bay's future. You can believe that."

"I do."

The moment stretched between them.

Jason could have stared at her forever, but in twenty minutes, half an hour tops, there'd be a horde of fishermen returning his boats, so he kept eating until his plate was clean.

"Thanks for making dinner. It was great."

"You're welcome." Her smile stretched from ear to ear. "But we're not finished yet. I made a cake last night. Coconut. Do you want some?"

"Silly question," he said.

She giggled.

"Okay, here it is." He stared at the confection she presented to him. Fully three layers high, covered in white icing and golden, toasted coconut, it begged to be sampled.

She cut a slice, laid it on a plate and handed it to him. "Tell me if I goofed."

He lifted a bit on his fork, placed it on his tongue and let his taste buds decide.

"Is it bad?" she asked, her brows drawn together. "I haven't made it in a long time. I guess I'm out of practice."

"Terrible," he agreed. Then he took another bite.

"You don't have to eat it. I'll throw it out." She rose, lifted the cake, her face drawn, slightly pale.

He grasped her wrist, lifted the cake away and took her other hand.

"Teasing, Piper. I was teasing. It's great. Light, fluffy. It's perfect."

"It's my grandmother's recipe." She stood, her wrists encased by his hands, and met his stare. "She always made a coconut cake every time I came home." Her voice dropped. "She said coconut is to celebrate happy times and being together."

"I agree with your grandmother," he whispered before he bent his head and kissed her. Forget the fishermen.

She froze for a moment, her slim body straight, unyielding. Then she was kissing him back. Her hands slipped from his to wrap around his neck. Jason shifted his grip to the narrow curve of her waist to ease her closer. The other hand he pressed into those tantalizing dark curls. She was light and fresh and he allowed his starved senses to revel in her.

When Piper drew back, she stared at him, her brown eyes huge in her face. She rested one hand against his chest, smoothing the fabric of his chambray shirt between two fingers.

"Why did you do that?" she whispered.

"I've been wanting to do that since the night of the Spring Fling," he told her honestly. He grazed a knuckle against her velvet cheek.

She chuckled. "Ida would be appalled."

He shook his head. "I don't think so."

She tilted her head to one side. "Oh?"

"Ida doesn't miss much." He shook his head, brushed his knuckles against her cheek. "Could we please forget about work?"

She nodded. Jason kissed her again. She was so beautiful.

"This has been brewing for a while," he whispered.

"Yes," she whispered.

When she nestled her head against his chest, he prayed, *Please don't let her shoot me down.* "What about you?"

"Me?" Her sigh drifted upward. "I think I've been running away for a long time."

"Why?" He tipped up her chin, struggling to read the emotions fluttering through her eyes.

"Love hurts, Jason. I'm not sure I'm ready to get involved again."

"Meaning you were before? In love, I mean."

"Yes. But he's gone now. Almost three years."

Gone—meaning he'd abandoned her? Or was it a mutual parting? Jason couldn't quite interpret her meaning. But he heard the tiny yawn she struggled to smother.

"You're tired. Come on, I'll—" Noises from the dock interrupted him. He glanced out the window, saw his renters returning. "Bad timing," he muttered. He brushed his lips across hers once more, then smiled. "I'm sorry, I've got to go sign these guys in."

"Go ahead. I'll clean up."

"No. I'll do that later. I insist," he said, holding up one hand when she would have protested.

"Okay." She moved away from him, found her shoes and slipped them on. "Mind if I go down with you?"

"Not at all." But he had no idea why she wanted to. Checking in rented boats filled with smelly fish wasn't exactly thrilling.

She followed him downstairs, stood to one side while he spoke to the men. After his introduction, she greeted them but added nothing else. Her attention seemed to be on the group of women and families waiting for their men. After a few moments she moved toward them and began chatting.

Jason wasn't stupid or naive. He could see the men's interest in her. In a green patterned skirt with a red top she was a summer rose, beautiful yet fragile at the same time.

His thoughts startled him and he ordered himself to concentrate on business. When the last of his renters was gone, he glanced around. Piper was still standing on the end of the dock but this time her gaze rested on him. After a moment she walked back.

"Can I ask you a question?"

"Sure." Her eyes narrowed in the way they always did when she was mulling something over. He waited.

"Do you ever get requests for rides around the bay? I don't mean fishermen, I mean regular people who just want some time on the water."

"All the time. Some rent the boats just to sightsee, but my fishing boats aren't the best for that sort of thing."

"Why not?"

He glanced at his fleet.

"Too shallow and too small. They're built to accommodate a guy trying to get his fish, not a lot of people. A tour boat is a different proposition. It can usually carry a bigger load— group outings, reunions, that kind of thing." He paused, then decided to tell her part of his dream. "I hope that in a couple of years I can expand to reach that market."

"What if I could guarantee you a full month of bookings if you had a boat that would sleep six?"

He smiled at her optimism.

"Piper, I appreciate the thought and it would be a great start, but it takes forever to get those boats. Peter has a waiting list a year long to supply three major outfits on the Great Lakes."

She didn't seem fazed by his comment. Instead she wrapped her hand in his arm and tugged him toward the door. "You do have a computer, don't you? And you're hooked up to the Internet?"

He nodded.

"Show me."

He led her to his office, opened his laptop. Piper said nothing, merely accessed her e-mail account.

"I had a phone call today just as I was leaving."

Where was this going?

"A gentleman from Pine Bluff has called several times, an older fellow. He's lived in the area for sixty-odd years but he's moving away now, going to live near his daughter on the West Coast. But he doesn't want to leave."

"Piper, what—"

"Mr. Higgins was wondering if I happened to know of anyone who'd be interested in purchasing his fleet."

Jason perked up, scrutinized her face and waited for the kicker. Piper watched him, giving nothing away.

"His fleet?"

"He sent me this e-mail. Read." She pointed to the screen.

"Two houseboats, a floater, two cruisers and three ski boats." His heart did a nosedive. "I can't afford all this, Piper."

"I know." She smiled, touched the corner of his mouth with her fingertip and pushed up. "Don't look so sad. I haven't quite finished."

"Okay." He straightened, slid his hands down her bare arms. "I'm interested. Hit me with the rest of it."

"As we've been developing the Bay, I've received a number of requests. Everything from an ice-cream shop to a place to board pets. I keep them filed by subject so that if I ever need to contact someone I have the information handy." She smiled slowly. "It so happens I have quite a large file on people seeking rentals on which they can overnight. In other words, a houseboat."

"But if I'm touring around in a houseboat, I won't be here and it's imperative that I be here. I can't leave everything to Andy."

"How old is Andy?" she asked, tracing his jaw with her fingertip.

"Eighteen."

"Does he have his boater's permit?"

He nodded, distracted by her touch against his skin.

"Couldn't he be trained to take a group out?"

"I guess."

"Mr. Higgins told me today that he'd consider some kind of partnership. He might even be persuaded to stay on for the summer. And of course, some houseboats are rented unaccompanied, meaning the renters drive themselves around the lake."

He burst out laughing at her smug look.

"What do you think of me now, Mr. Mayor?"

"I think you're a jewel beyond price." He kissed her, then set her away. "How do you feel about taking a trip tomorrow?"

"To see Mr. Higgins? I'd love to. I'll call him tonight, make sure it's okay."

"Good. After church we'll have a picnic on the way to his place. You can help me negotiate."

"You're going to do it?" she breathed. "Really?"

"I'm going to try. A houseboat or two would give the place

a boost and it's about time I did a little expansion." He brushed the tip of her nose with his fingers. "Thank you."

"No problem. I don't know why I didn't put it together before. Of course, I haven't seen his inventory, but tonight while I was talking to those families and they mentioned a houseboat vacation they'd taken in the Shuswaps, a lightbulb went on."

"I like your lightbulbs," he murmured. "And your dinners."

"Does that mean you're bringing the picnic tomorrow?" she asked archly.

"Of course. Do you like dill pickles and peanut butter?"

"No."

"Too bad. I love them."

Piper made a face and scooted upstairs to retrieve her jacket and purse. "I'd better get going."

"It's too dark to sail," Jason said when they were outside. A slash of lightning jagged across the sky as if to emphasize his opinion. In fact, high waves splashed against the dock as if to warn them. "I'll take you home in the truck."

Piper cast one look at the whitecaps dotting the bay and agreed. Five minutes later they were on the switchback.

"I hope you make it inside before the rain starts," he said, peering through the windshield. "You'll ruin that suit."

"Clothes aren't important. People are. I don't like that you'll have to drive back in what could be a deluge."

"I'll think about you. Time will fly."

They made it to Cathcart House as the first droplets began to splatter the screen.

"Come in and wait it out," she invited. "There's no point trying to negotiate the road when you can't see."

Because the black clouds looked ready to explode, and because he wanted a few more minutes with her, Jason nodded, climbed out of the truck and grabbed her hand. They raced across the yard with the wind whipping at their clothes and hair. Piper unlocked the door, stepped inside and flicked on the lights.

The heavens crackled, light blazed. A second later the power went out.

"Wouldn't you know it?"

"Is this a ploy to get me alone?" he teased, bending to whisper against her neck.

"You wish." Piper wiggled away from him. "Wait there. I've got some candles ready."

Jason closed the door behind him, waited until the faint flicker of a candle turned into the glow of several.

"Come on in. You can light the fireplace, if you want. That'll take the chill off things. I'm going to change." She disappeared.

Jason knelt in front of the fireplace, chose a match from the brass container and lit the already-set tinder. It caught immediately and he fed it with bits and pieces of wood until it was safe to add a small log, then two. Satisfied that the fire would not go out, he put the fire screen in front.

"That's better." Piper emerged wearing a red, bulky sweater and jeans that emphasized the length of her legs. "Fortunately my stove is gas so I can make tea. Or would you rather—"

The sudden break in her voice sent Jason hurrying to the kitchen where he found her staring at something on the table, her fingers clenched around the kettle handle.

He turned to look, reached out a finger to touch the tiny hotel model.

"Where did this come from?"

She sank onto one of the stools.

"That was the package in my car after the Spring Fling. I don't know where it came from or who put it there." Her dark eyes held secrets. "I'm pretty sure my car was locked that day, Jason."

"You're saying someone broke into your car?"

"And into this house." She scanned the room, shivered.

"What do you mean?"

Her attention shifted to the windows, to the yawning darkness beyond.

"Piper?"

She turned her wide-eyed gaze on him. "Yes?"

"What do you mean someone broke in?" He took the kettle from her, set it on the stove. "Tell me."

"I'd put the model in a cupboard," she whispered. "It wasn't on the table when I left this morning. I'm certain of that. Which means someone has been in my house when I wasn't here. Maybe they're still here." *Oh, God, why is this happening?*

Jason hugged her then reached for the phone to summon the police. He checked the main floor and upstairs. Nothing. He returned to the kitchen, found Piper hadn't moved. Her face was pale, her eyes robbed of their usual sparkle.

He filled the kettle and turned it on. Then he located the hot chocolate and made a cup, which he insisted she drink. By the time Chief Neely came she'd regained her equilibrium. But he lost his as she described several other incidents, none of which she'd discussed with him.

"Well, I haven't seen much evidence. It's useless to look outside with all this rain. And in here you say there's nothing out of place?"

"Not that I've noticed. Everything seems as I left it this morning. Except for that model." She kept staring at it, as if she could get a hint if she watched long enough.

"Not much point in dusting for fingerprints then. We wouldn't know where to look." Chief Neely offered a sympathetic smile. "Most I can do is have regular patrols go past, check things are okay. It might help if you changed the locks, and maybe look in to getting a security system."

"A security system?" She shook her head. "We never needed that before."

"Well, there's lots of folks coming and going these days. Could be someone on Lookout Point just snooping around, but I'd say it's a little more personal than that. Maybe someone doesn't like your ideas for the Bay." He stuck his pencil in his notebook, thrust it back in his pocket. "Even with a security system, if you were working in town and they broke in, you wouldn't get here in time to stop 'em, but at least you'd know when it happened. You'd feel safer coming home at night."

"I'll think about that," she told him. "But I'll definitely have the locks changed. I meant to do that a while ago."

"Okay then. That's the best I can do, ma'am." He started toward the door, then paused. "Say, you wouldn't know if someone's been buying land up here, would you?"

Jason caught Piper's start of surprise.

"Someone's buying property up here?" he asked.

"I'm surprised that as mayor, you don't know about it. Had a complaint about digging, reports of unusual traffic on the road. Thought maybe somebody was building a house."

"We'll look into it on Monday," Jason promised. "Thanks for your help."

"No problem." Bud left a few minutes later, after promising to check on the house throughout the night.

When he'd left Jason crouched to look into Piper's eyes. "Are you going to be okay? Would you feel better camping out at Ida's?"

"No, don't be silly. I'll be fine. It's just someone playing silly games." She offered a nervous laugh that didn't quite come off.

"You don't know who it is, do you?"

"No, I don't *know*. It just seems it has to be someone playing tricks. An ordinary thief would have taken something. Right?"

"Yes." She didn't sound sure of that.

"I guess."

"I'll be praying for you, Piper. Asking God to protect you. You can trust Him."

He kissed her good-night and left shortly after that, scanning the ditch and every side road as he returned to his place. Once inside he phoned to tell her he was home, but also to check on her.

"I'm fine, Jason. Don't worry about me. I'll see you tomorrow at church."

"You wouldn't prefer me picking you up?"

"Don't be silly. You'd come here and have to turn around and go back. I'll be there."

But after he'd hung up, he sat in the dark, watching out the big picture windows as the storm puttered out and the clouds scattered. A while later the stars emerged.

"Something's not right, Lord. I can feel it." He squeezed his eyes closed, trying to put his finger on the thing that had set his radar flashing. But he couldn't put the pieces together.

Neither could he get the picture of that model hotel out of his mind. He hadn't had much time to examine it, but at first glance it seemed to represent everything he'd been hoping for. Piper must have known that when she first unwrapped it. Yet she'd said nothing.

Trust.

"I'm trying, but please, don't let me make another mistake," he whispered, the sting of a past betrayal flickering to life. "Don't ask me to go through it all again, Father."

Piper closed and locked the front door, waiting till Jason's car lights were obscured by the valleys and hills. Then she walked to the table, picked up the model and turned it over and over, searching for the wooden *W,* Wainwright Inc.'s distinctive logo. It had been glued on the front, above the entry. Now it was not there.

She searched the cupboard where she'd hidden it, fingered everything in the drawer, wondering if it had fallen off. Nothing. That left just one possibility. Someone had removed it when they'd set the model here.

Her father?

What was it Jason said—that Wainwright had called *him?* Other than calling her father directly she knew only one way to check out her suspicions.

"Dylan? It's me."

"Hey, sis. How are you?"

"Okay. You?"

"Same as always. Running circles for the old man. Don't you wish you were back at Wainwright?"

"No."

He laughed.

"No, I don't suppose you do." She heard him talking to someone. "Listen, Piper, I've got company. Could I call you back, say tomorrow, sometime after sunup?"

"Sorry," she murmured. "I know it's late. I just need to ask you a question."

"Shoot."

"Where's Baron?"

"Why? You want to talk to him?" He sounded shocked.

"No. I just need to know if he's in town."

"Supposed to be in Montego Bay, but you know Baron. He does what he wants, when he wants." His voice grew softer. "I'm coming, Susan. It's my sister. I won't be long."

"So he's back from Britain?"

"Oh, sure. He's been all over North America in the past two weeks. We've had some company problems. Is that all you wanted?"

She drew a deep breath. "W-would he have come to the Bay, Dylan?"

"What bay?" He paused, choked. "You mean Serenity Bay? I doubt it. Why would he? I think he had dinner meetings scheduled in New York last night."

Relief. Piper swallowed, let out her pent-up breath. "Okay, thanks."

"Are you okay? Do you need to talk to him?"

"I'm fine. And no, I don't want to talk to him." She was about to hang up then thought of one more thing. "Dylan, is Wainwright working on a hotel project for the Bay?"

"We're interested but Dad called a halt until we can get to the bottom of some other problems. He's not in a hurry. He thinks there will be lots of time before you call for proposals."

"So you don't have an active, workable plan? And you're not buying up land around here?"

"Not that I know of."

"And you would know, wouldn't you?"

He laughed. "I'd better. Look, Piper, much as I love you, I do have another life besides Wainwright. I'll call you tomorrow, okay? We can talk then."

"No, it's okay. Take a day off. Goodness knows you deserve one with the pace he keeps you running at." She thought of her big brother. How she wished he could break free of Baron's grip on his life and walk away. But Dylan wasn't like her. He needed that approval.

"I took today off, Piper. That's the best I can do at the moment."

"I know," she murmured, understanding what he hadn't said. "If you need a longer break, come and stay with me. The Bay's great for reorienting your priorities."

"Is that what you're doing there?" Dylan didn't wait for her response. "Maybe I'll see if I can work something in later on but right now I have to go, Piper. You take care of yourself."

"You, too. I love you."

"Uh-huh."

She hung up, leaned against the counter and surveyed the model.

Either Dylan didn't know as much as he thought he did or someone else wanted her to think Wainwright was ready to pitch. Didn't matter which, though; she wasn't comfortable with knowing someone had been in her car, in her house, found the model and left it out.

Somebody was trying to tell her something. But what?

As she turned from rinsing her mug, Piper spotted the *W* sitting on the shelf over the sink, right beside the photo of her grandparents. She retrieved it, turned it over and over, thinking.

Had Jason seen it?

If so, why hadn't he said anything?

What's going on here, God?

Sunday's sermon echoed in her mind. How many times should I forgive my neighbor? Seven times seven? Seventy times seven, Jesus told him.

Forgive.

"I can't," she whispered.

Chapter Nine

"We can't stop Wainwright from approaching the town council with an idea, Piper. That wouldn't be fair. Anyway, why would we?"

"Because we've already ruled out Wainwright, Jason," she said, tired of the argument they'd wasted weeks debating. "Why bother?"

"*You* ruled them out," Jason said quietly. "I haven't. For all we know they may have come up with something we want, something that will meet all our needs." He held out a file. "These are notes from a brainstorming session the Chamber of Commerce held when you were away yesterday. I think you'll find some things of interest."

"Okay. Thanks. How are the houseboats working out?"

He grinned. "Purring like kittens. Higgy has tuned them purr-fectly. He's a great mechanic."

"Higgy?" she asked, one eyebrow raised.

"Andy calls him that and so do I. He prefers it." Jason sat down. "You look tired. Is everything okay?"

"No. I've been checking in to recent land sales. There have

been several transactions for property near Cathcart House. All to the same company. Ida and I have been trying to find out who owns it, but so far all we've got is a never-ending paper trail which looks like it leads to some offshore conglomerate."

"Well, they can't build anything without a permit and it's zoned residential. Since we haven't received a request to build, I don't know if you have much to worry about."

"Maybe not." Piper slid her hand into her pocket, felt the whisper of paper against her fingers. The Wainwright invoice she'd found in Gran's rose garden was burning a hole in her pocket, but this wasn't the time to blurt out her concerns. Besides, she didn't want to rehash the old arguments between her grandparents and her father, or get into his threat to someday buy Cathcart House and force them out of the Bay.

She'd tell Jason about her own past—sometime, but not now.

"We had another development yesterday."

The strange note in his voice brought her head up sharply. "Oh?"

"Wainwright asked to make a presentation at the council meeeting tonight."

"What?" Piper couldn't believe he'd said it. "Who called?"

"I don't know." Jason gave her an odd look. "Does it matter? Someone spoke to Ida, asked to be included on the agenda. So she did."

"At the last minute? Aren't there other important matters already scheduled?" Irritated, Piper glared at him. "You could have put them off."

"I told you. I didn't talk to them. Anyway, what's more important than a hotel for this place? You know how hard it's getting to house people who want upscale accommodations." He leaned forward, grasped her hand where it fidgeted with papers. "Piper, what's wrong?"

The concern in his eyes melted her heart. She grasped his hand, squeezed, then let go.

"Nothing. I'm sorry. It's just—you know my objections to Wainwright." She shrugged, tried to summon a smile. "I've been working so hard to coax Ted. I don't want him to be scared off just because Wainwright wants to make a play."

"Ted won't be scared off if he really wants it. Besides, isn't competition good for us?"

"Not necessarily. If Ted thinks we've been courting him and then learns we're also talking to Wainwright, he could feel like he's wasted his time."

"Who were you talking to yesterday?" he asked, then blushed at her look. "I'm not distrusting you, I just wondered if it was another hotel expressing interest."

"No. The corporate head of a fast-food company phoned me night before last to ask for a meeting. They wanted to know about available land within the town limits."

Jason grinned, slapped his hand on the desk. "Yes! I knew we'd start getting some attention. What's next?"

Piper shook her head, held up one hand.

"Whoa! Let's not get ahead of ourselves. This was an expression of interest. We talked possibilities but it's a long way from a done deal, Jason. You know how land development works. You were involved in locating parcels. You must know the ins and outs of negotiations."

"Uh-uh. I was never involved in any of that." Jason rose, moved to the window. His back was to her as he spoke. "I scouted locations, concentrated on finding the properties best suited to my clients. Once they were satisfied, I moved on to the next search."

"You never went back to see what had become of the property?" She frowned, sensing he was holding back.

"I did go back, once."

"And?"

"You could say the visit didn't meet my expectations. I saw my girlfriend there. With another man."

"I'm sorry." This was what Ted had hinted at that day by the elevator.

"Yeah, me, too." He turned, offered her a lopsided smile. "Shortly after that I quit and moved here."

"I'm glad."

"So am I." He touched her hair with gentle fingers. "Otherwise I'd never have met you."

"Did you care about her very much?" she asked.

"I'd planned to ask her to marry me the following weekend. It's a good thing I didn't. She married him instead."

"Oh, Jason." She rose, wrapped her arms around him and held him close. "I'm sorry."

"No, it's okay. I'm over it. I realized that I didn't really love her. I loved the idea of marriage." He pushed her bangs off her forehead, cupped her face in his palms. "That's why I'm paranoid about trust, I guess. In here—" he tapped his chest "—I know you're not like her. But it hasn't quite penetrated up here." He touched his head. "But working with you is teaching me."

He was telling her he trusted her, that he'd stopped suspecting her every move.

A flicker of guilt pinged inside her head. But Piper ignored it, lifting her face for his kiss.

A gentle rap on the door soon had them separating. Jason touched her cheek then walked to the door and opened it.

"This just arrived from Wainwright Inc. I thought you'd both want to take a look at it before council meets tonight."

Ida handed Jason a long tube, took one look at Piper and grinned before she hurried out of the room.

Jason removed the end and let a roll of papers slide out.

"Artists' renderings," Piper murmured as he unfurled them. She held her breath, stared down at the drawings. "They're not the same," she breathed.

"As that model you have? No, they're not." He looked at her with an odd expression. "Did you think they would be?"

Piper shrugged, avoiding an answer. She grabbed a pad and began making notes of changes to the hotel that would have to occur before it would fit in with the town's plans. There were many. An hour later, she leaned back in her chair, rubbing her forehead.

"It's too much. They'll never go for what we want."

"You don't know that."

He wanted it badly. She could see the excitement in his eyes.

"Why is this hotel so important to you, Jason?" She should have asked that long ago. But now Piper couldn't contain her curiosity about his answer.

"Because the town can't really move ahead without it."

"It's more than that, though, isn't it?" she said, noting the way he avoided her gaze. "You've been pushing hard to get one here ever since I came. Tell me why."

He sank down in the chair across from her. Silence stretched for a long time before he finally spoke.

"Have you ever wanted to be part of something really great? To see your ideas at work, watch other people benefiting and know that you had a big part in making it happen?" He grimaced. "Of course you have. That's what your job is all about."

"Never mind me," she said, realizing that until now he'd never really exposed his innermost feelings. "I want to know about you."

He sighed, leaning back in his chair.

"A while ago you asked me about Expectations. My job there involved a lot of travel and I loved that. But after I found my girlfriend and my best friend together, my world came crashing down. I realized that I'd never really taken in the whole picture. I'm not talking about my girlfriend."

He was quiet for a moment then spoke again.

"Maybe seeing them together forced me to realize that I wasn't committed to anything. I looked around that resort and thought 'I'm a part of this, I helped create this.' That experience changed the way I began to assess property. I decided I wanted to be more involved in the end result."

"I see."

"When I learned about Serenity Bay and began researching it, I couldn't help feeling that if I recommended it and some developer moved in, stuck in one of those cheap-lodgings-and-not-much-more places that would do little to help the town, that would be my fault, too." He rested his elbows on his knees. "I fell for this place the moment I laid eyes on it. Then things blew up at work. I quit and decided to come here, to see if I could help change things for the better, make a difference."

"To make it something more than just another cheap and tacky tourist town," she murmured with a smile. "Believe me, I understand. But I feel that way because I used to live here, because it was my refuge at a time in my life when things were really bad. What's your excuse?"

He studied her silently for several moments. When he spoke, his voice grew solemn, utterly serious.

"Because it's my fresh start." He searched her eyes, his face showing a defensiveness she'd only glimpsed before.

She knew there was more to it than he'd admitted.

"Why did you need one?"

"Because I'd made so many mistakes." A crooked smile lifted one corner of his mouth. "I doubt you could understand what it was like, Piper. You had your grandparents to love you. You never had to struggle to matter, to fight to achieve recognition, to be valued just because you're you."

If he only knew. Piper understood only too well.

"I didn't have terrible foster homes. They never abused me." He raked a hand through his hair, mussing it so he looked like a forlorn little boy. "But I was very aware that when I left, there'd be another boy to take my place, another kid to fill my shoes. I doubt if any of them even remembered me a year later."

"I'm sorry."

"That sounds like self-pity and I don't mean it to be." He rose, pacing the room. "I went to school on full academic scholarships, won the top prize offered. That got me a big mention, but there were a hundred other kids in college who'd accomplished the same thing. Big deal. It benefited me, but it didn't mean I'd contributed anything."

"And Expectations?"

"The debacle there was an awakening. I started to understand that I needed more to fill me inside than just finding a good piece of property. I wanted, needed, some personal involvement in any project I worked on." He shrugged. "I own a marina now, make half the money I used to. I don't have high-powered lunches or fraternize with the money guys. But I'm doing something important here. Or trying to."

What she'd heard had touched Piper deeply, but it also concerned her. She, more than most, knew the folly of looking for fulfillment in work. She'd seen it in her father, watched it overtake him, all in the name of helping God help him succeed.

"Jason, you don't have to prove yourself." She rose, walked

around the desk and stood beside him, her hand on his shoulder. "It's not what you do that makes you a good person. God loves you, He cares about you whether you put Serenity Bay on the map or not. It not about what you can do, it's about what He does," she reminded.

"Yes, yes. But surely what God wants is for me to succeed, to do the best for the Bay." He glanced at his watch. "I've got to get back. Andy's taking a group out to The Bowl."

The Bowl was the fishermen's name for a spot where some of the best and biggest northern pike could be found. Jason gave her a quick kiss then ran out the door. Piper watched him go, troubled by what he'd just said.

It was obvious Jason thought he had to prove himself, which made her wonder if that wouldn't contribute to his eagerness to accept Wainwright's proposal. She'd have to call Tina, find out what was going on.

But the afternoon slipped away too quickly. There was no time to do more than answer calls and make her notes in readiness for the meeting ahead. She ordered a sandwich to give her a few more minutes to prepare, ate it, then walked into the council chambers, hoping she was prepared to meet her father.

To her surprise no one from Wainwright was in attendance. The meeting proceeded without incident for an hour. Then a knock came at the door and Dylan appeared.

"I'm sorry I'm late," he apologized, the grin that had gotten him out of so many scrapes firmly in place. "It took a little longer than I expected to get here. I'm Dylan Wainwright."

"Come in." Jason introduced everyone. "We have nothing else pressing at the moment. Why don't we hear what Mr. Wainwright has to say?"

Since the council was in agreement, the pitch began.

Dylan didn't even glance her way, for which Piper was

glad. He lifted the huge portfolio he carried onto the table and began Wainwright's proposal.

"As you can see," he wrapped up twenty minutes later, "we've gone to a great deal of trouble to make this hotel a premiere jewel in the Wainwright chain."

"Our economic development officer, Piper Langley, and I took the liberty of examining the drawings you sent this afternoon. Perhaps she has some questions," Jason responded.

"Hello, Piper." Dylan grinned at her, his bad boy grin firmly in place.

"Dylan."

"You two know each other?" Jason asked.

"Of course." She looked at him, then refocused on her notes. "We've got a couple of problems with the concept, Dylan. The golf course won't work where you're indicating because we're hoping that in the winter we can use the greens for trails for cross-country skiing."

She listed the deficits one by one. Dylan took it gracefully, nodded occasionally, making notes for himself.

"You're asking for a lot," he said when she was finished.

Piper nodded. "But we're offering a lot of concessions. We want this hotel to fit exactly right with the Bay. The developer will be getting prime access, prime positioning and some lucrative tax breaks. In exchange we want a complementary structure."

The council members began to voice their own considerations. Lively discussions covered every imaginable topic until Jason called a halt.

"Order. Folks, we're way over time. I'd like to thank Wainwright Inc. and Dylan for taking the time to explain all that."

"No problem." Dylan began replacing the charts and drawings in his portfolio. "I'll get together with Dad and we'll come up with some changes." He glanced around the table, oozing charm. "Wainwright Inc. is committed to meeting your needs, folks. We want to hear your concerns, and if at all possible, we want to address them. When we make a commitment, it's for the long term."

"We appreciate that."

The meeting was adjourned. Piper caught up with Dylan outside a few moments later as he was loading his case into his SUV.

"Are you angry that I shot holes in the proposal?" she asked quietly. Their father was the problem, not Dylan.

"Of course not. All part of doing business." He turned to face her. "You don't think we get a contract on one presentation, do you?" He laughed. "Come on, Piper. You know better than that."

"Yes. But I also know how much time you put into each pre-sentation, especially when you told me you had nothing going."

"You know Dad. Pulls things out of a hat."

Or plans them way ahead. *Forgive.* Piper shook off the anger. "It's a great hotel, Dylan."

"Just not for here."

"No." She decided to be honest. "I'm not sure Wainwright can do the kind of hotel we want for here."

"My concepts aren't good enough for you, Piper?"

She was stunned at the bitterness she heard in those words and laid a hand on his arm.

"Your concepts are fantastic, Dyl, and you know it. I just meant that this is a poky little lakeside town—not your usual forte."

"I'm an architect with a master's degree in business admin-istration. My forte can stretch to anything it needs to," he said, his voice icy. "That's why Dad made me second in command of Wainwright Inc."

"I know. I'm sorry. I didn't mean anything. Please don't be angry," she begged, exactly as she had when they were children and she'd hurt his feelings with a snide comment about her father.

He glared at her, then like lightning, he was her big, charming brother again. "Sorry, sis. Put it down to the grueling drive here. You folks need some roadwork done."

"We're working on that." She stood on tiptoe, brushed his cheek with her lips. "Want to stay at Cathcart tonight, get an early start in the morning?"

"No."

The abruptness of his rejection dismayed her. But then Dylan had never appreciated the Bay and especially her grandparents' home. He'd hardly ever visited after she'd moved in with them, and then only with her father. Dylan had witnessed the same bitter feud she had.

"Okay."

He sighed. "I'm sorry, sis. I just meant I can't. I've got three early meetings tomorrow. I have to get back tonight."

"You should have flown."

"You should have an airport," he countered.

"We're working on that," Jason said from behind Piper. "She's got her finger in so many pies I'm amazed she doesn't get confused."

"She's a wonder all right. Best development officer in the biz." Dylan touched her cheek with one finger, squeezed her hand. "See you, Piper. Jason, it was nice to meet you. I'm sure we'll be talking in the coming days."

"I look forward to it." He stood beside Piper, watching as Dylan drove away.

"He seems nice."

"He is," she agreed. "I hope we didn't dash his hopes too

much. I know he put a lot of time into that proposal." She glanced at Jason. "What did you think of it?"

He held her gaze. "Do you really want to know? Or are you just being polite?"

Piper frowned. "What do you mean?"

"It's pretty clear you've already decided to throw a negative light on Wainwright's ideas, no matter what they are."

He was right. Even if Dylan had brought in that perfect model she had at home, Piper knew she would have found fault. But she couldn't admit it.

"That's not true."

"Sure it is." Jason thrust his hands in his pockets, but his gaze never wavered from her face. "There's something else going on here, Piper, and I'd like to know what it is. I'm not denying you might have a legitimate reason for distrusting the company, but we can't let that past experience impinge on what we're trying to do here."

"You thought the ideas he presented were what we wanted?" she asked, deciding a counterattack was better than defense. "You approved that plan? Because that isn't the impression you gave this afternoon."

"I didn't say I approved all of it. But there were some really good features. The ability to open out one side and make a patio café for the pool—that was excellent. The materials and the decor—they're very close to what we'd hoped for."

"Yes," she admitted.

"You never said that. You jumped hard on all the negatives." He glanced over her shoulder, lowered his voice. "It came close to an attack on Wainwright. I'll be surprised if he comes back to us a second time and that's not good for the Bay, Piper. We need a broad variety of interest and if Wainwright can give us what we need, I see no reason not to choose them."

I do, she wanted to scream. But she silenced that inner cry by gripping her briefcase a little tighter. A twist of anger coiled inside her stomach. Where was God in all of this? Did he honestly expect her to welcome Wainwright to her sanctuary?

"You're telling me to back off," she said.

"I'm *hoping* you'll get past whatever grudges you're carrying and see the possibilities in every presentation," he said softly.

"I was *hoping* we were aiming for top-notch and not settling for the first idea that came along," she murmured. "My mistake. Next time I'll note my concerns and hand them over for you to check before I say anything." She slid the strap of her bag over one shoulder. "I need to get home now. Good night."

But he wouldn't let her go so easily, insisting on walking beside her to where *Shalimar* was tied.

"What's really wrong?"

She ignored him, slipped out of her heels and into the deck shoes that would save the glossy wooden surface.

"Talk to me, Piper."

She straightened, met his scrutiny and decided to tell him.

"You hired me, presumably, because of my skills at economic development. But every time I offer an opinion, every time I try to do my job, for the benefit of Serenity Bay, you challenge me. Maybe I'm not the person you need to do this job, Jason."

He grasped her elbow so she couldn't leave.

"You're the only person who could do such a good job for us and you know it. But this—" he jerked his head toward the town office "—this wasn't about your job. It's about something else and I want to know what is going on." His voice dropped; he touched her hair, brushed it out of her eyes. "Tell me the truth, Piper. Maybe I can help. Is it Dylan? Was he the problem—something in you past?"

"No."

It would be so easy to release the memories that flooded back—dark, painful snapshots of seventeen-year-old Dylan begging her to go with them, angrily asking her to stop antagonizing their father, to stop causing a fuss. Her prayers that always went unanswered. Her secret fear that if she stopped fighting her father, she'd never be her own person again.

Piper could use words to describe the long days and nights after her father had taken Dylan away, the months he'd refused to allow him to visit, the long, lonely nights when she'd despaired of ever having her big brother close again—but words alone wouldn't help Jason understand how abandoned she'd felt. Letting him see the hole inside would only make her appear weak.

Dad needs you here with us, Piper. He needs his family. We haven't got anyone else but us you know. Wainwrights stick together.

But Baron hadn't needed her; he'd wanted to control her—just as he did everything else in his world. Just as he'd controlled and manipulated Dylan into becoming a replica of himself. Besides, Baron Wainwright had not been there when she'd needed him most.

Forgive.

How could Jason possibly understand that?

"Just talk to me," he whispered, reaching out to draw her closer.

But Piper backed away.

"I'm tired. I'm going home. You decide if you want me to stay or if you'd rather I left so you can get on with courting Wainwright."

She heard his hiss of exasperation but ignored it by casting off. Free of the dock, she revved the engine and took off across the water, in no mood to sail tonight.

The calm bay waters accelerated her progress and soon *Shalimar* was inside the boathouse. She climbed the stairs to the house. The lights were on, casting a yellow glow up the hill where Cathcart House lay waiting. Having the locks changed made coming home less of a worry, something the new security system enhanced.

Once she'd changed clothes and made herself a cup of mint tea, Piper curled up on a deck chair and searched the night sky for answers. Was it time to leave the Bay, to give up on the plan that had brought her here?

Why don't you ever help me when I need it, God?

I demand that you love each other as much as I love you.

"I do love him," she admitted at last, "but I hate him, too."

God is love.

"If you love someone, you will always believe in him, always expect the best of him, always stand your ground in defending him." She could almost hear him reciting the passage from Corinthians.

"He hurt me." She wept. "He hurt them. And he didn't come when I needed him. How can I forgive him?"

Let love be your greatest aim.

"I can't love. It hurts too much."

But that wasn't true. She thought of Jason, of leaving as she'd suggested. Of never seeing him again.

A soft sigh of sadness filled her at leaving the friendly souls she'd grown to care about. Abandoning her work plans wouldn't be half as bad as not seeing Jason again.

She was in love with him.

The realization surprised her, left her shocked.

Cared about him, yes. Wanted him to succeed, yes. But loved him?

She thought for a moment, comparing this love to her love for Vance. The soft, sweet rush of love she'd felt for him was nothing like what she felt now. With Jason it was different, more like a tiny fire that flared to life when he was near. Her breath caught whenever he walked into the room. Her heart skipped a beat when he winked at her in that audacious way he had. She found herself wanting him to wrap her up in his arms. To forget about Wainwright and hotels and the Bay and simply enjoy his presence.

But Jason was like Baron. He was consumed by his plans for the Bay, so much so that he was willing to cave on the rest of his dream if it meant getting the hotel he so desperately wanted.

She thought of Jason discovering the girl he'd cared about in the arms of another man, learning that his best friend had betrayed him. Perhaps he was coping with that betrayal by using the Bay to prove himself.

Hadn't her father used his work to compensate in the same way after Piper's mother had died?

Her parents had seemed close. Certainly her mother had never been shy about giving Baron her opinion on anything. They argued. They made up. Until he'd started that last project, the one that had overtaken his entire life. Nothing her mother had said then seemed to make a difference to him. He was gone for long periods of time and when he came home they'd argued. Then she'd died. Baron had become more controlling, more demanding.

And Piper had left home.

Tears trickled down her cheeks at the death of a family. Why had God let her mother die?

"Piper?"

She blinked. Jason stood in front of her. "What are you doing here?" He leaned down until his face was level with hers. He reached out to wipe the tear from her cheek.

"I had to come back," he whispered. "I'm sorry."

The simple words touched a spot deep inside that she'd thought long dead. Piper put her hands in his, rose and leaned into his embrace.

"I didn't mean to hurt you," he whispered, hugging her tightly. "I'd never do that. I only wanted to help. Instead I upset you. I'm so sorry."

She said nothing, simply laid her head on his chest and slid her arms around his waist, allowing his quiet words and gentle touch to heal. His kiss asked nothing in return but offered sweet comfort. How could she not love a man like this?

After a long time he turned her so they could both watch the stars.

"Why were you crying?"

"I was thinking about my mother, about how different things might have been if only she'd lived. I never understood why. Our lives were ruined."

"Sweetheart, your life isn't ruined." His words held a certainty she envied. "I know it hurt and I know the pain never totally goes away, but you coped, you kept going. You've made a difference. I'm sure your mother is very proud."

"Do you think so?" She watched a star skate across the sky. "I have a hard time believing that."

"Why?" He rested his chin against her shoulder.

"Has to do with my idea of heaven, I guess. Or rather God in heaven. I feel like he punished us and her by taking her too early, for no reason. I've always felt that God is sort of like a stern judge, sitting up there, peering down at us, waiting for one little misstep. In my head I know that's wrong. But inside—" She sighed.

Jason was silent for several minutes, then he coaxed her to sit down. He crouched down in front of her.

"Piper, God didn't punish you by taking your mother. He had other plans for her and for you, but He made sure you had grandparents who loved and cared for you. He gave you a wonderful place to live, and two very good friends. And then He brought you back here because He loves you. He has so much in store for you. You can't even begin to imagine." He touched her cheek. "He's not a God of hate. He's a God of love. He's your Father."

She made a face. "Maybe that's my problem. God as a father is one analogy that doesn't work for me. My real father is bad enough."

"Tell me about him."

"What do you want to know? He's driven, arrogant, controlling, demanding, pushy, manipulative if he has to be, and he thinks he does." She shook her head, tossing away the pain. "I don't think he ever saw me as anything other than an extension of his own ambition."

"Now tell me about your grandfather."

She smiled, closed her eyes and tipped her head back against the chair.

"Papa wasn't any less demanding than my father, but he had little time for arrogance. He was interested in everything and everyone. Any time you wanted to talk, if you needed a story or a hug, he had time. He listened, really listened. And he never told you what you should or shouldn't do. He'd hear you out, then help you put things in perspective. You know?" she asked, blinking to look at him.

Jason nodded. "You felt as if he really cared about helping you achieve your goals?"

"Yes! I miss him so much." Tears ran down her face. "I have no one to talk to."

"Oh, Piper." A sad little smile lifted his lips, and his eyes rested on her in a comforting way. "That isn't true. You can always talk to God."

She frowned, trying to understand what he was telling her.

"Don't you see? God knew your father wasn't what you needed, so He moved you into a position where you'd know and love a man like Himself, a man who taught you God's ways. A man who loved you and, more than anything, wanted what was best for you. If you need an analogy for God, use your grandfather, think about his open arms, his welcoming smile. God is just like that—always there, always ready to listen, offering His love."

"I never thought of it like that before," she whispered, staring at his hands holding hers. "But you're right. Papa was the way the Bible describes a loving father."

He smiled, patted her cheek, then rose. But he stood there watching her.

"Can I say one more thing?"

"Sure."

"Don't hang on to your bad feelings against your father."

"You don't understand—"

"No, I don't," he interrupted. "Nobody can know what drove him but your father. He lost his wife. His daughter left his home. I'm not saying he didn't deserve what he got, I'm just saying that maybe it's time to cut him a little slack. Who knows what he was thinking of, or how your mother's death affected him. Maybe losing her hit him harder than anything he'd ever experienced."

"He threatened my grandparents, you know." She glared at him, the pain alive and burning in her heart. "He actually told them he'd take this house and all the land from them."

"He never did it, though. He was hurt and angry, lashing out at someone in his pain." Jason shook his head. "Can't you forgive him after all these years?"

For that—maybe. But there was something for which Piper would never forgive Baron—not as long as she lived. She tried but—

"Think about it, Piper. Think about what hanging on to the hurt does to your life." He tugged on her hand, drew her up. "Believe me, I know what I'm talking about. Having your best friend try to ruin your name and then marry your girlfriend isn't easy on the ego. But they love each other very much. I wasn't the man she needed. I have to believe God knew what He was doing."

She stared into his eyes, saw the same gentleness she'd glimpsed in her grandfather, a respect and care for others that was more than merely words.

"Thank you," she said, reaching up to brush his cheek with her lips. "You didn't have to come all the way over here. I would have come in to work tomorrow."

Jason chuckled. "Yes. But I would have missed this."

He wrapped her in a snug embrace and told her without words that he cared about her. And Piper kissed him back.

When he drew back, his eyes sparkled.

"That was definitely worth the trip." Jason glanced at his watch. "But I'd better get home."

Suddenly he bent, lifting something.

"What's this?" he asked, holding out a book.

Piper caught her breath.

"It's my grandfather's diary. It's been missing since I moved back. Someone must have returned it."

Someone like…Baron Wainwright?

Chapter Ten

"About time, boss!" Andy's voice bellowed above the roar of the houseboat motor as Jason eased the craft into its mooring.

"I hope you enjoyed your trip, folks. Step carefully now." He gave the boy a warning look, nodding when Andy held out a hand for the ladies to grasp as they stepped off. "I believe your lunch is waiting for you, if you'll follow Mr. Higgins. Come again soon."

The small group of day-trippers was the third that week. Jason hoped there would soon be many more boat tours. They took time, but they more than paid for themselves in word-of-mouth publicity among seniors' groups in the area.

Once they were out of earshot, Andy captured his attention.

"What is it, Andy?"

"Ms. Langley wants you up at the town office, ASAP."

"Did she say why?" Jason asked, stifling his groan. Not that seeing Piper was a hardship. But the day stretched ahead with a hundred things to do and none of them included the town office until the council meeting at seven tonight when Wainwright Inc. would address them again.

Maybe Piper's call had something to do with Dylan's re-appearance. After last week he wasn't sure what to expect.

"Couldn't really understand what she was saying but I think it's important. She came down here herself a few minutes ago. Wanted to know why you didn't answer your cell."

"Okay, thanks." He finished tying off the boat. "Can I leave you to clean her up?"

"Of course." As Jason walked away Andy muttered sotto voce, "If it were me, I'd be moving a little quicker than that to see a babe like her, but I guess when you get that old—"

"Hey!" Jason threw him a withering glare. "I'm not deaf, you know. Not yet."

Andy didn't look the least bit daunted.

"She's got a good-looking guy with her. Holds her arm when she walks, smiles at her constantly. I wouldn't waste my time talking to me if I were you."

"You're right. I won't." Jason strode up the dock and crossed the street, heading for the town office. He rapped once on Piper's door before entering. "Piper?"

She looked flustered, totally unlike cool, competent Piper.

Jason crossed the room to stand beside her. "Anything wrong?" he asked, keeping his voice low.

"Everything's just fine," she said gaily, her fingers touching his in the lightest brush. "Jason, I'd like you to meet Quint Gilroy. Mr. Gilroy, this is our mayor, Jason Franklin."

They greeted each other. Jason glanced at Piper, discerning from her carefully modulated tone that this man was important to them.

"Mr. Gilroy would like to speak to the council tonight, Jason. He's interested in purchasing land in town to build some rather lovely condos." Excitement glittered in her eyes.

Jason didn't blame her. It was more than they'd ever hoped

for. Immediately his mind swung into overdrive as a mental picture blossomed.

"Wonderful," he enthused, shaking the other man's hand. "Let's sit in the boardroom. We've a wall map there that might help us. What kind of land are you looking for?"

He listened as Gilroy described his project, struggling to keep his mind from blowing everything out of proportion.

"I don't do huge projects," Gilroy stated. "I'd like to start with two buildings of ten units but have enough room to expand down the road by adding more complexes as the idea takes off."

Piper waited, but when Jason didn't offer any suggestions, she drew attention to a parcel of property that had been empty as long as Jason could remember.

"Jason has a lot more experience with the needs of your kind of development than I, Mr. Gilroy. But this particular plot does offer the benefit of a water view on three sides."

It was enough to get the ball rolling and as ideas mushroomed Jason took over, falling back into an old pattern as he emphasized the location, the amenities and the possibilities. He wasn't sure how much time had passed before he noticed Piper's glare.

"I'm sorry. Was I rambling?"

Gilroy rose, grabbed his briefcase as if he couldn't get away fast enough.

"There's no way I can accommodate that kind of development," he said hurriedly, edging toward the door. "I appreciate that you once worked with the big boys, Mr. Franklin, but I haven't got that kind of money. I'm a small investor who happens to own a construction company. We could have begun immediately but your ideas are a little too rich for me." Gilroy gulped, glanced at Piper and forced a smile. "I'm sorry to have bothered you."

Jason tried to backpedal, caught the tiny shake of her head Piper gave him. He shut up while she did damage control. In the end Gilroy calmed down enough to go with her to the site she'd proposed to look around.

"I know you're very busy, Jason," she purred sweetly, "so we won't detain you. Mr. Gilroy and I can talk at our leisure." The look in her eyes told him not to argue.

"Nice to meet you, Mr. Gilroy. I hope you find what you're looking for." He watched them leave, Piper soothing as she walked with him.

"What happened?" Ida asked, her head tilted to one side like a curious bird.

"I think I just blew it." How many times had Piper warned him to slow down, not to push so hard?

"A little aggressive, were you?" Ida's snort earned his glower. She didn't back down. "When are you going to relax, Jason?"

"I don't know what you mean. Developing Serenity Bay has been my first priority for quite a while now. I thought you knew that."

"I do. But does it all have to happen this month?" Ida poked her pencil tip into the automatic sharpener on her desk and let it whir until the pencil was just a stub. "You're grinding us down with your pushing, Jason. Piper's lost about five pounds since she got here, from stress. When are you going to learn to trust?"

"I trust Piper!" Indignant at the accusation, he leaned his elbows on the counter and glared at her.

"I wasn't talking about Piper, though some other time I might dispute that comment—like when you're pressing me about her whereabouts." She let him digest that for a moment, then sighed. "I was talking about God."

"God?" Now that didn't make sense at all. God was the only one he did trust.

"You act as if He's out to wreck whatever you do," she said. "If you trust someone, you have to have faith in them. Doesn't the Bible say that God will give you the desires of your heart if you devote yourself to Him?"

He nodded. His Bible study this morning had been about that very verse.

"Isn't developing the Bay your heart's desire?"

Yes, it was. Proving himself was a deep-seated need that grew whenever he thought about the past.

"Don't you believe that God wants this place to progress, that He'll work all things together?"

Did he? Jason searched his inner heart and realized she'd hit on the truth. Maybe he wasn't so sure he had God's approval, maybe he knew, deep down, that success with the Bay had more to do with shoring up his own shaky self-esteem. It was time to examine his motives.

"Does Harold know he married such a smart woman?"

"He should. I tell him often enough." She laughed.

"You keep telling him." He checked his watch, then made a decision. "Ida, I'm unavailable until the council meeting tonight. If somebody needs me, send them to Piper or put them off."

"You've got it, boss," she said, then she winked.

As he walked back to the marina, Ida's words reverberated through his mind. He gave Andy his jobs for the rest of the day, got in his truck and took off for the depths of the forest where nothing and no one could interfere with his thoughts.

Piper had tried to warn him but he wouldn't listen. He'd wanted the Bay to flourish so badly that now he was risking losing investors by pushing them too hard for what they couldn't or wouldn't give.

But if he didn't, if he just sat back and waited, what would change?"

Maybe nothing. And that was his biggest fear.

So what was he trying to prove here—that the foster kid who'd never mattered to anybody was important, that the Bay couldn't get along without him at the helm?

He delved deeper into the truth, then finally faced it head-on.

It didn't matter what level of success he achieved for the town. He could never erase the hurt that came from knowing she'd chosen someone else above him.

He'd told Piper he'd never loved Amber, that he'd realized she wasn't the woman for him. That much was true. But the realization had only come after she'd dumped him for Trevor. And it had come on the heels of learning that Trevor had chosen money and achievement above their friendship.

Jason claimed he'd accepted God's will in that matter. Was that true?

Not really. He saw that he'd clung to the pain of it, searched for a way to erase it. What he hadn't done was let God wash it away.

Who was he to talk to Piper about letting the past go?

He'd thought he'd dealt with it but it'd been there, underneath, eating away at him all this time.

What about Piper?

He thought of her now, her gorgeous face surrounded by that mop of unruly curls that expressed her mood of the moment. Gorgeous, confident, accomplished. She answered to nobody and forged her own path, depending on herself to achieve her goals.

Piper was everything Amber hadn't been. Was that why

he'd found her so attractive, because she outshone his former girlfriend?

Jason hated the thought, hated what it implied about him— a shallowness he'd never imagined. But he faced the possibility because what he needed now more than ever before was to face the truth.

Was Piper important to him because of what he felt for her, because of the place she filled in his life? Or because he needed to prove that a beautiful, strong woman could care about him, that he wasn't unlovable?

He closed his eyes and tried to imagine Serenity Bay without Piper, but a thousand images filled his brain. Piper at the helm of *Shalimar,* her face utterly serene as the wind whipped past. Piper struck with a fit of the giggles in the middle of a snowball fight at Spring Fling. Her melted-chocolate eyes darkening black with temper when she took him to task for interrupting her meetings. Tears plopping from those black lashes onto her silken cheeks hiding a wealth of hurt she kept tucked inside.

The Bay without Piper? It didn't compute.

He loved her.

Jason leaned back against a tree and let that sweet knowledge flood over him. It wasn't about comparisons. With Piper he'd found something he'd never known before—acceptance. She hadn't flinched when he'd told her his sad little story, didn't seem to care that he was only a glorified mechanic. When he was with Piper he felt at home.

So what was he going to do about it?

Nothing.

Oh, he'd be there, as much as she'd let him after today's debacle. He'd make sure she knew that he cared for her. But he wasn't going to push her, force her into something she might regret.

This time, Jason decided, he was going to sit back and let God take over.

Even if it killed every plan he'd ever made.

Where was he?

Piper kept her seat, forced her hands to remain still and scanned the notepad in front of her but every nerve in her body was attuned to the sounds around her and the expectant faces waiting for Jason to appear at the town council meeting.

Dylan wasn't here, either, but she knew he'd show. Once her father decided on a project, he was like a dog with a bone. He'd keep pushing until he got his way. Rather like Jason, she mused grimly as she smiled reassuringly at Mr. Gilroy.

"I'm sure he'll be here momentarily."

A rush of footsteps outside the room signaled Jason's arrival. He burst into the room, tousled, slightly dusty and meekly apologetic.

"Sorry. I was out in the forest and I got a flat tire. Shall we begin?" He picked up the agenda. "Mr. Gilroy is here to talk about his desire to build some condos in Serenity Bay. Go ahead, Mr. Gilroy."

Piper swallowed her surprise as the condo builder rose and began a halting speech. Jason asked several questions which soon loosened the man's tongue and his presentation became much more interesting. Asked for her opinion, Piper reinforced what Gilroy had said. At the end the council's interest was palpable and an offer was tabled.

Satisfied with that development, she glanced around, realized Dylan had arrived while she was speaking. He smiled at her, but she could tell his focus was elsewhere. She found herself gripping her notepad a little too tightly as Jason called on him next.

"Wainwright Inc. has taken your concerns under advisement and made significant changes to our proposal. We are hopeful that what you see today will offer you greater perspective into our future plans."

Piper studied each aspect as Dylan presented it, wishing she'd seen it first. Several things sent up immediate red flags and she scribbled notes to herself for later comment. She couldn't help studying Jason during the presentation. He seemed remarkably calm. Perhaps too calm?

His disappearance this afternoon left a lot of questions, and the possibility that he'd met with Dylan. Jason's aggressive stance on the hotel was no secret, so it wouldn't be surprising if he'd sought an opportunity to meet outside of the council.

But he said he'd been in the forest. Doing what?

"We'll now open the floor for questions. Piper, anything you want clarified?"

Surprised that Jason had called on her first, she gathered her composure and rose.

"It's a good proposal," she said, her focus on Dylan. "Well thought out and carefully planned. But there are still several issues that run counter to our plans for development of the beachfront and the immediate area." She listed the problems, illustrating how they would alter plans already moving forward for other aspects of development.

As she spoke, Piper waited for Jason's rush of argument. But he remained silent. It was Dylan who pressed her.

"We have to have some leeway to fulfill the needs of the hotel," he argued. "We can't build something this massive only for the town's benefit. Wainwright has an investment to recoup, after all."

"Naturally," she said quietly. "But our investment is also

great. In two or three years, when Serenity Bay is ready to pursue another phase of our plan, we don't want to be in the position of having to reorient some of our projects, or perhaps even cancel them, because we didn't plan for the contingencies I've noted."

"So what you're saying is that we're close, but still not quite there yet," one of the councilors muttered.

"Yes." She met Dylan's glare, knew he was frustrated and felt a twist of shame that she'd hurt him. But if that's what it took to defeat Wainwright…

"Okay then." Dylan began taking down his work. "I'll take that as a no. I should warn you that I'm not sure Wainwright is prepared to come back with another offer. We do not usually accept such a large amount of—er, guidance when we submit a project and we have already made a number of concessions to fit your needs."

"I'm sorry we've been so difficult," Jason chimed in.

Piper could hardly believe he had said that. She'd expected him to be furious but he looked almost resigned as he thanked Dylan for his work. As Dylan left the room, Jason called the meeting back to order and suggested they go in camera— retire to privacy where the general public was not present— to deal with the rest of the issues.

Thus excused, Piper left, caught up with Dylan as he placed his briefcase inside his car.

"You're not in a rush to get back again, are you?" she asked quickly, needing to make him understand her position.

"Why?" He paused, turning to look at her.

"I put a chicken in the slow cooker. I thought you might share a meal with me." She widened her gaze. "You haven't eaten, have you? You never used to before a presentation."

His brows lifted as if he was surprised she'd remembered.

"Come on, Dyl. It'll be just us two. I'd like a chance to catch up with you."

After several moments he shrugged. "Sure. Why not?"

"Do you want to come with me, or follow me to Cathcart?"

"I'll have to leave and for that I'll need my truck. I'd better follow you. It's been so long I'm not sure I remember how to get there."

"You'll remember once we get going." She reached out and hugged him. "I'm across the street." She pointed.

"You're still driving that thing?" he asked, but a hint of softness lay underneath the words.

"I couldn't get rid of my little roadster. Vance loved it. So do I. Besides, it runs like a dream." She grinned, then hurried across the street, thanking God for the opportunity to reconnect with her brother outside of the business arena.

She drove quickly, eager to share what little time they had together. At the house Dylan told her he'd been up since five and asked if he could take a quick shower. By the time he returned Piper had everything ready.

"I remember this meal," Dylan murmured as he served himself more of the golden chicken. "We'd come back here after church for Sunday dinner," he guessed.

Piper nodded.

"Then you and I would run outside to play."

"Yes." She smiled at the memory of that happy time before her mother had died. "You used to tease me with garter snakes you found in Gran's garden."

"And you never told. Why?"

Piper shrugged, smiled. "I thought you wouldn't play with me anymore and I loved playing with you. You were always the best big brother, Dyl. Nobody could have had more patience."

He ignored that, concentrating on his food. But the furrow between his brows grew deeper.

"Why did you come back here, Piper? Why didn't you sell the place and get on with your life?"

"I tried," she told him honestly. "After Vance died I buried myself in work, took on way too much and pushed myself to keep going. But I lost my joy." She pushed at the two peas left on her plate. "Gran and Papa were gone so I came back here, spent a weekend clearing out, dealing with stuff. When the day came to leave, I knew I'd rather stay. I felt a peace here, a certain comfort of happier times that I wanted to hang on to. So when I saw the want ad for economic development officer—" She shrugged. "That was my chance."

"Dad tried to contact you in Calgary," he told her.

Piper gaped. "Why?"

"He's had some health concerns, Piper. He's not as young as he was the day you walked out."

The anger in his voice shocked her until she recalled those visits her father had made to Cathcart demanding she return home. Dylan had begged her to come back. Baron had made both of them miserable.

"Oh, Dyl." She reached out to grasp his hand. "I'm sorry I had to leave you alone with him, but I just couldn't take it anymore. You were older, starting college. I doubt if you knew just how overbearing and demanding he'd become."

"Are you kidding?" An angry smile lifted the corners of his mouth. "I took the brunt of it the day you disappeared. I still do."

She tried to console him but Dylan shook her off. After a moment she coaxed him into the living room and served coffee there.

"Why don't you leave, Dyl?" she asked quietly. "You're smart. You could sell your stock, work for someone else, or set up your own company. Why do you keep taking it?"

"Why?" He barked out a laugh. "Because one of these days Dad is going to retire. You don't realize how much he's aged, how much I actually do around there, Piper. Every day he depends on me more and more. And one of these days I'll be taking the reins. I deserve it. I've worked long and hard, and I intend to be CEO of Wainwright Inc. Then I'm going to implement some of my own ideas."

"Good for you." But she didn't think the benefit was worth the price he'd paid.

"You don't care?" Dylan asked, obviously puzzled by her attitude.

Piper shook her head.

"Wainwright Inc. has only ever meant unhappiness to me. He insisted I work there and I tried, really tried. But I had no autonomy. I couldn't think for myself. It was stifling. Far better for me that I left. For Vance, too," she reminded.

"Funny how Dad never took to him." Dylan shook his head. "I guess he never forgave him for stealing you."

"If it hadn't been Vance, he would have found another reason. Now tell me about some of your projects, something you're really excited about."

His eyes lit up and he began to discuss an idea he hoped to present to their father soon. But as Piper watched him her mind drifted back to Jason and his face when Dylan's hotel idea had been scotched. He'd looked forlorn, as if someone has just kicked him. She vowed to redouble her efforts to find a developer.

Before Dylan returned with an idea that she couldn't punch holes in.

* * *

Jason secured his boat to Piper's jetty, then climbed the stairs, anxious to share his decision to let God take control of everything now that his meeting was finally over. He slowed his steps as music wafted down the hill, the sound of voices laughing, teasing.

Piper had company.

Two more steps and he'd reached the rose garden. He looked in through the big windows. Shock held him immobile.

Dylan Wainwright lay sprawled in her grandfather's easy chair, his face wreathed in a smile as he stared at a picture Piper held up.

"I can't believe you kept that after all these years," Jason heard him say.

They shared an intimate chuckle, then he saw Dylan glance at his watch.

"I've got to get moving, Piper. It's a long way back."

"I'm glad you came for dinner, Dyl. It gave us a chance to catch up." She reached out and hugged him. "Don't be such a stranger."

"I'll try." Dylan hugged her back as if he was used to it, brushing a hand over her hair. "I like it like this. Makes you look younger."

"I feel better than I have in a long time. You should try living here for a while."

He couldn't hear any more. Jason turned on his heel and moved back down the slope, not caring that he was going too fast and could slip. He jumped into his craft, gunned the engine and took off across the water, turning the words in his mind over and over.

What did it mean?

"You two know each other?"

"Of course."

He should have figured it out earlier. It wasn't her father Piper had been waiting for during the Spring Fling. It was Dylan—a man she clearly cared about. So why was she so determined to shoot holes in his project?

And if she cared about Dylan, what was going on between himself and her?

Nothing made sense. Jason eased into his slip at the marina, secured the boat then took the stairs two at a time up to his perch. He didn't bother with lights, simply sat there, staring into the black water.

I said I'd turned it all over to You, but— The idea stole in as silently as the mist that now began to creep across the water.

Maybe it had all been a test. God only wanted him to surrender to show he could give up control. Now that he had, maybe Jason was supposed to act, do something to ensure Wainwright would come back to the table with something new.

Only, what could he do?

When the mist turned to fog, then a light shower, Jason finally moved inside. But the mental snapshot of Piper laughing with Dylan, her hand on his arm, kept Jason awake all night.

By morning he'd come up with a plan. He went to the office at the crack of dawn, searched Piper's Rolodex and came up with a number. Once Andy was busy with his duties for the day and the fishermen had left, Jason locked himself in his office and made a call.

Piper was great at her job, no question. But some things you just had to do yourself.

Chapter Eleven

"I appreciate the appointment, Mr. Wainwright. I know you're a busy man."

"Nonsense, Jason. I've always got time for you." The firm grip closed around his with a strength the almost-white hair belied. "You look better, my boy."

"I feel great."

Baron brought him up to speed about Expectations and they talked freely about his time there.

"Have a seat, son. I know I'm going to."

"Thank you."

"Now tell me what brings you here."

"I was hoping we could discuss your ideas for Serenity Bay. You've shown us two projects, but neither have quite met our hopes. I'm wondering if there's something I can do to ensure the next one is a winner."

"Serenity Bay." Baron shook his head. "That's Dylan's department. I don't have anything to do with it." The tanned fingers clasped and unclasped his custom-fitted pant leg, the dark brown eyes never quite meeting his. "Perhaps I should call him, though I don't believe he's in the office today."

"It's not necessary. I was hoping we could just talk for a few moments."

"I'm mostly a figurehead at Wainwright Inc. these days, Jason. The old man getting ready for the pasture. You should have made an appointment with my son."

He said it with a laugh but Jason could hear the pain behind the words.

"Wisdom doesn't age, sir." Jason took a deep breath. "Besides, I'm sure Dylan has other things to do. He's given us such a lot of his time already. Maybe you and I could brainstorm for a few minutes without him."

He laid out the diagram Dylan had forgotten on the board table two nights ago.

"This is the last conception we looked at."

Baron Wainwright leaned forward, traced the building with a fingertip. "It's a beauty, isn't it? The boy has real talent. I don't tell him that enough. What's your concern?"

"Do you know Serenity Bay, sir?"

Baron smiled and his whole face transformed.

"I should. Spent almost every summer there for many years. My wife grew up there. She loved it." The smile faded, the eyes dimmed. "But that was a long time ago. I don't go back anymore."

"Maybe you should, sir. You could see how much it's changed."

"I like to remember it the way it was when my wife was alive." He pointed to the drawing. "So what aren't you happy about?"

Slowly, precisely, Jason laid out each of Piper's points. And with a sharpness he wouldn't have imagined, the head of Wainwright solved every one. Though Baron looked somewhat older than he remembered, his mind was obviously as sharp as ever.

"It's a matter of perspective, primarily. No doubt Dylan

believes the restaurant is best located here. But if it was shifted, you could get what you're after and we'd free up another vista point without ruining your beach."

It was so simple. Jason couldn't believe they hadn't thought of it before.

"I can't thank you enough, sir," he murmured, staring at the lightly penciled lines the old man had drawn in. "I think this is something everyone will approve."

Wainwright rose, motioned to the coffeepot his secretary had just set on his desk. "Are you in a hurry, Jason?"

"Actually I'd love a cup. I didn't get my morning dose."

"Got up too early, I suppose. It's a long drive in to Toronto." He handed Jason a porcelain mug.

Jason took a sip, turned to sit and found himself staring into Piper's face from an eight-by-ten glossy framed in gold. She was younger, her hair was long, but it was definitely her.

"Will Piper approve of this change?" Baron Wainwright asked, sitting down behind the desk. "I can't imagine my daughter is exactly thrilled about doing business with my company, especially not in Serenity Bay."

"Your...daughter?" Every ounce of breath left his lungs.

"You didn't know?" Baron inclined his head to stare at the picture. His whole face seemed to sag with sadness. "No reason you would, I suppose. We don't exactly communicate anymore. Piper hates me."

"I—" Jason struggled to recover. "I'm sure that's not true, sir."

"Yes, it is. And I deserve it. After her mother died—well, let's just say I made some mistakes."

This was the man Piper loathed? Jason couldn't get it through his brain. Baron Wainwright was decent, honest and not above standing up for what he believed in. Something must have changed him.

The door burst open.

"Dad, Tina's not at her desk and—hey, Jason. What are you doing here?" Dylan thrust out his hand, glanced from one to the other. "Everything okay?"

"Of course. Don't fuss." Wainwright's gruff tone surprised Jason. "We were just talking turkey."

"I was worried that after our last meeting you'd be tempted to toss your ideas for Serenity Bay in the garbage and get on with your life," Jason interrupted. "I couldn't reach you so I contacted your father. He's come up with a brilliant idea to satisfy both our needs."

"Indeed."

Jason caught the dark look of pure anger Dylan tossed his father's way, though he recovered quickly.

"Well, let's see what you've got," he said, moving toward the table.

"It's your concept, of course, and I wouldn't dream of asking you to change it except that I thought we might save each other a whole lot of frustration and time," Jason remarked diplomatically.

"Does Piper know you're here?" Dylan asked.

"No, I'd prefer to tell her about this trip myself, in my own way." He saw Dylan understood.

"She's not going to be pleased you went behind her back, you know," Dylan mumbled, his attention on the drawing.

"That's an understatement."

Dylan glanced up, grinning.

"In fact, she's going to tear a strip off you a mile wide. Piper is very independent. You can't believe how long Dad and I debated even presenting a Wainwright idea."

"I'm very glad you did, because this idea is one of the best hotel concepts I've ever seen."

"Thank you." Dylan glanced at his father, rose quickly and moved behind the desk. "Dad? What's wrong?"

"Nothing, son. I'm fine. Just a bit dizzy. Don't fuss," the old man barked. "I'm fine, I said."

"Okay. Okay."

The tender tones of care and compassion in Dylan's voice surprised Jason. He'd always seen the man as hard-nosed, fixated on business. Yet the other night with Piper, and now with his father, his feelings lay exposed on his face.

Dylan lifted his father's cup, sniffed it.

"You're not supposed to be drinking coffee, Dad. You know what the doctor said."

"Phooey! At this age, what am I saving myself for? It's not like you're providing me with grandchildren." Baron glared at Dylan. He brushed his fingers against the picture of Piper.

Dylan took away his cup, moving to stand beside Jason.

"I'll get the changes to you at your next council meeting," he murmured. "I think it would be better if we left my father now. He's been overdoing it and he's tired."

"Certainly. I'll just say goodbye." Jason thanked the older man then quietly left.

Outside the office, Dylan plunked down the cup on the secretary's desk and gave her an angry glare before turning back to face Jason.

"I'm sorry to involve you in family problems, Jason. I'm not sure what my father told you but he and Piper haven't spoken for several years. I'd prefer it if you didn't mention that you came here and saw him."

"But surely she should know that he's failing?"

"I've told her." He frowned, then continued. "Dad will rebound. Baron Wainwright always does." A lopsided smile added to his sad look. "What I don't want is a confrontation between them. It's better if things go on as they have for now."

"You *don't* want them to reconcile?" he asked with a frown.

"I'd like nothing better. This position as go-between isn't fun. But every argument, every hurtful word only diminishes him more. For now it's best that they live their own lives." He sighed, raked a hand through his hair. "I'm trying to shield Dad as much as I can, take the load from his shoulders, though he doesn't like it. But both of them have hard heads."

"I understand. I won't lie to her, but as far as is possible, I'll keep my meeting here to myself." He walked beside Dylan to the elevators. "You'll be up next week with the revisions?"

"Count on it."

"Maybe when the hotel's done, your father will come and see it."

Dylan shook his head, his eyes dark and foreboding. "Don't count on that, Jason. Going back there—it could kill him."

Then he walked away.

All the way home Jason could think of only one thing— Piper Langley was Baron Wainwright's daughter. He'd trusted her completely and she'd kept that one most important truth from him. The woman he'd come to trust, to care about.

To love.

Pain at her deceit boiled inside, but he tamped it down, told himself to remain calm. Better to go along as if nothing had happened, find out what else she was willing to lie about. Then he'd expose her—and she'd leave.

That was for the best, wasn't it?

As Jason rolled down the last hill into town, a new question bubbled up.

When and why had she changed her name? Was that all part of the plan?

* * *

Something was wrong.

Though she couldn't put her finger on it exactly, Piper knew that Jason had changed. What she didn't know was why, or how she could fix it.

He was unfailingly polite, he listened to every idea, worked with her on each project as willingly as she could have asked. But all the time there was a barrier between them, a chasm that, no matter how hard she tried, she couldn't breach.

She longed to hide out at Cathcart House. But the council meeting lay ahead of her tonight. According to the agenda, Dylan would be there with a new idea. She wondered how many more times she'd have to shoot down her brother's ideas, watch the haunting sadness of disappointment fill his eyes, and know that she'd put it there to protect herself. What kind of a sister did that?

Not that she didn't have the best interests of Serenity Bay in mind. She did. Tweaking his last idea would have been easy. She could have made the suggestions herself if she hadn't been too afraid to allow Wainwright to build here.

For the tenth time today she wondered about her father. Last night during dinner, Jason had alluded to an article he'd read that claimed Baron was declining in health, that he'd begun to leave more details to Dylan. At first she'd thought he was hinting at something, but that feeling had been chased away by a flurry of new ideas they'd worked on. Then he'd calmly wished her good-night.

Piper pushed away her half-eaten sandwich and asked the waitress for her check. Fifteen minutes and then it would start again.

You don't have to hurt Dylan. Why not trust Me?

The chiding of that still-small voice had grown louder in

the past week, reminding her that once she'd believed that God would work all things together. What had become of that faith? When in all the pain and hurt had God become synonymous with Baron Wainwright?

Piper didn't know anymore. All she knew was that a lump sat in her heart and every time she thought of her father, it ached a little more. Why couldn't he have been a real father, loved her the way a man was supposed to care for his own daughter? Failing that, why couldn't she have continued the life she'd loved in Calgary, the one Vance's death had ended?

Discontented with questions that had no answers, Piper left the restaurant and strode down the street to the office. Inside she stored her bag in her desk, gathered up her notes and, after combing her hair, took her usual seat in the council room. Jason and Dylan arrived together a few moments later, teasing each other about their fishing abilities.

When had they become so friendly?

The evening started out badly as a council member pointed out the mistakes in two ads that had run last week. Piper tried to explain it was a printer's error but the member wouldn't let her finish a sentence. Finally, after waiting to no avail for Jason to intervene, she gave up and remained silent.

After making short work of the rest of business, Jason then asked Dylan to present his new ideas.

"I think you'll agree we've hit the nail on the head this time," her brother said, passing around artists' renderings of the newly revised hotel. He went into great detail explaining the changes and how they aligned to each problem she'd outlined last week.

Tension inched up her spine as Piper scrutinized the plans for problems. There were a few but they were minor and she knew it. She offered her half-hearted objections but they were quickly shot down. Everyone seemed to favor this new proposal.

Piper felt as if the sand were sinking beneath her feet. Relief swamped her when Jason finally adjourned the meeting. She rose, intent on escape.

"Hey, Piper, we're going for coffee. Want to join us?" Dylan sounded happy, probably buoyed by his good presentation.

"I can't, thanks. I have to get home." She rose on tiptoe, kissing his cheek. "I'll have to take a rain check."

He shook his head at her, his fingers trailing down one cheek. "You can't live in the past, sis. You've got to look ahead."

She smiled, hugged him, then left without saying anything more.

Jason stood on the sidewalk, watching *Shalimar* push across the blue water.

"She didn't look well. Is everything all right, do you think?"

Dylan turned from the truck where he'd stowed his belongings.

"With Piper? She's all right. Her problems have more to do with the date."

"The date?" Jason searched Dylan's face for an answer. "July 22 is a bad day?"

"For Piper it is. Her husband died on this day three years ago."

Husband? She'd been married?

"Vance was a nice guy, and they really loved each other. Then he got brain cancer. They tried every treatment but nothing helped. By the time he died, it was a blessing to everyone. He suffered terribly. That's one of the reasons Piper and Dad don't speak."

"Why?" Jason choked out, his anger rising. "What did your father do?"

"As far as I know, nothing. I don't really understand it, but after Vance's death, Piper refused to ever speak to him again. And she hasn't."

So she'd lost her mother, her grandparents, her husband and cut herself off from her father. Why?

"Dylan, I'm sorry, but I'm going to have to take a rain check on that coffee. Do you mind?"

"No, no problem. To tell you the truth, I should go straight back, anyway. I'm up to my ears at work."

Jason waited until he saw the taillights of Dylan's truck fade away, then he climbed into his boat and raced across the water, uncaring that he soaked himself by pushing against the waves too hard.

How could he have been so stupid? How could he have let it happen again—duped by the only person he'd dared trust? Anger seethed in his soul, fueled by the pain that stabbed far deeper than anything Amber had caused.

Once his boat was tied to the jetty, he took the stairs two at a time, stomped across the deck and pounded on the door. It opened seconds later. Backlit by the kitchen, Piper stared at him.

"Jason? What's wrong?"

"Why didn't you tell me you were married?" he shouted, clenching his fingers around the door frame.

Her mouth opened in surprise, her eyes darkening to huge pools that threatened to draw him in, drown him in their depths.

"Why? Because my husband died a horrible, painful death that upsets me to think about, and because it's nobody's business but my own." She stepped outside onto the deck, glaring up at him, the oval of her face lit by the fairy lights dancing in the breeze. "If divulging personal information was a job prerequisite you should have included it in the application process. Does your knowing about Vance make me less capable at my job?"

"Stop that!" He knew she was angry, but so was he. "It's not the knowledge. It's the secrets. I don't understand why you couldn't have said something."

"Like what? 'Oh, by the way, I'm a widow'? Why should I have to? I came here to start over. I haven't cheated you of anything, haven't worked against the Bay."

"Haven't you?"

She looked so innocent, standing there in her bare feet, her hair tumbling over an unmade-up face. Jason dropped his voice, trying to hide how deep her dishonesty had cut. "Why didn't you tell me you're Baron Wainwright's daughter, Piper?"

She looked stunned by the question. "But I—I assumed you knew. I thought you understood that Dylan's my brother."

"You didn't think there might be a tiny conflict of interest there?" he snapped, infuriated that she offered no argument.

"Conflict of interest?" A rueful smile twisted her mouth. "Hardly. I've deliberately avoided anything to do with Baron Wainwright for ages. I'm trying to stop my father's company from building in Serenity Bay, Jason, not gouge a big profit for them. Where's the conflict?"

"The conflict arises, Piper, because you deliberately worked against me," he growled. "I thought we were both trying to do something special for Serenity Bay."

"I am!" She clamped her hands on her hips, met his stare. "In every way that counts I am *not* my father's daughter, Jason. What I've done, I've done for the benefit of the Bay. Wainwright is wrong for us."

"Why? Tell me that." He leaned in so his nose was mere inches from her. "What do you have against Wainwright Inc. aside from an old feud with your father, Piper? And don't give me any garbage about them not serving our interests. That's nonsense. The hotel Dylan proposed tonight will fit our needs perfectly."

"So you've decided, have you? You know enough about hotels to know what will work best in this town, what will help achieve the goals we've set?" She laughed bitterly. "Be careful your eagerness to get your name on the map doesn't trap you into trusting the wrong man."

"You don't trust Dylan?"

"I'm not talking about Dylan." She turned her back to him to stare into the night. "My brother does his best, but whatever he promises, he is unable to fulfill without my father's backing. And Baron Wainwright cannot be trusted."

"Why Piper? Tell me why."

"Leave it alone." She whirled around, her eyes flashing with anger and pain and a thousand other emotions he couldn't decipher.

"I can't." He touched her arm, waited for her to meet his gaze. "I don't understand why you did this, Piper. I trusted you. I believed you when I haven't believed anyone for a long time." He lowered his head, touched her lips, unable to break free of the magnetic pull he always felt around her. "I care about you," he whispered.

"If you care about me, drop Wainwright." She didn't move, didn't flinch under his stare.

"I can't. You know how important the Bay is to me. I can't just write off someone as big as Wainwright Inc. without a very good reason." He settled his hands on her shoulders. "Tell me why, Piper."

Her shoulders sagged under his grip. He felt trembling course through her and knew she couldn't take the stress much longer.

"You want to know why you shouldn't trust Baron Wainwright?" she whispered so quietly he had to lean in to hear.

She drew back, settled herself on one of the chairs perched on her deck and motioned for him to do the same.

When he was seated across from her, she spoke.

"Baron Wainwright let my husband die."

Chapter Twelve

"His name was Vance Langley. He was a decent, honest man who wouldn't hurt a flea. He taught track in a high school. He loved kids, poured his heart and soul into helping them train, fulfill their potential, reach their goals. You couldn't have found anyone who was healthier. At least that's what we thought."

Piper prayed for the composure that would let her get through the story without breaking down. She kept her focus on the floor in front of her and forced the words out.

"My husband contracted a rare form of cancer. It progressed very fast. Vance was in horrible pain and there was not one thing I could do about it."

Her voice broke but she cleared her throat and pressed on.

"We'd almost given up the day I learned of an experimental treatment that had worked on other patients in a situation as desperate. It was being offered in Italy but it cost a great deal. Our insurance had run out, I'd spent our savings, borrowed from friends, done everything I could. We had nothing left. Even our house was gone."

"Dylan?"

"He helped out as best he could but he's on a salary and he didn't have a lot of ready cash." She pushed her hair off her face. "I couldn't stand watching Vance suffer any longer. I hadn't spoken to my father at all since I left Wainwright Inc."

She caught his surprise and managed a faint smile.

"I'd worked there for almost a year, trying to mend fences between us. But my father wouldn't accept that I was an adult, that I could contribute to his company in my own way. The third time he went behind my back to change a deal I'd made we had a huge argument. I left, and I never went back."

"But surely—"

"Vance was in agony. I had to do whatever I could to stop that, so I phoned my father. Baron didn't answer so I left a message. I begged him to loan us money so I could get Vance to Italy." She twined her fingers together, staring at them, reliving those hours of waiting, praying, hoping. "He never called me back."

"I'm sorry, Piper."

"I couldn't understand why he didn't call back. I tried again. After the third message I phoned Dylan, begged him to talk to my father, ask him to help. My father never called us back. Vance died soon after."

She looked up through a wash of tears.

"Do you understand, Jason? He let him die. He could have helped, he could have talked to me, visited Vance, anything. He chose to ignore us, to punish me for leaving his company. That's how I know he isn't to be trusted."

Piper rose, walked to the door and pulled it open.

"If that's the kind of person you want to do business with, go ahead. But understand that I won't be a party to it. I can never forgive him."

She was almost through the doorway before the hand on her shoulder stopped her.

"You have to forgive, Piper."

"How can you say that?" Bitterness welled up inside her. "He was my father and he couldn't be bothered to help the man I loved."

"I understand what you're saying, sweetheart." Jason gathered her into his arms and held her as the sobs racked her body. "I know you went through agony. I don't pretend to understand it. But I do know you have to forgive Baron Wainwright or it will suck the life from you. I couldn't move on until I forgave Amber and Trevor. That's the way God made us."

"It isn't the same," she argued, easing away until the night air replaced his embrace. "God wasn't there. Only my father was. He's supposed to be there for me, no matter what. He didn't care enough. How do I get past that?" She pulled open the door. "I don't want to talk about it anymore. Good night, Jason."

"Good night."

She didn't watch him leave, didn't wait for the sound of his boat or pick up the phone when he called and left a message that he'd arrived home safely. Instead, Piper slipped on her swimsuit and immersed herself in the soothing waters of her hot tub.

She'd never felt so alone.

Jason read the hastily scribbled note left on his desk the next morning, wishing he'd ignored the querulous renter who'd kept him occupied for too long. He hurried out to speak to Ida.

"When did she go?"

"I'll assume you're speaking about Piper?"

He inclined his head.

"I have no idea. There was a note on my desk when I came

in saying she'll be out of town for the next three days. If I have questions I'm to contact you." Her stare narrowed. "I have questions."

He did not want to face Ida's acerbic wit today. But escape wasn't an option now. He leaned his elbows on the counter.

"What's the problem?"

"Piper's notes say there's a delegation from a tour company coming today. She wants you to host a barbecue on the houseboat after you take them on a tour of the bay." Ida tapped a pencil against her notepad. "Apparently she's been coaxing them to come out here with their tours and they perked up when she mentioned you had houseboats for rent."

"Really?" The news stunned him. To be included on a prepackaged tour was a coup he'd never imagined happening so soon. Piper had mentioned nothing about interest from a tour company.

And he knew why.

A wave of shame rushed over him as the knowledge penetrated. She'd been afraid he'd mess it up, get too aggressive and turn the prospective clients off. It had happened before, though she'd warned him over and over to relax and let people get a feel for the area.

"She says that if you can't handle it, I'm to figure out something else. I need to know if you can handle it, Jason."

Last night came back with a vengeance. He'd accused her of pursuing her own agenda yet here was proof positive that Piper Langley was committed to getting Serenity Bay on the map.

"I can handle it," he muttered through gritted teeth. "What time?"

They sorted out the details then Jason left to get Andy started on cleaning the houseboat to within an inch of its life.

Piper had given him a chance to prove himself. He wasn't going to mess it up.

Now if only he knew that she'd be coming back.

"Thanks a lot, Row. I don't know what I'd have done if I couldn't hide out here for a few days."

"Like you haven't done the same for me a hundred times. I just wish I hadn't been so tied up with work and we could have spent more time talking." Rowena slammed the trunk. "You're really going to call Baron?"

"Already have. He wasn't in so I left a message. I guess he'll call me when he gets it." Piper shrugged. "The Bible tells us to forgive as we want to be forgiven. At this point, I'm not sure I can do it, but I have to try."

She searched her friend's face, saw the doubts rush across it. Rowena reached out and hugged her, then stepped back.

"Of course you do. Don't mind me, Pip. You already know I have a problem in that department."

"I realize now that part of what Jason said is true. I have been letting my anger and hurt toward my father cloud my life, until it'd begun to take over. My focus has been sidetracked from God. I don't want to become a bitter old woman hiding away from life."

"You won't." Rowena trailed behind her, waited till she had the car door open. "What about Jason?"

"I don't know." The sting of his accusations burned too deeply to brush off. "He doesn't trust me, Rowena. It's pretty hard to have a relationship with someone who constantly suspects you."

"You want to have a relationship? With him, I mean?"

"I love him," Piper admitted.

Rowena nodded.

"What's happening with the hotel?" she asked.

"I haven't been able to find out much. Tina's on holiday so my source is dried up for the moment."

"Dylan?"

"He's been unreachable." She decided to confide something she'd kept to herself. "The morning I was leaving Serenity Bay to come here, I could have sworn I saw his truck parked on a side road."

"Dylan? What was he doing—camping?"

"He hates camping." Piper shook her head, checked her watch. "There must be lots of those trucks around. It probably wasn't him at all. Anyway, I've got to get on the road." She took a deep breath. "I'm going to stop by my father's before I leave."

Rowena's eyebrows rose high on her forehead. "You're kidding?"

"No. I want to get it over with. If he doesn't want me there, he'll have to say so. Then I'll know I've done the best I can. Then I'll be able to put it to rest."

"Call me," Rowena ordered after hugging her once more. "Let me know. And don't take any of his garbage."

"Thanks, Row. You're a good friend," Piper said as she climbed into the car. She prayed silently as she wove her way through the streets, deserted at this early-morning hour.

Sunday morning. Baron should be having breakfast on the terrace by the pool about now.

The house looked the same. Elegant, stately. Two massive pots burgeoned with cascading flowers—pansies, babies' breath, lobelia. Her mother's favorites.

Forgive.

"I'm trying, God."

Piper swallowed the lump in her throat, climbed out of the

car and walked to the massive door. Whispering one last prayer, she lifted her hand and pressed the buzzer.

The door swung open, but it was Dylan who stood there.

"Piper? What are you doing here?"

"I came to see Dad," she said simply.

He stared at her for a moment. His eyes flashed with surprise but he quickly recovered.

"I wish you'd phoned first. He isn't here."

Somehow she hadn't prepared for that. "Oh."

"Do you want to come in? I'm just leaving but I could manage another cup of coffee."

"No, thanks." She couldn't face the memories right now. "I'm on my way back to the Bay. I guess I might as well get on the road."

"Okay." Dylan closed the door behind him and walked with her to the car. "Did you like my idea?"

"The hotel is great, Dyl."

"Not the hotel." He frowned. "Didn't Jason tell you?"

"No, why don't you tell me?"

"I gave him a concept for a community center. It would be perfect at the edge of town on that vacant plot by the bush."

Piper listened as he went on and on, detailing his ideas of concerts and events that would tax the little town. Her heart sank as she realized Dylan had drawn Jason into his dream.

"We're nowhere near that stage yet, Dyl. We haven't even got enough accommodations right now."

He glared at her. "Why do you always have to pour cold water on everything, Piper? Are you mad because you didn't think of it first?"

"No! I'm sorry, Dyl," she apologized. "I didn't mean to do that. It's a great idea. We're just not ready for it yet."

She'd hurt him again and now he was pouting. Piper

sighed, stood on tiptoes to kiss his cheek, then got back into her car. Home was the best place for her.

"I love you. Tell Dad I want to talk to him, will you?"

He nodded, rocking back on his heels. "Sure. Soon as I see him. Take care, Piper. The roads will get busy with all the cottagers coming back after the weekend. I don't want to hear about my sister in an accident."

"I'll be fine," she said. She waved then left, eager to escape now that the confrontation with Baron had been averted. The more she thought about it, the stupider the idea seemed.

Anyway, the ball was in his court now. If he wanted to talk to her, all he had to do was call.

The rest was up to God.

Jason stood inside his marina and watched Piper dock *Shalimar.*

Two weeks and nothing had changed. She was still keeping him at arm's length.

She laughed and joked with Andy while retrieving her briefcase from the hatch of the boat. On the surface everything was fine. But he didn't miss the way she tossed a quick glance toward him, as if she knew he was standing there, watching her. Or the quick, hurried walk that got her away from him.

He prayed endlessly about her, apologized several times, until she'd told him to stop. He'd done everything he could think of but the chasm remained there between them—a widening gap of distrust that had cost him more dearly than he'd ever imagined.

For once Jason was tired of the endless round of tourists that swarmed the Bay. He was putting in eighteen-hour days just to keep up with things. Higgy was an answer to a prayer. He took on most of the houseboat tours now. But yesterday he'd pulled a muscle in his back, leaving Jason to manage on his own.

He checked his calendar. Today looked relatively clear, thank goodness. Maybe he'd have time to take a break after lunch.

But it didn't happen that way. Piper's summons had him curious and anxious at the same time. He walked into the town offices at ten after one and found her on the phone.

"I can make that," she said, beckoning him inside. "It's not a problem at all. What information will you need?"

No cheery smile to warm him. Jason missed that. He closed the door behind him, sat down in front of her desk and waited for the call to finish.

"All right. I'll see you tomorrow morning. We'll count on talking for the full two days. Thank you." She hung up, leaned back in her chair and rubbed the corner of one eye.

"Tired?"

"Not really. Just a little frazzled."

Jason kept his lips shut. If she wanted to explain, she would, but he sure wasn't asking.

"That was a man from Toronto who develops strip malls. They've been looking around Serenity Bay apparently, though no one contacted me until today."

A strip mall? He almost let out a yell of excitement. Until he caught the look in her eye and reminded himself that it was just a phone call.

"Do they need more information?"

"No. Apparently they've almost decided to begin purchasing land." She rose, moved to a town map. "Here," she said, indicating a block that would coincide nicely with structures already there. "I'm to meet with them tomorrow to answer more questions about the town's future plans."

"Great!" He kept an eye on her, trying to assess her. It wasn't easy. Piper had always kept her emotions under wraps, more so now. "Do you want me to come along?"

She shook her head.

"It's not necessary, thanks. I'm assuming that if and when they have something to decide, they'll approach the town council."

His heart sank. He wanted to be included in the discussion, but how could he say that without making her think he was shadowing her?

"I'd really like to go, Piper. I promise I'll let you do the talking. I'll only answer what I'm asked. But I'd like to hear what they have to say."

A sad little smile tipped her mouth.

"Still don't trust me, eh, Jason?"

"Of course I trust you." He leaned in, held her gaze. "Can't you understand what a shock it was to learn you were a Wainwright and that you'd been married? I thought we were beginning to share our lives."

"I never deliberately kept either from you," she murmured, her face pale. "I assumed you knew my maiden name, but even if you didn't, I never thought it would matter. I left that behind a long time ago."

"Really?" He watched her closely. "I think you're still carrying it close to your heart. I think that's why you never came right out and asked me if I knew—because you're afraid to face the truth."

Piper shook her head.

"I know exactly what I feel for my father," she told him, her tone icy. "I even thought it was my duty to contact him, to try and repair the rift. I thought that's what God expected me to do." She stood in front of the window, peering out.

"It is."

"Is it?" Piper whirled around. "That was two weeks ago, Jason. Since then I've heard nothing. My father hasn't even so much as left a message for me, that's how little he cares about me."

"I don't believe it." He frowned as he rose, holding up a hand to stem her protest. "I'm not calling you a liar, but something must be wrong. Have you spoken to Dylan?"

"This morning, as a matter of fact. Dad is fine. He's quite capable of picking up a phone. In fact, he's been working long hours trying to get the London project up to speed. It's just his daughter he doesn't have time for."

"I'm sorry." He wrapped his arms around her and drew her close, waited for the shower of tears to abate. "I'm so sorry. I thought for sure that if he—"

"You know a different man than I do, Jason. You know the charismatic businessman who swings the big deals and spreads his charm on everyone around." She drew back, sniffed. "I know the man who doesn't have time to waste on the girl who wouldn't do as he wanted."

"But it doesn't make sense."

"Let it go, okay?"

He nodded, snuggled her head against his chest and let her recover, but his mind couldn't synthesize the two men. Baron Wainwright had known the name of every single locator at Expectations. If they were married, he knew their spouses' names and often asked after them. He remembered illnesses, anniversaries and any other information you told him. He'd taken pains to make each encounter warm and personal.

Could someone just shut that off when it came to his own family?

"You said you used to work with him," Piper said, lifting her head to look into his eyes. "How come you didn't know Dylan?"

Jason shrugged. "I don't know. He never came to Boston

with your father, I guess. I never made any trips to Wainwright's offices so I wouldn't have seen him there. But I've gotten to know him better since."

"What do you mean?"

"He was here on Saturday. We went for a boat ride, barbecued some steaks, talked. He stayed at my place."

"What did you talk about?"

"Dylan has big ideas, Piper. I get the feeling that he never really discusses them with anyone else. He knows Serenity Bay very well. He's given me a couple of ideas."

She tilted her head to one side.

"Why the funny look?" he asked, tugging one of her curls.

"I always thought Dylan hated the Bay. He wouldn't come here much after I left home. Now you're telling me he knows it? I just find it odd."

"I find it odd that you're in my arms and I'm not…"

Jason leaned his head down and kissed her gently.

He hoped he'd convinced her that he loved her, but Jason decided he wasn't leaving anything to chance. He couldn't go through another two weeks of agony.

"Piper?"

She blinked at him, as if her mind had been elsewhere. "Yes?"

"Will you forgive me? Will you believe me if I tell you I love you, that I have for a long time? That I want to go back to the way we were?"

She wore a troubled look.

"I don't know if we can." She met his stare. "You didn't trust me, Jason. Even after all the time we've spent together, after all the things I've worked on, you actually thought I'd betray you. It's hard to rebuild."

"No, it isn't. You just trust that I've learned my lesson, that I know I was wrong and that I'll never make the same mistake again. I'd trust my life with you, Piper. That's how much I believe in you."

She wanted to believe him. He could see that. But she was holding back.

"What can I do to prove I trust you?"

"I don't know."

"Would it help if I said I have no intention of going to that strip mall meeting you're holding?"

She chuckled. "You can't. You have town council tonight, remember?"

"But it's supposed to last two days. I could go tomorrow." Her expression changed and he hurried to correct himself. "But I'm not. You're the person who handles development for the Bay. When you're ready to talk to me about it, I'll be here."

The phone rang. She answered it, jotted down notes, said she'd call back. Then she looked at Jason, her eyes dancing with excitement.

"What?"

"I don't think you can go tomorrow, either."

"Why?" It was something good, he could tell that much.

"The Freemont Society just phoned to say they want to talk to you about an idea they have. They want a conference call with you tomorrow morning at nine. You're to call them back at this number to set it up."

"Shouldn't you be in on that?"

She shook her head. "They're interested in working with Franklin's Marina, not Serenity Bay."

"The Freemont Society—don't they run that summer camp for disabled kids?"

"Yes."

"So what do they want with me?"

"You'll have to ask them tomorrow. I've got to get busy assembling packets for my meeting." Piper picked up a file from her desk, then turned to look at him over one shoulder. "You're sure you're okay with not coming?"

He forced his head to nod. "You go get 'em."

"I will." She opened the door, paused, then quietly asked, "Do you want to have dinner tonight?"

Jason shook his head.

"I'm sorry, I'd love to but I'm hired out for a seniors' picnic cruise this evening and Higgy is off. His back is still bad."

"Okay, well another time then." She smiled then followed him out of the room.

Lunch would have been good, too. Any time that they could spend together would have. Jason decided to phone her tonight, after he got back.

As it turned out Jason did have a dinner partner. Dylan dropped in just as Jason's pizza delivery guy left.

"Want to share?" he invited.

"Yes. I'm starving," Dylan said.

They shared the pie, consuming every last bit as Jason told him about the possibility of an outside tour company taking him on.

"Sounds like you're going to make some people very happy."

"I hope so. It could mean a great deal to the Bay if we had regular tours."

"Of course." Shortly after that Dylan left.

Jason picked up the phone, glanced at the clock and hung up again. Too late to call Piper now. His questions would have to wait.

He loved Piper. He'd told her that.

One of these days he was going to find out if she felt the same way about him.

Chapter Thirteen

If the first day of meetings hadn't gone well, the following morning rated as a major disaster.

Piper excused herself for the lunch hour, picked up a sandwich and drove to a nearby park to take a break.

She was putting off calling Jason and she knew it.

Her cell phone rang. It was him.

"Hey! How's it going? I'd hoped to hear from you last night." He sounded in a good mood.

"We talked till midnight. I thought it was too late to call." Suddenly no longer hungry, she put the sandwich back in the bag and sipped her coffee.

"So?"

Truth time. "Don't get your hopes up on this one, Jason."

"What's wrong?"

"Nothing's *wrong*," she said, bristling. "They're asking too much. They think that because we're small, we should concede on every point. I'm trying to illustrate the benefits of the first location but now they're asking for the waterfront. We just can't do that."

"Maybe I should come down."

Fury lit a fire in the pit of her stomach. *Here we go again.*

"No, Jason, you should *not* come down. This is my job. This is what I do. Remember? But I don't expect to win everyone I talk to. We may have to walk away from this, wait until we're further along." She drew a calming breath. "What did The Freemont Society want?"

"They'd like to take some kids on a houseboat cruise tomorrow morning. An all-day thing. If it works out well they'll book once a week for as long as their camps run. It's a kind of reward for the ones who push through their rehab."

Piper frowned.

"You don't sound that excited. It's quite an opportunity, isn't it?"

"Yes, of course. The steady income will be welcome."

"But?"

"But the opportunities from that mall would be even more welcome," he said quietly.

Piper gritted her teeth, rose and tossed the uneaten sandwich and half-finished drink in the garbage.

"You're doing it again," she complained. "I leave for one day and you're right back second-guessing me. When are you going to stop trying to control the world, Jason?"

"I'm concerned, that's all. This is a big thing for the Bay. If we lose them we don't know when the next opportunity will come along. It could be years."

"It could be tomorrow." Inside the car now, Piper closed her eyes and leaned her head back against the headrest. "Look. You've been teaching that boys' class at Sunday school about God's plan for their lives. Well, don't you think he's got one for yours? Do you really believe what you're telling those kids—enough to follow it in your own life?"

Silence. He was probably furious.

Tough. So was she.

"Trust is a two-way street, Jason. If I can't trust your faith in me, if it fluctuates with the circumstances, what kind of a relationship are we going to have? You said you care about me."

"I do," he insisted.

"Prove it. Have some faith that I'll do the right thing, whatever it is." She swallowed hard, then gave him the ultimatum. "More than that, have some faith that God didn't bring you this far to kill your dream because of one strip mall. In fact, I'd say He's trying to give you your dream."

"What do you mean?"

"You'll have a heaven-sent opportunity waiting on your boat dock tomorrow morning. What are you going to do— blow it off to race here and try to persuade a group of men to do something they don't want to? Or grab what your Father has given you and make it work?"

Piper waited a moment then closed the phone. It was time to go back to work.

"They're all wearing life vests?" Jason waited for Higgy's nod. "Okay then. Let's cast off."

He left Higgy to steer out of the bay while he made sure everything was secured. Andy waved goodbye and the kids waved back, in high spirits and ready to savor this new adventure.

"Couldn't have asked for a better day," one of the group leaders said.

"It is gorgeous out here, but I hope you've got lots of sunscreen. This sun can be hard on the skin."

Assured that each child was protected, he moved into the galley and started preparing the hot dogs they'd roast later on the beach. The atmosphere was stifling hot down here with barely a whisper of air despite the open windows.

Peals of laughter echoed across the water.

Too bad Piper wasn't here.

Her call yesterday had caused him a sleepless night of soul-searching. By five he'd admitted the root of the problem—he wanted to tell God how things should go and God wasn't listening.

As Higgy said, "If you want to hear God laugh, tell Him *your* plans."

It wasn't about Jason Franklin, though. It wasn't his plans that were important. With the dawn's early light had come the last vestige of surrender. God was in control.

He heard the engines slow as he finished his prep. That meant they were at The Bowl. The kids would need help with their rods and reels.

For the next three hours he baited hooks, removed fish and took snapshots. If this continued they'd have enough fish to fry for dinner.

Complaints of hunger had them moving on toward Carroll's Cove, a pretty picnic spot easily accessible for the children with wheelchairs and those with locomotion issues. Jason pulled, tugged and lifted while Higgy went ahead and got the fire going. Then there were coolers of supplies to be transported. Everybody was hot and thirsty.

"I never would have imagined I'd enjoy the day so much," Higgy murmured later as the supervisors helped those who wanted to swim into the water. He held the soda can against his cheek trying to cool it. "Looking at these kids. It makes me feel shame to know I don't give thanks enough for my life. Look how hard they work just to get to that water."

He was right. Once they'd packed up the food, Jason and

Higgy relaxed on the banks under a willow tree and watched the impromptu water volleyball game. Then it was time to push toward Fairview Falls.

It was four-thirty before Jason thought to check the weather report. The news was not good. He motioned Higgy in.

"Tornado warnings are out."

"Makes sense given the heat and humidity," Higgy murmured. "But I've never heard of the Bay being hit before."

"One touched down five miles out last year. Close enough for me. I think it's time to head back."

"Gotcha."

They got everyone on board and Higgy steered them back toward Serenity Bay. But they were a long way out when the wind picked up and began tossing waves that pushed them too close to shore.

Then the motor died.

"What's wrong?" he asked Higgy.

"I think we're out of fuel."

"Impossible. Andy filled her last night. I checked to be sure." Jason did his own check and couldn't believe what he saw. "The spare?"

"Empty. I'd say someone doesn't want us going home."

They looked at each other for several minutes.

"Find a place along the shore. The waves will push us in and we can dock. Then we'll get the kids off. We can probably shelter them on board, but I'd feel better if we found a cave or something off the water," Jason said.

A crack of lightning had Jason reaching for the radio. He issued a distress call while Higgy edged them inward. Suddenly he realized the radio had died.

Reality stung. He was on the water, in the midst of a storm, with a group of kids who would need a lot of help to get off the boat. By the looks of the sky, the houseboat was about to be deluged, perhaps even tossed onto the rocks.

Jason pulled out his cell phone and dialed. No signal.

The distress beacon—they could set it. He opened his mouth to tell Higgins, saw the open panel, the empty space. The beacon had been removed.

They were on their own.

The weather bulletin ended as Piper parked her car. Her skin prickled with warning. Jason's houseboat trip was today.

She climbed out and raced for the marina. Her heart hit her toes at the sight of the empty berth. The houseboat was not in its mooring.

Inside the building, Andy was on the phone.

"I'm telling you, I can't reach him and he's two hours overdue. There's no response on his radio and his cell phone isn't working."

She pulled out her own phone, called Ida.

"He's not here, Piper. I've already called for help."

"Good. He's got that group of disabled kids with him. If they've had mechanical problems we'll have to pray they made it to shore. Who's searching for them?"

Ida's silence sent a shiver through her.

"What's wrong?"

"Water search and rescue was called over to the next county to help there just after lunch. We've got a couple of launches out looking but I'm pretty sure Jason intended to take the group a long way down, make it a real tour. If that's the case—" Ida didn't finish.

She didn't have to. Piper understood exactly what she hadn't said. He'd never make it back in time before the second storm hit.

"Is there a way to get someone up in the air? If they could fly over, spot them, we'd know exactly where to send the boats. The wind is dying down, I think," she added, studying the wind sock Jason had fastened to the end of the building.

"We don't have air support up here, Piper. It will take at least three hours to get something from the city. My other phone's ringing. I have to go."

Piper hung up as the truth sank in. At best, Jason was stranded. At worst, he could be lying somewhere hurt, unable to protect his passengers.

Have some faith that I'll do the right thing.

Her angry comment returned with haunting clarity. She'd told him to trust her. Now it was time for her to prove that she was worthy of that trust.

There had to be someone with a plane or a helicopter who could help them.

Like a dream, an old memory of her father landing his helicopter at Cathcart House flew across her mind. He still had one. She knew that. She'd seen a news clip in which he'd climbed down from the powerful beast.

Maybe—

This was no time for hesitation. They needed help and they needed it fast. Piper pulled out her phone and dialed the office. Baron was at home. She dialed the house. Dylan answered.

"Dyl, this is an emergency. I need to talk to Dad."

"He's not here, Piper. Did you try his cell?"

"Not yet."

"What's wrong?"

She explained the situation as quickly as she could.

"It's urgent that I talk to him. The winds are down for now but the weather station says they'll pick up later. The Bay is going to get lashed by a very heavy storm. I've got to find Jason and those kids."

"Okay. Well, if I hear from Dad I'll get him to call you."

She nodded, hesitating.

"Anything else, sis?"

"You couldn't come, could you? Just to be here. I'm so scared."

A static-filled pause hung between them.

"I would if I could, Piper. You know that. But I'm too far away. I'd never make it there before morning."

"Of course. I should have thought of that. I'd better go, Dyl. I want to keep the line free."

He said goodbye and she hung up.

Though Piper kept the line free, her father did not call back and hurt sent a deeper root into her heart. She'd told him it was urgent, explained how badly they needed his help. Why didn't he answer?

"I tried, God. I tried to forgive him. But this is exactly like before, with Vance."

She turned her attention to the group of volunteers who'd gathered at the marina to help organize the search effort. Most of them had friends or family on the water, searching. But nobody had reported a sighting.

"Waiting's the hardest part," Andy told her as minutes ticked into hours. He handed her another cup of coffee though she hadn't finished the first one he'd already given her. "We've only got a small window of opportunity here, according to the weather forecasts. If we could just get something in the air to search…"

Piper's cell phone rang.

"Dad?"

"Piper?" The beloved voice sounded faint.

"Jason! Where are you?"

"…help. Boat…ran out of fuel…stranded. Send help."

"It's coming," she promised. "Just hang on. Jason?"

But there was only static, then the line went dead.

She couldn't lose Jason, too. She hadn't even told him that she loved him.

Two more boats chugged toward the marina. The room fell silent as the men walked inside, shaking their heads at the unasked questions.

Piper knew then what she had to do. The past could not be repeated. She wouldn't let it. The old arguments and bitterness had prevented her from pleading, begging, doing everything possible to get Vance what he needed. She'd caved in, let anger and hurt interfere when she should have demanded help no matter what the cost to her pride.

She clicked open her phone and dialed. When one avenue didn't work out, she tried another. Dylan was still no help but after seven calls she finally reached Tina.

"Thank goodness! Tina, I need to speak to my father. I've been trying his cell, the house. I can't find him. Do you know where he is?"

"We've just come out of a meeting, honey. He's right here. Hold on."

"Piper?"

The sound of his voice grabbed her heart and squeezed until tears pooled in her eyes. She loved him. She couldn't fix the past, couldn't undo what he'd done. Right now it didn't matter that he'd hurt her and maybe would do so again. This was her father and she needed his help. No matter what.

"Daddy?" she whispered.

"I'm here."

"I need help."

A soft, slow sigh, then the voice came back. "Tell me what's wrong, sweetheart."

Piper quickly poured out her story.

"It's really bad, Dad. Jason's got kids on the boat. Disabled kids. We've got to rescue them."

"I have an old friend who lives about an hour from the Bay. He's got a big chopper he uses to bring his family to their lake home. Let me see if I can reach him."

"Will you let me know, Dad?" she asked softly.

"As soon as I do. And Piper?"

"Yes?"

"I love you."

Joy sprang up inside her, a fountain of happiness she couldn't suppress.

"I love you, too, Daddy." She closed the phone and found Andy at her elbow.

"Was that the answer to a prayer we've been waiting for?" he demanded.

"I hope so." She hugged him, whispering a heavenly plea. *Please, God?*

Jason tied off the lines as best he could, hoping it would be enough to keep the boat from ramming against the rocks and destroying the hull. But that was the least of his worries.

"Did you find anyplace we could shelter?" he asked Higgy.

"A cave, of sorts. If we can get everyone off before it starts really pouring, those with wheelchairs might have a hope of making it. Otherwise, we'll have to carry each of them. I started a fire already in case we need to dry some things out."

"Good enough for me. Let's see if we can get a ramp ready.

You man the controls, try to keep us steady while I help unload everyone."

"Okay."

A clap of thunder had some of the kids whimpering.

"Hey, this is just another part of the adventure," he told them with a grin. "Don't you worry. Cap'n Higgy and I have everything under control."

What a joke. He was utterly powerless and Jason knew it. No matter what he did, it was only a stopgap measure until—*if*—help arrived. The arrogance of trying to impose his will on the universe hit him full force. He was no more in control than a flea controlled the dog it sat upon.

He looked into the trusting faces of his passengers and turned to Someone who knows all things.

God, forgive me for thinking my way is best. Show me what to do.

"Okay, mateys. We're almost ready for our first expedition. I want you all to pay attention to your leaders. They'll give you each a number. When your number is called, it's time for you to get off this boat. There's a storm coming so the waves will bounce us around a little, but don't you worry. You're all going to be just fine."

"Are you sure, Captain?" A little redheaded boy who looked about nine tipped up his freckled face and peered into Jason's eyes. "Certain sure?"

"I'm positive, son. You're number one," he said, then glanced at the supervisor to be sure she'd heard. She nodded and Jason went back outside.

He jumped off the edge into the water and secured the ramp as well as possible with the waves lashing against him. They'd have to move fast.

But with that thought the storm seemed to intensify.

"You are in control here, Lord. But if you could give us ten minutes, I'd sure be grateful. Give us a break in the weather for ten minutes so we can unload these kids and get them safe."

Nothing happened. The wind continued its raging, the water soaked his pants, splashed his face. Then a soft whisper inside his head asked, *Do you trust Me now?*

"All the way, Lord. Your will be done."

A quiet sense of calm filled him. God was here. All Jason had to worry about was the task before him. Rain pelted his upturned face, but he ignored it.

"Number one. Come on down."

Chapter Fourteen

The chopper blades whipped the bay into a frenzy. To Piper it was a glorious sight.

She stood under the eaves of the marina building, watching for the pilot to emerge. To her surprise her father stepped out of the cockpit and jogged across the parking lot.

"Daddy?" She tumbled into his arms and hugged him back. "What are you doing here?"

"I came to help." He grinned. "Had to fly to Don's house. He's away but he said we could use his chopper. So I brought it. Are you ready to go?"

"We have some supplies—blankets, extra clothes, stuff that might help if the kids have been exposed to the elements. Also a nurse, just in case." She didn't want to even think about injuries.

He nodded. "How far out is he?"

"We're not sure. Probably a long way since no other boats have spotted them."

"Okay, let's get loaded. It's going to get worse before it gets better."

Less than ten minutes later they were airborne, carrying an extra passenger, a volunteer who'd insisted on coming, in case Jason needed help. The other two sat in the back. Piper sat across from her father, watching as he touched the controls that carried them over the water.

"Thank you for doing this," she said quietly, knowing the softness of her words would carry through the headset.

Baron reached out and touched her hand.

"Sweetheart, I've been waiting for so long for you to ask me for something. Your call today was an answer to a prayer."

"It was?" She adjusted the earphones to be sure she wasn't dreaming this.

"Of course." His smile reached out to warm her. "I've wanted to talk to you for a long time but you would never listen."

"But I phoned you and you never answered." She cut herself off, holding up her hands at his protest. "No. You know what? Let's not do this. Vance wouldn't have held a grudge and neither do I. I've forgiven you. Let's just move forward."

"Vance?" Baron's head jerked around from his scrutiny out the side window. "What grudge?"

"Forget it, Dad. Let's just concentrate on finding Jason."

She turned to stare out the window as the angry feelings threatened to take over again.

"I am concentrating. But I want to know what you meant that Vance wouldn't have held a grudge?"

"That you didn't help," she said simply, swallowing down the tears.

"Vance never asked me to help him."

"No, he didn't." She lifted her head, looked at him. "I did. I begged you, Daddy." She could barely squeeze the words out. "You never returned my call. Vance believed you'd call, Dad. He died waiting."

"Piper, listen to me. I never got a call from you. Not once." His face had paled, his eyes swirled dark with turmoil. "If I had, I would have sent whatever you needed, done whatever you asked."

"But you must have. I left a message with Dylan. He said he'd passed it on to you."

Baron glanced at her, then stared through the windscreen.

"This message—what exactly did you tell Dylan to say?"

"That I needed your help. That Vance would die unless we could get him to Italy for a new treatment. You must know."

He shook his head, his face haggard.

"Don't you think I would've come if I'd known my own daughter needed me?" he grated. "I thought you hated me."

"I thought I did, too. I was wrong. But this doesn't make sense."

Baron nodded.

"I remember—I was in Europe then. I never even knew Vance was gone until two weeks after his funeral. If I'd known you needed me—" He frowned at her. "You told Tina you'd been trying to reach me today."

"Yes. I left messages at the office, at the house, on your cell. I even called Dylan, begged him to tell you." She stopped, touching his arm. "You're very pale. Are you ill?"

"No." He dropped several hundred feet to get a better look at something on the water's edge. "Piper, I spoke to Dylan about ten minutes before you called me today. He said nothing about your call."

"But that doesn't—" She leaned forward, peering down at the tiny island off to her left. Her heart leaped to life, sending a rush of joy.

"There, Daddy! I think that's Jason's boat. Higgy painted the top just the other day."

"I need a patch to land on. See if you can spot a clearing." Baron's voice was stronger now, his face purposeful as he concentrated on his machine. "And Piper?"

"Yes?"

"Pray."

The noise echoed into the cave. The kids looked up, eyes wide.

"Is that the elephant you were telling us about?" the smallest asked.

Everyone burst into laughter.

"I think it might be. I'll go check. Don't let those marshmallows burn."

Jason motioned to Higgy to wait then he stepped outside, scanning the sky. A helicopter was circling the island, preparing to set down on the grassy knoll fifty feet away.

Piper had come through for them.

He hurried back inside to tell the supervisors what was going on.

"Didn't I tell you the adventure wasn't over yet?" he teased the children.

Their laughter had Jason thanking God that none of the day's events had traumatized any of them. He was certainly in control.

He returned to the cave opening, watching as the massive machine came to rest. Rain fell in sheets of gray but he could make out the figures of four people moving toward him.

"Piper?" He wrapped his arms around her and held her tight. "You didn't have to come all this way."

"Yes, I did." She kissed him, then leaned back, her wet hair hanging in her eyes. "Are you all right? Is anyone hurt?"

"No. But I'd like to get them out of here while they still

think it's a game." He blinked in surprise at Baron's appearance. He reached out to shake his hand. "Thanks for coming, sir. I take it the transportation is courtesy of you?"

"A friend," Baron told him. "But that's not important." He pointed up. "I asked some friends to follow. I hope you don't mind. Let's get your passengers loaded as soon as they're landed. We're going to have to do it in one trip. The wind is getting too high to risk another trip back."

Jason nodded, squeezing Piper's hand.

"I'm glad you called him again."

"There's something you should know, Jason." Piper stopped speaking when Higgy interrupted.

"Gale force winds are predicted."

"The storm looks like it's worsening," Jason told her. "We've got to get moving. We'll talk later, okay?"

Piper nodded. "Go and do what you have to," she whispered.

With Baron's help, Jason soon had teams formed. Together they moved all the kids aboard the three choppers. After a last look at the houseboat, he joined the others, motioning for Baron to follow them home.

Piper tried to give him her seat but he shook his head. "Tell them a story," he said, then moved to the second chopper. He'd keep the kids calm, make it an adventure. Hopefully they'd never realize the perilous situation they'd been in. To keep them busy Jason launched into another story that left them hanging until the helicopters finally landed at Serenity Bay.

"Hey! How are we gonna find out what happened?" his carrot-topped friend demanded.

"Guess you're just going to have to come back next week." Jason grinned. "Okay, the ride's over." He glanced at Piper, who stood waiting.

"Everyone's to go to the community center," she explained. "We've got a chicken dinner and lots of games. With prizes."

The excited kids could hardly wait to exit the helicopter before hitting the power buttons on their wheelchairs and zooming off, supervisors jogging to keep up. While Piper was busy with one of them, Jason turned to Baron.

"Thanks hardly seems enough."

"Forget that. What happened with the boat?"

"I'm pretty sure somebody sabotaged it." He explained the problems. "Higgy checked the beacon last night. Everything was fine." He swallowed, hating what he had to say. "I've been trying to think who could have done it. Dylan was here, Baron. We had dinner then I got a phone call. He said he was going to wait outside."

"I was afraid of that." Baron looked upset.

"Why?" Jason frowned, his surprise deepening as he heard about Piper's attempt to reach her father through Dylan. "But why? Why would he do that?"

"I don't know. But you need to speak to the police. Now. They'll want to examine the boat."

"And Piper?"

"She and I have some talking to do," Baron told him. "I love my daughter, Jason. Even though I've acted like a jerk, I always did. It kills me that I wasn't there when she needed me." His eyes clouded. "For her to lose Vance like that—" He shook his head.

"You're here now. I think that means a great deal."

"I messed up, Jason. I messed up a lot."

He patted the tired father's shoulder.

"We all did. But we serve a God of second chances."

Baron nodded but he said nothing more, content to feast his eyes on Piper, who was speaking to several officials. She looked over one shoulder, winked at them and grinned.

Jason longed to hang on and never let her go, but he couldn't. Not yet. Not until he'd apologized to the Society's director, not until he talked to Bud Neely.

Then he'd find her. And with God's help he wouldn't let her go.

Piper slipped her arm into her father's and walked beside him to her car. She could hardly believe he was here, that he loved her, that he always had.

"Where's Jason?"

"He had some things to do." Baron pressed the hair out of her eyes. "I need to talk to you, honey. Can we go for a coffee somewhere? I could sure use one."

"Get in. I'll drive you." She switched the heat on then steered out of the parking lot toward the town's only drive-through. After she'd ordered and picked up two coffees, she pulled into an empty space on the lot. "I'm so thankful you came. I don't know what we would have done."

"God would have worked something else out." Baron sipped the steaming liquid. "Piper, I need to apologize. I acted like a boor and an oaf after your mother died. A hundred times I've wished I could take it back and a hundred times I've prayed for God's forgiveness. Now I'm asking for yours."

"Why did you do it, Daddy? What changed?"

"Everything." He tilted his head back, closed his eyes. "I always thought I'd die first, never her. When she was gone I couldn't accept that God would do that. I got bitter and very, very angry."

"You were hurting," she agreed. "We all were."

"It was worse than that. I let fear take over."

"Fear?" Piper had never imagined her father was afraid of anything. To hear him say it shocked her. "Fear of what?"

"Of messing up. Of not doing the right thing. Of being a horrible parent." He dragged one hand through his hair. "She was so good at it, a natural-born mother. I should have let her teach me but I got caught up in making money. As if that mattered after she was gone."

"You did your best," she offered quietly, wondering at the anger that had faded now that he was here.

"No, Piper, I didn't. What I did was try to dictate every move you made."

"Why did you do that?"

"Because I was stupid. Because I was stubborn, too stubborn to know your grandparents were exactly what you needed. Because I was terrified something would happen to you and you'd leave me, too. Just like her." He blinked rapidly, then stared into her eyes. "I loved your mother more than my life, Piper. But in those days I was young and brash and I scorned God. I certainly didn't think I needed Him. I'd decided I was going to raise you all by myself, my way. I was going to turn you into a woman your mother would be proud of."

"Oh, Daddy."

He reached out to touch her curls, laid his palm against her cheek.

"She would be proud, Piper. So proud of her brave, strong, true little girl." He patted her shoulder. "Even though I took my loss out on your grandparents, accused them of taking away my daughter, even though my incessant demands drove you to them and kept you from the home your mother had made, even though I wasn't there to help you as she would have wanted, you've come shining through. Your mother would be so proud of you. Just as I am."

Piper set her cup into the holder, leaned over and wrapped her arms around him.

"I didn't understand, Dad. I wanted you to hug me and hold me and you were trying to live through your own grief." She relaxed in his embrace for a few moments, then risked a look into his eyes. "But you were much harder on me than Dylan. Why?"

He let her go, and shrugged.

"I felt that Dylan was older, that he'd already made so many decisions, chosen his path. I didn't think he was as vulnerable."

"Dylan needs to know you love him, Dad."

He nodded. "I should have told him more, I know. Instead I've taken him for granted. And now there are problems."

"What problems?" The concern etching his face sent a shaft of fear to her heart. "Dad, is there something wrong at Wainwright?"

He nodded.

"There have been a number of—irregularities—all involving him. That's why I've been traveling so much. I've been trying to catch them before—" He paused, refusing to say any more even though Piper begged him to continue.

"I've got to go, honey. I promised I'd finish what I started and I can't stop now. Can you drive me back to the helicopter?"

"Of course." She swallowed the last of her coffee, switched the engine on. "But you'll come back, won't you? You'll come and stay so we can talk and get caught up with each other. I have so many things to tell you."

He smiled. "I'll be back, honey. Nothing in the world could stop me."

Satisfied, she drove them back to the marina. The rain had stopped for the moment. They stood together on the windswept lot and embraced, saying without words everything that needed to be said.

"Take care, sweetheart," Baron murmured, kissing her cheek.

"You, too, Daddy." She hugged him tight, then let go. "Come back soon."

"Yes." He turned to walk away, then paused, turned back. "When Dylan shows up, find a reason to keep him here and then call me, will you?"

She nodded. He gave her one last look, then walked to the helicopter, climbed in and was gone.

Piper checked Jason's shop, but he was not inside. They needed to talk but it looked as if that would have to wait. Once she'd made sure the children had left and she was no longer needed, Piper returned to her car, intending to head home. But when she was inside, she remembered her father's words and puzzled over them.

Why would Baron ask her to keep Dylan here when Dylan wasn't even in town?

She'd have to ask him when next she saw him.

Piper turned her thoughts to Jason, a tiny smile lifting her lips. She wanted to see him, to tell him how much she loved him.

But not like this.

She decided to go home to Cathcart House. She'd cut some roses, fill the house with their heady scent. A bubble bath, fresh clothes and then she'd start dinner.

And maybe, if everything worked out just right, Jason would show up. Then she'd tell him what she'd been afraid to say before.

Now she knew why God had brought her to Serenity Bay.

"I forgive," she murmured. "Please forgive me."

The rush of peace assured her God did. She could hardly wait to tell Jason.

Chapter Fifteen

❧

Jason huddled in his chair, desperately praying for God's help. Once more his life was out of control.

Outside a car stopped, a door clicked. Footsteps padded to the door. It opened.

"Dylan? Hey! What are you doing here?" Piper paused with one hand on the screen door, scanning her brother's lounging form in her grandfather's chair. Her gaze rested on Jason, widened at the gag in his mouth, the ropes binding his hands and feet. Her body sagged, her shocked whisper carried across the room on the wings of fear. "What have you done?"

"*Me?* What have *I* done?" Dylan lurched out of his chair, his voice a notch too high, speech a tad too quick. "Shouldn't that be what have *you* done?"

A gun appeared in his hand. He waved Piper into the room.

"I don't know what you mean." Piper moved forward, dropped her bag on a chair but kept going until she stood in front of her brother. "Dad said you never passed on my message, Dylan. Not today when Jason needed help, not when Vance was sick. Why?"

"Why?" The stark pain brimming in his voice echoed around the room.

"Do you really have to ask, Piper?"

"Yes." She sat down in front of him, ignoring the gun barrel aiming directly at her midsection. "I have to ask because I don't understand why you'd do such a thing. I love you, Dyl. You're my big brother. I thought you loved me, too."

"I did." For a moment the dark eyes softened. A wistfulness flickered across his face. "I do. But it costs me too much. I'm sick of paying. Now it's your turn."

Jason knew the exact moment she realized the truth.

"It was you! All those incidents, the model hotel, the chlorine in the tub, the plans so conveniently dropped. You did all that. Even the salt in *Shalimar's* fuel?"

Dylan nodded and Jason wished he could spare her this. But there was nothing he could do except pray.

"Jason's boat?" Her eyes flared with anger at the response.

"Yes!"

"Why?"

"Do you know what it's like to be second best? To always fall short, to never feel like you've quite managed to meet the bar? That you'll never be able to do enough, say enough, work hard enough to get your father's approval?" He shook his head, snorted. "Stupid question. Of course you don't. How could you? You were always the apple of Dad's eye. 'Piper this. Piper that. When Piper comes back.' Blah, blah, blah. On and on he went. I could count on one hand the number of times I heard my own father say, 'Good work, son. Well done. I appreciate your effort.'"

"Oh, Dylan." Tears washed down Piper's face as the hate-filled words poured out. "You have no idea."

"Don't I?" He jerked his head, scanned the room. "Look

at this place. Even here you were the favored child. I got cold, hard cash. You got the place they loved."

"Because they thought you didn't like it here, Dyl. You took Papa's diary. Did you read it? He loved you, they both did. But you never seemed to want to stay at Cathcart. Not after Mom died."

"Why would I? To compete with Perfect Piper?" He glared at her, his face red. "I read the diary, read all about how proud they were of you. You're right there. I kept as far away from this place as I could."

"I'm far from perfect." She shook her head. "But why Vance? What did my husband do to you that you would stop Dad from helping us?"

"He would have bled the company dry looking for a miracle. I knew there wasn't one. Not for him. Not using the company I'd been breaking my back to keep on solid ground." Dylan touched her arm. "I was sorry about Vance, Piper. But in reality his chances weren't good, anyway. According to my information he wouldn't have made it through the treatments. And when he died, Dad would have felt he had to console you by offering you a job at Wainwright. I wasn't going to allow that."

"I feel like I don't know you at all," she whispered.

"You don't."

"And Jason? What is his crime? How did he threaten you?"

"He didn't. But you fell for the guy. His business is here. That meant you'd be staying. I couldn't have that." He jerked the gun toward Jason. "I figured that if he died on the water somewhere, you'd get out of here fast. Then I could get on with my plans."

"Your plans?"

Jason had never seen Piper so white. Her fingers clenched around the arm of her chair as she struggled to remain calm.

"Your *plans* could have killed innocent children, Dylan. Your greed and hate could have stolen their lives. You would have been a murderer!"

Dylan paced, agitated and angry.

"I didn't know they'd be on that boat! He never said anything about them. He only said he was going out in the morning. How was I supposed to know? How could I know?"

The plaintive wail hit a nerve. Jason felt a wash of pity for the boy so desperate to gain love he'd resorted to such extremes.

"It couldn't have been just jealousy, Dylan. What you did to me, to Jason, to those kids—there has to be more to your actions."

Dylan nodded, his eyes emotionless, his face very calm. "There is."

Piper rose, moving forward until she stood directly in front of him—as if she intended to protect Jason from that gun. His blood ran cold and he wiggled hard, thumping the chair on the wooden floor.

Piper's eyes begged him to be silent. Dylan grew agitated.

"Shut up or I'll shoot you." He turned back to Piper, grabbed her arm. "You want to know why? Look. I'll show you. Then maybe you'll get it."

He pulled a folder lying on the table toward him, flipped it open.

Piper bent, staring at the contents.

"This is the hotel model you left in my car," she whispered. "It's beautiful, Dylan. But what—"

He didn't let her finish.

"I own all the land around Cathcart House, Piper. All of it. Once you sell me Cathcart I'll be able to start construction. The hotel in town will look like a dump compared to this place. *My* place. When you're gone and construction is complete, then everyone will know, especially Baron, that I'm worthy of the Wainwright name, that I deserve to run the company."

"When I'm gone?"

Jason knew how hard she struggled to keep calm, to say the words through the fear. He'd never felt more proud or more grateful to God for giving him a chance to love this woman. If only—

"I don't want to kill you, Piper. I won't have to if you'll promise never to come back here. Never."

"Why? You could have built this in town, Dylan. You could have brought the model in to the council. They would have passed it in a heartbeat." She touched a finger to the file. "It's beautiful, the most fantastic work you've ever done."

"Really?" He was like an eager boy, his smile hopeful, begging for a soft word.

"I didn't tell you, Dyl, but I've kept track of your work. You have an amazing talent. *Builder's Digest* was right when they said your work will only gain more accolades." She smiled, but it was a sad smile, one filled with regrets. "You could have done it in town. So why here, Dyl? To ruin what Gran and Papa built? To spoil my dream?"

He lost his smile; his eyes burned with anger.

"Isn't it only fair? You've managed to ruin mine."

"How?"

"After Christmas last year, the old man had a physical. His heart isn't right. He got scared about dying and had a new will made out." Dylan's face altered into a hardened mask of fury. "He left you half of Wainwright Inc. Half of everything I've worked so hard to build. Half of what you walked away from and left me holding the pieces. I had to show him I was worth loving, worth holding on to."

"I do love you, son." Baron eased into the room and

stepped forward, one hand held out. "God has been dealing with me about the way I've treated you."

"God!" Dylan jerked away from Baron's touch. "Mom used to say God is love but after she was gone I never felt it. I used to come home at school breaks wishing she'd be there to hug me. I was all alone, Dad."

"I know." Baron nodded. "You shouldn't have been. That was my mistake. I have to ask your forgiveness, Dylan. I was not the father you deserved. You are the best son a man could have asked for and it took me too long to appreciate that. I love you. With my whole heart I love you, son."

"You can't." Dylan bit his lip as his father removed the gun from his hand, dropping it onto the floor. "I did some things at Wainwright, Dad. Bad things."

Baron nodded. "I know. I forgive you. Because I love you."

"Are you sure?" Dylan murmured, hesitant yet to believe.

"Positive." Baron drew his son into his arms and held him as Dylan wept, clinging to his father like an anchor. "I love you more than my life."

"I love you, too, Dyl," Piper added a few minutes later, wrapping an arm around his waist. "You're my big brother. I'll always love you."

Jason's heart got stuck in his throat as he watched a family reconnect bonds that had been ripped apart by hate and anger and jealousy.

If ever he'd needed proof that God was in control, he had it now.

Baron signaled and Chief Neely and another officer stepped through the door. Bud picked up the gun, tucked it into his belt. Then they cut Jason's restraints. Jason rose, stretching his limbs.

"We have to go with the police now, Dylan. But don't

worry. I'll go with you. I'll be there to help you. I don't know what we'll face, but we'll do it together." Baron met his son's gaze without flinching. "We have to tell them the truth now, son. All of it."

"I know." Dylan lifted his head, nodding at the officers. He glanced at Jason. "I'm sorry." He held out one hand. "Forgive me?"

Jason took it, squeezed hard. "Of course. After all, God forgave me."

"Thanks." Then it was Piper's turn. Dylan's face fell as he stared at her. "I'm so sorry, sis."

"It's okay." She hugged him, then sniffed. "You go with Dad. He'll take care of you. I love you."

The police walked him out of the room to a waiting squad car outside. Jason moved to one side, giving father and daughter space.

"I've got to go with him, honey. He'll probably go to jail but I have to help." Baron's eyes begged her to understand.

Piper smiled, touched his cheek. "I know. You go, Daddy. Do what you can. When you want to talk I'll be here. Waiting."

They embraced then Baron hurried away. Jason stepped forward, eager to get Piper to himself. But the police had other ideas.

"If you'll come with me, Jason, I'd like to get your statement. Piper, you go with this officer."

"Sure." She looked at him directly, summoned up a smile. "Talk to you later?"

"Count on it," Jason confirmed.

Epilogue

By ten o'clock, Serenity Bay lay in a pool of darkness with only a small, yellow flicker here and there.

Seated on the deck, Piper's gaze rested on the surrounding forest. She ignored the chilly breeze whispering across the land.

Waiting was the hardest part.

"Piper?" The warm hand on her arm made her smile. "Are you all right?"

She turned her head to look at Jason and nodded. "Yes."

"What are you thinking about?" he asked, sinking down beside her.

"God. My father and Dylan. Love. Forgiveness. His leading."

"God led me here to teach me how to trust." His fingers grasped her chin, urging her to face him. "I believe He led you here, too."

She nodded.

"I came for the wrong reason," she murmured. "But He turned that into good, showed me a side of fatherhood I'd never seen before." She threaded her fingers with his, staring out across the water. "God is like the bay, I think. Ever changing, ever new. Sometimes demanding but always there, always waiting to wrap you up and hold you close."

Tears rose but she ignored them.

"I saw God in my father today. Tina's been filling me in on what Dylan's done to Wainwright. To my father. Dad knew everything, Jason." She blinked away the tears and smiled. "And yet when the time came he wiped it away, loved my brother in spite of it all."

"He did the same for you," Jason reminded.

"Yes. I misjudged him so badly and yet he forgave me. Dad was there, waiting for me all along. Just like God. Only I couldn't see it, I couldn't experience the love because I wouldn't trust in it. I guess He brought me here to teach me trust, too." She smiled at him as the peace settled like a blanket on her heart.

"I love you, too, Piper. I think it began the first day you showed up at the town office. You looked like a winter rose to me."

"A rose?"

"Mmm." He laid his index finger against her cheek, let it glide across the skin. "You were wearing red and I remember you reminded me of a long-stemmed rose, the kind a man gives a woman he loves."

Jason leaned over, plucked a deep-burgundy rose from her grandmother's arbor and brushed it against her cheek.

"I love you," she whispered, sitting very still as he tucked the bloom in behind her ear. "When I thought there was a chance you might drown out there, I knew I couldn't go another day without telling you how much you've meant to me these past months. Everything I've worked to achieve, I couldn't have done any of it if you hadn't been there."

"Even though I pushed you too hard?" he asked with a lopsided grin.

"Even though you constantly challenged me to try harder," she agreed.

He slid an arm around her waist, drew her so close only a whisper separated them.

"We make a good team when we work together, Piper. Will you keep working with me, keep reining me in, keep teaching me to trust? I think God has lots in store for Serenity Bay. Together we're strong enough to accomplish whatever He sends." His lips brushed hers. "Someday soon I'm going to ask you to marry me, be my partner for the rest of our lives."

She tilted her head a fraction to the right, tracing the lines of his face with her eyes.

"Someday soon I'm going to say yes. After we help Dad with Wainwright Inc. Think you can work with me there?"

"Think I'll love it." They kissed, sealing the promise of a thousand tomorrows. Across the bay a shower of gold sparks lit up the night sky.

"What's that?" Piper asked, blinking as one after another, an array of fireworks dazzled them.

Jason groaned.

"I forgot to tell you. We were invited to Ida's for ribs again. She caught me just as I was coming over here. She knows I love you, Piper."

Piper burst out laughing.

"After today, I'm pretty sure she knows I love you, too."

Another boom resounded across the valley and the sky filled with a soft, golden glow. Jason picked up Piper's hand and squeezed it.

"What's next on your Serenity Bay calendar?"

"The Summer Splash will be over soon, but then we've got the Fall Fair." She reached up, pulled his head down and told him wordlessly how much she loved him. "Then it will be time for the Winter Festival."

"Piper, the mayor probably shouldn't say this, but you are the number one priority on my to-do list."

She laughed, snuggled her head against his shoulder and thought how wonderful it was that God had planned for her to love this man.

"I think I might be free on New Year's Eve, Mayor Franklin. Does that fit in with your schedule?"

"It's pretty far away." His chin rested on her head. She could hear the rumble of laughter from deep down in his chest. "But I'm learning that good things come to those who wait. I'll wait for my winter rose."

* * * * *

Dear Reader,

Welcome to Serenity Bay. Though this pretty tourist town is a total figment of my imagination, it's as real to me as my own backyard. That's because it's not so much a physical place on the map as it is a destination for the soul, a place where wounded hearts can run to find healing, help and friends who will be there no matter what.

I hope you've enjoyed Piper's search for forgiveness and the revelations it brought. Jason had his own quest to learn to trust. That's not an easy thing when those to whom you're committed most have betrayed so deeply. Isn't it good to know that no matter how many mistakes we make, our loving heavenly Father is there with open arms and a heart brimming with tenderness to show us He never gives up on us?

Please join me next month for Ashley's story in *Apple Blossom Bride.* Until then, I wish you peace in your relationships, joy in your everyday life and the fullness of a love that grew in the heart of God to be shared with His children on Earth. I pray you find an abundance of it, enough to pass on to those you touch today.

Blessings,

Lois
Richer

QUESTIONS FOR DISCUSSION

1. Piper moved to Serenity Bay for two reasons. What were they? Discuss moves you may have made and the reasons behind them. What hopes did you have before you moved? Did moving change your life for better or worse?

2. After a major disaster at his job in Boston, Jason decided to move to Serenity Bay. Discuss events that have led to major changes in your own life.

3. On the surface Serenity Bay seems like a town where we'd all like to live—peaceful, friendly. But everyone carried his own set of problems. Talk about ways we deal with our problems and their effectiveness.

4. As a teen, Piper rebelled against her father after her mother's death. What events triggered rebellion in your life? How did you deal with it? Did you have grandparents to run to? List ways you can make it easier on the teens in your life, whether it's at church, or at home.

5. Dylan saw himself as the one who was passed over. Find a biblical character who experienced the same sense of being forgotten. Describe roles parents play in such situations.

6. When her husband died, Piper chose to keep herself isolated from her father because she couldn't forgive him for abandoning her. In the

end she realized she'd made a mistake. Consider your own life and instances where you held on to blame rather than made peace with it. Was it worth it?

7. Piper never deliberately kept her family name a secret, but she also never told Jason why she was so against Wainwright Inc. Do you keep secrets in your relationships? How can we keep from doing so? Is this a time to houseclean with God?

SUSPENSE

RIVETING INSPIRATIONAL ROMANCE

Don't miss the intrigue and the romance
in this six-book family saga.

THE SECRETS
OF STONELEY

Six sisters face murder, mayhem
and mystery while unraveling the past.

FATAL IMAGE
Lenora Worth
January 2007

**THE SOUND
OF SECRETS**
Irene Brand
April 2007

LITTLE GIRL LOST
Shirlee McCoy
February 2007

DEADLY PAYOFF
Valerie Hansen
May 2007

BELOVED ENEMY
Terri Reed
March 2007

**WHERE THE
TRUTH LIES**
Lynn Bulock
June 2007

Steeple
Hill®

Available wherever you buy books.

REQUEST YOUR FREE BOOKS!

2 FREE INSPIRATIONAL NOVELS
PLUS 2
FREE
MYSTERY GIFTS

YES! Please send me 2 FREE Love Inspired® novels and my 2 FREE mystery gifts. After receiving them, if I don't wish to receive any more books, I can return the shipping statement marked "cancel." If I don't cancel, I will receive 4 brand-new novels every month and be billed just $3.99 per book in the U.S., or $4.74 per book in Canada, plus 25¢ shipping and handling per book and applicable taxes, if any*. That's a savings of 20% off the cover price! I understand that accepting the 2 free books and gifts places me under no obligation to buy anything. I can always return a shipment and cancel at any time. Even if I never buy another book from Steeple Hill, the two free books and gifts are mine to keep forever.

113 IDN EF26 313 IDN EF27

Name _____ (PLEASE PRINT) _____

Address _____ Apt. # _____

City _____ State/Prov. _____ Zip/Postal Code _____

Signature (if under 18, a parent or guardian must sign) _____

Order online at www.LoveInspiredBooks.com

Or mail to Steeple Hill Reader Service™:

IN U.S.A.: P.O. Box 1867, Buffalo, NY 14240-1867
IN CANADA: P.O. Box 609, Fort Erie, Ontario L2A 5X3

Not valid to current Love Inspired subscribers.

Want to try two free books from another series?
Call 1-800-873-8635 or visit www.morefreebooks.com

* Terms and prices subject to change without notice. NY residents add applicable sales tax. Canadian residents will be charged applicable provincial taxes and GST. This offer is limited to one order per household. All orders subject to approval. Credit or debit balances in a customer's account(s) may be offset by any other outstanding balance owed by or to the customer. Please allow 4 to 6 weeks for delivery.

Your Privacy: Steeple Hill is committed to protecting your privacy. Our Privacy Policy is available online at www.eHarlequin.com or upon request from the Reader Service. From time to time we make our lists of customers available to reputable firms who may have a product or service of interest to you. If you would prefer we not share your name and address, please check here. ☐

LIREG07